The Last Swan
in Sacramento

G·K
Hall
&Cº.

Also by Stephen Bly
in Large Print:

Red Dove of Monterey
Miss Fontenot
The Marquesa
Sweet Carolina
I'm Off to Montana for to Throw the Hoolihan
My Foot's in the Stirrup . . . My Pony
   Won't Stand
Stay Away From That City . . . They Call It
   Cheyenne
Where the Deer and the Antelope Play
One Went to Denver and the Other Went Wrong
It's Your Misfortune and None of My Own
Son of an Arizona Legend
Final Justice at Adobe Wells
The Lost Manuscript of Martin Taylor Harrison

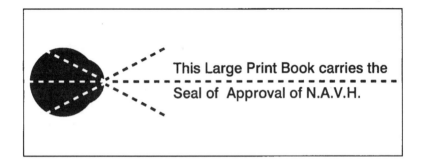

This Large Print Book carries the
Seal of Approval of N.A.V.H.

Old California Series
—————— *Book Two* ——————

THE LAST SWAN IN SACRAMENTO

Stephen Bly

G.K. Hall & Co. • Thorndike, Maine

Published in 2000 by arrangement with Crossway Books,
a division of Good News Publishers.

G.K. Hall Large Print Western Series.

The text of this Large Print edition is unabridged.
Other aspects of the book may vary from the original edition.

Set in 16 pt. Plantin by Rick Gundberg.

Printed in the United States on permanent paper.

Library of Congress Cataloging-in-Publication Data

Bly, Stephen A., 1944–
   The last swan in Sacramento / Stephen Bly.
     p. cm. — (Old California series ; bk. 2)
   ISBN 0-7838-9127-X (lg. print : hc : alk. paper)
   1. Married women — Fiction. 2. Large type books. 3. Sacramento
(Calif.) — Fiction. I. Title.
PS3552.L93 L38 2000
  813'.54—dc21   00-033461

For
Jan, Julie, and Tammy —
Sacramento girls

"And the Lord said unto Joshua,
Get thee up; wherefore liest thou thus upon
thy face?"

Joshua 7:10 (*KJV*)

One

Sacramento, California . . . September, 1865

Martina Patricia Merced Swan stared reluctantly into the mirror.

The reflection hadn't changed from the previous day.

In fact, it hadn't changed in years.

Her face was still narrow. Chin pointed. Eyes brown and a little sunken. Ears a little too large. Lace-collared neck a little too long. Her bust still tight in the dress, as it had been since baby Christina's birth.

She applied a soft pink lip rouge and tied two thin turquoise ribbons in her hair.

"Why, Martina, you look exactly like . . . ," she hesitated, "your father!"

Daughters should look like mothers. Sons should look like fathers. Isn't that the way it's supposed to be? Walter, Joseph, and Edward have Mother's red hair, Mother's fiery eyes, Mother's magnetism. I get the plain looks of a man who spends his life punching cows. Rather handsome on Father, but . . . quit your sniveling, Martina. You've known that for twenty-two years!

She scooted to the side of the crib and gazed down at the sleeping one-year-old with the

7

shock of silky red hair. Martina's long, pale fingers latched the double row of tiny fake pearl buttons with the speed of one who had worn this dress often. Her decision had been quite simple. Wear the light blue dress.

Since the day she was married, she had a weekly schedule for her dresses. There were only three fancy dresses then. But one advantage of marrying into a family that owned a clothing store was seven fancy dresses. One for each day.

Tuesday was always blue.

Martina tugged at the waistline to get the dress to hang straight. *I like things orderly. A good routine means no surprises. I like to know how a day's going to be before it happens. I like plans.*

Of course, nothing has gone according to my plans since the day I married.

Except baby Christina.

Thank You, Lord, for my beautiful little girl.

She stabbed on small, oval turquoise earrings that dangled just below her lobes. They were the only pair she had owned before she married.

Fussing at the high lace collar and cuffs, Martina plucked up a chipped ivory-handled brush. After two dozen strokes with the brush through the waist-length, almost perfectly straight, dark brown hair, she turned around to look again at the mirror.

Nothing had changed.

She laced up her shoes, made the bed, and straightened up the storeroom that served as their bedroom, kitchen, and parlor. Then she sashayed across the room again to the crib and whispered, "Well, baby Christina, you are a sleepy girl this morning. It's no wonder. You wanted to play most of the night. Mommy's going down and open up the front door of the store for Mr. Chambers. I'll be right back."

Wm. Swan & Son — Clothing, Dry Goods, & Such was one of Sacramento's landmarks. When her father-in-law had arrived at the confluence of the American and Sacramento Rivers in early January of 1849, the town was no more than a congregation of tents scattered in the swampy lowlands. In those days, boats were unloaded wherever they could dock, and goods were often sold where they sat on the Embarcadero.

Like all the others, William Swan, Sr., had gone to the diggings. He panned for gold for all of three hours and claimed it was the most worthless three hours of his life. He immediately returned to the tent city of Sacramento and opened a warehouse where shippers could store goods before distributing them to the various gold camps. The 100-foot tent made of canvas sails from abandoned ships soon gave way to a two-story wooden building for not only wholesale but also retail business.

Like most of the rest of Sacramento, Wm. Swan & Son burned to the ground in 1852. And like most, Swan quickly rebuilt only to face the flood of 1853. For the next eight years Sacramento and Swan & Son boomed. But at 8:00 A.M. on December 9, 1861, the boiling American River plowed through the levee on the city's eastern edge, sweeping in with the power and devastation of a hurricane. Even worse, on January 9 heavy rain and snowmelt in the Sierras flooded the already saturated town.

Some said they should abandon the site. But others, like William Swan, Sr., had a better idea. He brought in dozens of mechanical jacks and raised his entire store a few inches at a time until it was ten feet higher than before. The city brought the streets up to that height, and soon other business owners followed Swan's lead.

Sacramento lived on. As did Wm. Swan & Son. The two-story brick building on the corner of 5th and J remained a landmark. The retail business was run on the bottom floor, the wholesale from the upper floor.

But business changed. Some companies, such as Huntington & Hopkins Hardware, Crocker's Dry Goods, and Stanford's Groceries chain, got bigger. Small family operations like Wm. Swan & Son began to suffer. Their wholesale business had shut down before Mr. Swan, Sr., died. And the posh Swan family home, once a social hub, had been sold by his widow to finance her move back to upstate New York.

That left William Hays Swan, Jr., with a business past its prime. He made his living quarters in the storeroom above the store, assuring Martina it would be their home for only a few months. He was almost right. In their two years of marriage, William had only been "home" for a few months.

The stairs swept right down into the heart of the store and fanned out toward the tall oak-and-glass front doors on J Street. It was a convenient arrangement when the wholesale business flourished upstairs. Now it was difficult to convince customers that upstairs was a private residence. On more than one occasion patrons had burst into her room when she had slipped upstairs to nurse the baby.

Seven o'clock daylight illuminated the room through the large front windows, and tiny particles of dust were suspended in the air over neatly organized rows of merchandise. When Martina reached the first floor level, she recalled the comment of a recent woman patron: "What nice, wide aisles and roomy shelves!"

That's because I can't afford to buy more inventory. Soon there will be nothing left except roomy aisles and empty shelves.

Martina glanced at the oak clock that had graced Swan's entrance since January 1849 as she headed to the door. Through fire and flood the clock had survived.

Mr. Chambers is going to be late. He's always here at 6:55. I trust he isn't ill.

She spied two long brown envelopes on the clean gray-painted wooden floor where they had been shoved under the door.

Messages already? Maybe someone brought word from Billy.

The handwriting on one was unfamiliar; the other she knew. It was a faded handbill with lead pencil writing on the back.

Dear Miss Merced,

I surely am sorry about the store. I guess it can't be helped. Don't worry about me. I'm going up to Grass Valley and work for my sister's husband. Send my wages in care of Nevada County Feed & Grain.

I trust you'll get this letter. If I don't hear from you in a week or so, I'll stop by Rancho Alazan and see you when I get a chance to come out of the mountains.

Yours sincerely,
Winifred Chambers

Martina read the entire letter again word for word.

Winifred has quit? But he's worked for Swan's for ten years. . . . What does he mean, "sorry about the store"? Things could certainly be better but . . . Rancho Alazan? Does he think I'm moving home to be with my parents?

He can't quit. I need help. He knows I can't . . . Why didn't he come talk to me?

Why did he scribble something on the back of a handbill and shove it under the door instead of talking to me face to face?

Lord, I didn't need this. I need a good break — something nice to happen. This isn't it.

The return address on the second envelope

12

read Delta State Bank. She shoved it into her big, deep pocket unread.

An impatient banker is the least of my worries at the moment. Winifred sounded like he expected me to close up the business and go running home to Mama and Daddy. Who has he been talking to? Mr. Clayton at the bank?

She scurried up the wide stairway to the landing on the second floor, opened the chipped light-green-painted wood door, and propped it open with a used brick.

Baby Christina, this would be a very good morning to get some extra sleep. Oh, how I'd love to have some extra sleep.

She turned and dashed back down to the store.

We have opened on time since 1849. If the fires couldn't put us out of business — or the floods — I'm not going to let a fickle employee keep us closed either. It won't be the first time I've swept the porch and opened the store, Mr. Winifred Chambers!

Martina stooped down and spun the dial on the cubical black safe that stood behind the counter. She pulled out the gray tin box. With a key from her bracelet, she opened the cash register and then the money box. She counted out thirty dollars' worth of change, stuck it into the cash register, and shoved what was left back into the safe, spinning the brass dial.

She glanced around the peaceful store with its worn wooden floor. Row after row of identical wide wood shelves, stacked six feet high under the twelve-foot ceiling, greeted her eyes. Each of the pale green-painted shelves had seen tons of merchandise come and go. Everything was folded and neatly stacked in its proper place. Without customers Martina thought the store looked more like a museum than a retail business.

All right, we will open up. The clerks will be in soon. Until then it will be just me and Christina.

"And you, Mr. Broom," she mumbled as she snatched up the worn straw sweeper with its chipped blue-painted stick.

Martina stooped and tugged open the floor deadbolt on the right side of the ten-foot-tall double doors. She dragged the unpainted wooden chair by the mirror over to the front door. Carefully balancing herself, she twisted the lintel deadbolts open.

Her ankle twisted slightly as she banged back to the floor and scooted the chair back into place. Then she released the deadbolt by the large polished-brass door handles and glanced back into the store.

Lord, this is a good day for William Swan, Jr., to come home.

A very good day.

Martina almost fell through the etched opaque glass of the front door when she shoved it. The door swung open about two inches and then caught on something and came to a sudden stop.

Not the door! Don't tell me the front door is broken!

The right door also opened only two inches, then jammed. Her small, thin mouth drooped when she spied a heavy piece of chain strung between the outside door handles.

A chain? Very funny. What kind of sick vandals would think it's a joke to chain a business closed? I don't think I've alienated any customers. . . . My word, we haven't had many customers. I'll bet it was those men who were sitting on the curb yesterday. They were obviously loafing about. I should have had a lawman run them off. That kind should not be allowed to loiter in the business district!

Martina marched to the back of the room and carefully hung the broom on its hook. Then she dashed to the rear of the building. *This is absolutely absurd to have to go out the alley door of my own store,* our *store, just to see what vandals did to the front!*

A shudder of despair hit high in her chest and sank to her stomach as the solid oak back door opened only an inch, to reveal a similar chain.

Lord, this is macabre. Someone is trying to lock me in my own store. Why? What do they want? There's not much money in the safe, and if they locked themselves out, how can they . . . unless they are inside. . . . It's just me and baby Christina!

The feeling Martina had was like the last scene in a nightmare, that horrible despair and hopelessness that is so severe the person wakes up.

She ran up the stairs, listening to the pounding of her shoes and feeling the pounding of her heart. With red curls shooting out every way at once, the year-old infant slept peacefully in her bed.

Martina stormed around the room, her mind flitting from terror to anger. *Billy, I need you here. I need you here right now! A married woman should not have to face this alone. No woman should face this alone.*

Martina rushed to the dresser, dug through a stack of men's shirts, and pulled out a model 1849 Colt pocket revolver.

I don't know when this was loaded or if the powder is still dry, but if there's someone in this building, I'm going to pull the trigger and find out!

Martina marched back to the second-story landing, the pistol in front of her. She stopped to survey the silent store below.

Bolts of cloth.

Stacks of ready-made children's clothing.

Trousers and work shirts.

Linens and towels.

Quilts and comforters.

Dresses and hats.

Undergarments and shoes.

Ribbons and lace.

She searched for something more.

For an intruder.

No one could come in and chain the door shut from the outside. Unless it was a big gang. But then they couldn't get out. It doesn't make sense.

She sat down on the top stair and brushed her thick, full skirt in front of her. She glanced down at the gun in her hand and took a deep breath. Then she shoved the revolver into her pocket. Her hand brushed across the bank letter, and she jerked it out and tore it open. Her eyes narrowed as she followed each line.

September 15, 1865
Dear Mr. Swan:
Pursuant to loan #1289
1st extension — June 30, 1863
2nd mortgage — August 30, 1864
60-day final extension — June 30, 1865
2-week grace period — Aug. 30-Sept. 13, 1865

Having exhausted all avenues of contacting you, the bank is forced to impound your known assets at J and 5th Streets, Sacramento, California, pursuant to California Civil Code, section 33b-16.2. This property, known as Wm. Swan & Son — Clothing, Dry Goods, & Such, is to be sold at auction to the highest bidder on November 1, 1865, at said location. Until that time no assets may be removed except for personal belongings.

We have posted this notice on said building and sent a copy to your last known address at Virginia City, Nevada, as well as this copy. Unless proper satisfaction of this loan is received by October 1, 1865, we will at that date publish notification of auction.

Yours sincerely,
Landel Clayton, President
Delta State Bank

Martina Merced Swan gritted her teeth. There were no tears in her eyes. No abnormal heart palpitations. And no sense of doom. Instead, there came a familiar resolve.

Mr. Swan? You wrote a foreclosure notice to my husband. Mr. Swan has not been around for over a year, and you know that. I've been to your office, Mr. Clayton, three times in the last month. Not once did you mention padlocking our store. His last known address is Nevada? Billy's last known address was right here!

I've been right at this store for the last two weeks. You could have contacted me any day! No assets may be removed? How on earth can I pay a loan if I can't sell my inventory?

This is crazy. I've run this store almost single-handedly for two years, and you act as if I don't exist. Well, I do exist, Mr. Clayton, and you are going to have to deal with me face to face!

Martina stomped down the stairs, the weight of the revolver in the dress pocket rubbing on her leg. As she reached the middle of the store, she heard a knock on the glass of the front door. Even through the opaque glass she could see the familiar long white bib apron and white bonnet.

"Miss Merced?" a young woman's high voice called out. "Are you home? Miss Merced!"

Both store clerks had known her before she had married William Swan, Jr., and to avoid confusion with her mother-in-law, they continued to call her by her maiden name. Martina's protests had had little effect.

"Miss Merced?"

Martina shoved the front door a couple inches until the chain pulled tight. "Good morning, Doraine," she called out.

With her pale forehead creased by the door edge, the clerk peered into the store. "Miss Merced, what is happening?"

Martina rubbed the bridge of her long, thin nose. "I believe it's the handiwork of Mr. Landel Clayton at the bank."

"Can he do this?" Doraine tugged on the chain.

"Not to me, he can't. Stand back, Doraine, I'll . . . eh, unlock the door." Martina kicked at the immovable door and felt pain shoot up her right leg.

"Should both of us stand back?" There was almost a tickle in Doraine's voice.

"Both of you?" Martina leaned forward, her forehead against the door. "Is Evie with you?"

"No, we have a customer, a Mr. —"

Martina heard a deep voice mumble several words, and she spotted a one-inch strip of a man that included boot, trouser leg, vest, shirt, tie, clean-shaven face, dimple, eyeball, and tilted gray hat. "What do you want?" she asked him.

A slightly puzzled but rolling baritone voice answered, "I'd like to talk to Mrs. Swan. Could you tell me where she is?" She could tell he was trying to look her over.

"Stand back," Martina commanded.

He pulled off his hat and held it in front of him. His neatly trimmed dark brown hair showed a hat crease, his forehead a tan line. "Do what, ma'am?"

She waved her hands at both of them as if they could actually see her and called out, "Will both of you stand around the corner from the door, please?" Boots shuffled across the wooden sidewalk.

"We're around the corner," Doraine's muffled voice called out.

Martina pulled out the Colt, jammed the barrel through the crack of the door until it rested against the link of steel chain, and pulled the trigger. The explosion echoed across the room and sent a cloud of gun smoke into Martina's face. She staggered back, coughed once, and then hollered, "Yank off that chain, Doraine!"

Within a moment the two tall front doors were propped open with rocks the size of small pumpkins. Doraine LaFlor carefully held the chain away from her clean white apron.

A man around thirty, wearing faded but clean blue denim trousers and a starched white cotton shirt and vest, looked at her from head to toe. As Martina fanned the gun smoke with her hand, she noticed his stove-top black boots, floppy-brimmed gray hat, and the Colt army revolver in his belt holster.

"Miss Merced, this is Mr., eh —," Doraine stammered.

"Loop Hackett, ma'am." He tugged off his hat

and rolled it in his hands. His dark brown hair was a little long and edged with a hat curl. "I don't believe I've ever heard of someone locking their store every night with a chain on the outside and them on the inside." His deep blue eyes danced above a wide, easy smile.

At least he has clean teeth. I like a man with clean teeth. "How I choose to secure my store is no business of yours, Mr. Hackett," she retorted.

He hesitated as Doraine LaFlor clanged the chain on the floor inside the front door and returned with the broom. "Where's Mr. Chambers?"

"I believe he just quit," Martina snapped, not taking her eyes off the man with the sheepish grin.

LaFlor's hand raised to her smooth white cheek. "Why on earth would he do that?"

Martina, pistol still in hand, folded her arms across her chest. "He had the mistaken idea we were going to close the store."

"Would you like me to sweep the boardwalk, Miss Merced?" Doraine asked.

"Yes, that would be fine . . . no . . . no . . . Doraine, please go to the hardware store and borrow Mr. Gammon's bolt cutter." Martina took the broom from the clerk's hand.

Miss LaFlor brushed her bangs out of her eyes. "Bolt cutter?"

Martina put her hands on her hips and felt the thick material of her full dress. "I want to unlock

21

the back door, and there's no need to waste another bullet on that chain."

Mr. Hackett's thick eyebrows raised as he studied the gun in her hand.

Teasing you, Mr. Hackett, is the most enjoyable time I've had in weeks. She slipped the gun back into her deep pocket. The barrel felt warm against her leg.

Another white-apron-clad young lady swished up to them just as Doraine crossed the wide, dusty street. The newcomer's long black hair was neatly stacked on the back of her head and tucked under a starched black straw hat. "Am I late, Miss Merced? Oh, I hope I'm not late. I try so hard to get ready, and then the table is crowded at the rooming house, and by the time a chair next to Mr. Mendes opens up — he's the one with the very handsome mustache — anyway, am I late?"

"Relax, Evie — we're just opening up. I sent Doraine on an errand, so you'll have to run the counter this morning."

"Yes, ma'am." Evelyn Norman moved toward the back of the store and then called back. "I hope I didn't miss anything exciting. I always miss the good parts. Did you shoot someone?"

"Not yet," Martina replied. "I'll be in and explain it all in a minute."

"Did you know baby Christina's crying?" the unseen Evie called out. "It's not her panic cry — just sort of her 'where's my mama' cry."

"I'll take care of it. Thank you." Martina

looked around and shoved the broom into the hands of Loop Hackett.

"Say, are you Miss Merced or Mrs. Swan?" he quizzed.

"I'm called both. My mother-in-law was always called Mrs. Swan. So for clarity some use my maiden name, even though the senior Mrs. Swan has moved to New York state." She turned to waltz into the store.

Loop Hackett stood at the doorway and peered in. His broad shoulders blocked most of the morning light. "I do need to talk to you," he called out.

Martina stopped at the base of the stairs, her hands folded in front of her. "Yes, I imagine you do. Are you a creditor?"

He stepped into the store and swung the broom over his shoulders and gripped it with both hands. The muscles in his arms outlined the white cotton shirt. "Oh, no . . . not exactly."

"Well, that's a positive beginning. I'll be back in a few moments," she announced.

He held the broom out in front of him. "What do you want me to do with this?"

"I suggest you sweep the front sidewalk." Martina glanced over at Evie Norman who was listening to every word. Martina turned back to him and dropped her chin. She thought of it as her forcefully demure look. "Unless you'd like to go upstairs and nurse my baby."

"I'll . . . eh, I'll sweep the sidewalk." The words toppled from his startled face.

23

"Thank you, Mr. Hackett. I will talk to you in a few minutes."

Neither the clerk nor the man with the broom could see the sly smile on her face as she scooted up the light green stairs toward the sound of infant distress.

The few minutes lengthened as Martina not only cleaned up and fed Christina but recombed her hair and sparingly applied lilac water. With the baby happily sitting in the middle of the big bed playing with an old shell necklace, Martina dabbed rose water on her neck and wrists.

Lord, my store manager quit, the bank put chains on the doors — this is not a good day. I'm due for a good day, and You know it.

With the long dark blue dress hanging from her chin to her tiny laced-up black shoes, Christina smiled and flashed bright, alert hazel eyes around the room.

"Punkin, you are going to look exactly like your Grandma Alena when you grow up." Martina plucked the infant up and waltzed over in front of the full-length mirror.

"Me!" Christina squealed.

"That's you, young lady. Look at that beautiful wavy auburn hair. You'll captivate them all, just like my mother. And that's good, little darling. I ought to know. I grew up thinking my mama was the most beautiful woman in the state of California. I still think so, but you'll give her a run for it someday. Lord knows, I never did."

24

"Mama!" The word seemed to bubble out of the baby, surprising both her and her mother.

"You're right, darlin'. It's you and Mommy . . . just you and Mommy."

Martina brushed the dark brown hair back off her eyes. It was tied behind her ears by double ribbons and draped straight down her back past her waist. "Did I ever tell you what it was like growing up as the daughter of La Poloma Roja de Monterey? Strangers and dignitaries would stop by Rancho Alazan just to see Mama and talk to Daddy. 'Are you Doña Maria Alena's daughter?' they would ask in disbelief.

"But Mama always called me her 'beautiful Martina.' And Daddy? Well, your Grandpa is a pushover for Merced women. How I loved to come down to Sutter's Fort . . . and then later on to Sacramento . . . just me and Daddy. Everyone would say, 'You must be Wilson Merced's little girl. You look just like him!'

"That's nice when a girl is five or six. It was wearing a little thin when I was sixteen. But, young lady, you won't ever have that problem. You do not look like your daddy or your mommy, for certain."

Martina felt tears slip from the corners of her eyes.

Billy Swan, I have cried for you for way too long. If you are alive, you are a scoundrel — a deserter of your family. If you are dead, may the Lord have mercy on your soul. But I need to go on. I am twenty-two years old. I will not have all joy in life depart at such an age as this.

She shifted the baby to her other hip.

Lord, I know You dwell on high. I know You dwell at Rancho Alazan. I know You dwell in the hearts of my father and mother. But sometimes . . . it seems like You have deserted Sacramento, especially Wm. Swan & Son. It would be a wonderful sign to me if You would chase off the creditors, like that ruggedly nice-looking Mr. Hackett. I would give You great praise if I could walk down the stairs and he would be gone.

Carrying Christina at her side, she strolled down the stairs into the middle of the store and was delighted to see both clerks busy assisting the half a dozen customers who milled about. Her perfume covered the normally musty smell and hinted of springtime, even though it was the middle of September.

Doraine LaFlor scooted up to her quickly. "Miss Merced, perhaps you want to assist Mrs. Arden." Doraine raised her sandy-blonde eyebrows. "She wants to purchase material for all the dresses for her daughter's wedding. She doesn't want to speak to one of us lowly clerks."

Martina glanced across at the robust middle-aged woman wearing a small black velvet hat with large turquoise feather. "Oh, my, that sounds promising. How many dresses?"

"Twelve." Doraine smiled showing her white, yet slightly crooked teeth. "Can I take Christina for you?"

"Thank you."

The contented baby showed no hesitation to leave her mother for the strong arms of Doraine LaFlor. Martina took a pencil and notebook from the counter and turned to the baby-toting Miss LaFlor. "Did the Lord send us the deliverance I asked for and chase off that man, Mr. Hackett?"

Doraine's wide, full-lipped mouth opened, but for a moment no words came out. "Deliverance? I, eh . . . oh, he's still here."

Martina's heart sank. *Lord, it was only a small request. And it could have been such a blessing.* She surveyed the store. "Where is he?"

"He cut the chain off the back door and then returned the bolt cutter to Mr. Gammons." Doraine ran her pointed pink tongue around her lips as if it helped her to think. "I believe he's carrying some packages for Mrs. Galt."

"Mrs. Galt came to town? It's not even the last of the month."

"Yes, and she bought the entire bolt of that horrid green-flowered print," Doraine whispered.

"Well, that is good news! I'll help Mrs. Arden. If Mr. Hackett returns, tell him I'll see him as soon as I'm finished."

"For a handsome man, you're sure stalling him," Doraine said. There was a suppressed giggle in her voice that reflected her dance-hall past.

"Handsome?" Martina scoffed. "You certainly wouldn't expect a married woman to notice that!"

Two

Mrs. Abner Arden's voice was deceptively soft. As a little girl, Martina used to think this was a sign of a shy, hesitant woman. But as she grew older, she understood that it was more sly than shy — and highly determined, not hesitant.

"Martina, dear," Mrs. Arden greeted her, "how are you, and how's the world's prettiest baby?"

"We are both well, Mrs. Arden. Thank you for asking."

"And how is your dear mother?" Mrs. Arden gushed. "We spent the summer in Europe, you know . . . and I haven't see Alena in quite some time."

Nor have I, but I will never admit that to you. "She's busy at the ranch this time of the year." Martina imagined her mother galloping across the rolling hills on her morning ride.

Mrs. Arden put her fleshy hand on Martina's arm. "Those brothers of yours are almost grown."

"Yes, it's hard to believe that I once towered over them. They are all taller than Father."

"And they have that beautiful hair like their mother's." Mrs. Arden patted Martina's hand.

"They will be very sought-after young men, I suppose."

"Yes, ma'am. They are handsome and men of integrity. I'm very fortunate to have such brothers."

Mrs. Arden let loose of Martina's arm. "I assume Doraine told you what I wanted. With Lucida's wedding coming up in only three months, I thought it time to do a little planning. Naturally, I thought of Swan's. Do you still have the silk from Paris?"

"Yes, we do. I certainly appreciate your considering us. We'll work diligently to get everything you need."

"Oh, I know you will, dear. Why, I was just talking to Mrs. Clayton . . . Do you know the Claytons?"

"The banker?"

"Yes."

"I know him, but I haven't met his wife."

"Well, Mrs. Clayton said she thought your store was closed." Mrs. Arden parked herself in front of the ribbon rack and held a deep purple one against the back of her hand. "I said, that's ridiculous. Sacramento has always had a Swan's. Oh, of course, you don't have the selection that you once carried, but there is no finer or more knowledgeable staff than here."

"Thank you for that compliment. We hope to build the stock back up soon."

Mrs. Arden stepped across the aisle and ran her ring-covered fingers across a bolt of deep purple silk. "Now that the war's over, Mr. Arden says they will make more progress on the railroad. When the day comes that you can ride a train from Omaha to Sacramento, well, all the businesses will certainly boom."

"The prospect of a transcontinental railroad is exciting," Martina replied. *But I'm not sure I can stay in business until then.*

"And how is young Mr. Swan? Has he returned home from the Comstock?"

"Not yet, Mrs. Arden."

"Well, business must be brisk over there. How long has he been gone? Is it six months?"

"Over a year, Mrs. Arden."

"Someday I want to go over just to say I've been there. I hear it's quite . . . lively. I must ask Mr. Arden to take me. Do you like Nevada?"

"I've never been there. I've never been out of California."

"That is so marvelous," Mrs. Arden bubbled. "An adult woman who was actually born in the state."

"Actually when I was born, California was still a part of Mexico."

"That makes it even more romantic! The story of your mother and father's romance — it is so thrilling! Why, you should write a book about them."

Martina tried to smile. "Perhaps, someday. Right now I'm a little busy running a business and raising my baby."

"Oh, well, certainly. And young Mr. Swan

runs a business in Virginia City, I hear. I certainly admire a young couple who work so hard to succeed. It must be very gratifying for both of you."

I have no idea if it's gratifying to me, let alone to a husband I haven't seen in over a year. I don't even know if he's running a business . . . or merely running. "Yes, ma'am. Now how can I be of assistance today?"

"Well, dear, let's start with this bolt of purple silk . . . and . . ."

Purple silk.

White silk.

Pearl buttons.

Black velvet.

High-heeled shoes.

Hats from Brazil.

The list continued.

By the time Martina packaged the goods and accepted Mrs. Arden's bank draft for $325, it was well after 11:00 A.M. She stared down at the check. *Forty dollars each for Doraine and Evie, sixty to Winifred for severance. If baby and I can get by this month with thirty, that's over $150 for new inventory. That's not much but better than what I had an hour ago. Thank You, Lord . . . and Mrs. Arden.*

Martina sent Loop Hackett to help Mrs. Arden load her goods in the carriage. When he sauntered back into the store, she carried baby Christina on her hip.

"Mr. Hackett, you have been excellent in your

31

assistance this morning. Other than the fact that I couldn't afford to hire you, you would make a nice addition to our staff."

Hackett's grin was hesitant, embarrassed. "I'm not actually looking for employment. At least, not as a clerk."

"Mr. Hackett, do other women tease you incessantly? Or am I the only one?"

Hackett blushed. "Actually I seem to make a fairly easy target."

Martina took a deep breath and sighed. *I suppose I cannot postpone this any longer.* "Well, Mr. Hackett, just what do you need to talk to me about?"

He shoved his hat to the back of his head. "Have you heard from your husband lately?"

"Let's get to the point." Her brown eyes narrowed. "Just how much money does Billy owe you, Mr. Hackett?"

"No, no, that's not it," he explained. "I was wondering if you had seen him lately."

Even though the bright September sunlight burst through the windows, the store seemed dark and dull to Martina. "I don't believe it is any business of yours how often I see my husband."

Hackett took a step back. "No, ma'am, I don't reckon it is. I take it from the tone of that answer that you haven't heard from him in quite a spell."

She threw her shoulders back and raised her chin, bracing for an expected emotional assault.

"Is this conversation going anywhere, Mr. Hackett? I really do have a business to operate." Martina bounced baby Christina into a smile and a string of uninterpretable sounds.

"Miss Merced?" Evie interrupted, her small hands clutched tightly in front of her. "I'm sorry to intrude, but there's a gentleman who wants to pay in gold dust, and you know how I don't like to weigh it out. Such folk always intimidate me. I just know I'm going to sneeze or drop it or something!"

"Mr. Hackett, would you visit with Christina for a moment while I handle this matter?"

He looked straight at the grinning dark-haired clerk. "Eh, well, sure . . ."

"She's Evie," Martina clarified. "This is Christina." She handed the twenty-five-pound infant to the flustered man.

Martina and Evie scurried to the back of the store.

"You let him hold Christina?" Evie whispered.

"Keep an eye on him," Martina urged. "I just wanted to disarm him."

Evie Norman glanced back at the man who stood frozen in place with an inquisitive baby tugging at his suspenders. "He's not doing anything at all, Miss Merced. He reminds me of a man I dated once. And he certainly is not taking his gun off."

"Believe me," Martina flashed a quick, wide grin, "he's nearly defenseless."

It took only a couple of minutes to weigh out

33

the two ounces of gold dust and safely contain it in the cork-stoppered glass beaker. She swooped back across the store and plucked up Christina, to the obvious relief of Loop Hackett, who hadn't moved a muscle.

"You did very well, Mr. Hackett."

"She's a pretty baby."

"She's a beautiful, spoiled, little one-year-old angel. Now, Mr. Hackett, what is the purpose of our conversation?"

"I have a message I needed to bring to you."

Martina glanced out at the sidewalk on J Street. Two women peered through the window into the store. She didn't look back at him. "From whom?"

Loop Hackett cleared his throat. "From your husband."

As if she had jumped from a pier into the cold water of the San Francisco Bay, every muscle in Martina's body convulsed, then stiffened to ward off the sudden pain. Christina squirmed to get down, and Martina again began to bounce her on her hip.

"You know my husband?" The words fell out of her mouth like eggs dropping on a brick road.

"You are married to William Hays Swan, aren't you?"

"Junior."

"Yeah, that's him," Hackett said. "He told me to tell you —"

Martina stepped forward and leaned into Hackett's face. "Where did you see my husband?"

He leaned closer, their eyes only inches apart. "In Virginia City."

She grabbed hold of his arm. "When?"

Hackett freed himself, then stepped back, and glanced down at his boots. "See, here's the thing, Mrs. Swan — I regret to report that I haven't seen him since right after Christmas, but he gave me a message and I —"

She hugged Christina tight. "That was over nine months ago."

"Yes, ma'am. I got delayed."

"Let me get this straight. You were supposed to bring a message to me last Christmas, and you are just now arriving. Why bother with it now?" Martina tried to read his eyes. She discerned sorrow but not guilt.

He rubbed the back of his tanned thick neck. "Well, that's the very thing I've been debating all week."

"You've been in Sacramento a week?" she challenged.

He rocked back on his heels. It made him look even taller. "Eh, a month actually."

Martina began to storm in circles around Hackett. "You have a message from my husband. You've been here a month, and you just now decide to come see me?"

"Well, ma'am, here's my story." Hackett followed her path like a pup. "I crossed the Sierras last January, but that big blizzard dumped seven feet of snow in one day. I got lost and staggered into a cabin almost dead. A widow lady and her son nursed me to health through the winter."

"Mr. Hackett, I'm sorry for your misfortune, but that hardly explains —"

"Let me finish, Mrs. Swan." She caught the aroma of spiced shaving tonic. "I was ready to leave the mountains in late March, but the widow lady took sick . . ."

Martina stopped her pacing and looked at his imploring blue eyes. *I bet she did. She wasn't about to let a handsome man leave her cabin.* "So naturally you had to stay and doctor her?"

"Yes, ma'am. I didn't leave the mountains until August."

Martina noticed that his cheeks were a shade paler than his forehead, as if he had recently shaved off a full beard. "So did she become miraculously healed?"

He brushed the corners of his eyes with the back of his hand and looked away. "No, ma'am . . . she died."

Martina's heart sank. She bit her tongue. *Lord, forgive me for being a presumptuous, heartless cynic.* "Oh . . . I'm sorry. I'm truly sorry for my cavalier attitude," she muttered.

Hackett took a deep breath, then continued. "So when I finally got to town, I figured I was too late to deliver the message. I was too humiliated to show up."

Martina readjusted the baby on her hip. "And what made you change your mind?"

Hackett blushed. "That's even more embarrassing than being late." He stepped to the side of the aisle to allow two women to proceed toward the back of the store.

Martina watched the women size him up as they squeezed past. He was now standing right next to her.

"More embarrassing?" *You'd really be embarrassed if you knew what those two ladies are thinking.*

"Ma'am, don't take this wrong." He turned away and looked at the door. "I'm not good at talking like this, Mrs. Swan, especially to a married woman."

"Talking like what?" She released her gaze and let her eyes wander across the store. "You haven't said anything yet."

"Well, ma'am, here goes. I was at the bank a couple of weeks ago when you came in, and frankly, ma'am, you turned my head and troubled my mind."

Her head whipped back around to face him. "I did what?"

"You're a beautiful lady, ma'am. That's all I'm tryin' to say." He let out a deep sigh. "There, I said it. I'm sorry. Now at the time, I didn't know you were a married woman. Don't be judgin' me too harshly."

"Mr. Hackett, those are kind words, and I take no offense. Obviously, you've been isolated in the mountains too long. But what does all of this have to do with my husband?"

His hands hung straight down at his side and fidgeted with his denim pockets. "I asked the clerk at the bank who you were, and he said Mrs. Swan, so naturally I drove them thoughts from my mind."

Martina rubbed the bridge of her nose in order to cover her smile with her hand. *Just what were those thoughts, Mr. Loop Hackett?* "What did you learn about me from the clerk at the bank?"

"That they hadn't seen William Swan, Jr., in over a year and that you were trying to run the business by yourself."

"Not merely 'trying,' Mr. Hackett — I *am* running the business by myself."

"Yes, ma'am. That's what I meant. Anyway, when I heard that, I surmised that maybe you hadn't heard from your husband in a while."

"That was two weeks ago?" She tapped her finger on the spotless empty shelf next to her.

"Yes, ma'am."

"And you are just now coming to see me?"

"I was scared to death of having a mortifying conversation," he admitted.

Try as she did, Martina could not hide her smile. "Like the one we're now having?"

"Sort of," he said.

"Please tell me what the message was. It might be that it's something my husband hasn't told me." *Since I haven't heard from him in months, anything will be an improvement.*

"That's why I'm so flustered. He told me to tell you he needed $500 by the first of April. That's why I hesitated. The message is so outdated, it's useless, I suspect."

What — $500! You abandon your pregnant wife, never bother to come see your daughter, and you send for $500 we don't have? That is detestable, Mr. William Hays Swan, Jr. Hold your tongue, Martina Patricia. Don't say what you really feel. You are never allowed to say what you really feel. Cultured and controlled. It's the mark of Merced women. Yes, Mother. "I imagine the emergency is long past. Tell me, Mr. Hackett, do you happen to know why he gave you this message instead of writing me a letter, or better yet, coming home to make the arrangements?"

"All I know is, he figured I was coming to Sacramento and would reach you before the mail did."

"Well, I'm afraid he underestimated the post office . . . or overestimated you."

"Yes, ma'am. I reckon he did."

She rubbed her palms back and forth and then held her clutched hands to her chin. "Saying that I had the money, exactly what did he want me to do with it?" *Billy Swan, you do not get a penny until you come home!*

"I was to bring it back to him in Virginia City."

"How nice of you."

He tipped his head as if failing to hear the sarcastic tone. "Thank you, ma'am."

"Mr. Hackett, why in the world should I ever believe a story like that? Any drifter in California could come into this store with the same story and theoretically walk out of here with my $500, could they not?"

"Yes, ma'am, that's just what I said. I told him you'd need some proof that he sent me. And he told me I should just give you this." Hackett pulled a rawhide necklace out of his coat pocket. It had ten grizzly bear claws interspersed with ten silver beads.

Martina yanked the necklace out of his hand and clutched it to her chest. She could feel tears trickling down her cheeks. "Doraine," she cried out, "come take Christina for me."

The sandy-blonde clerk scurried toward her. "Are you all right, Miss Merced?"

"I believe I need some fresh air. Mr. Hackett and I are going for a short walk."

Doraine's eager arms surrounded the plump infant. "Yes, ma'am. Come on, little darlin', Aunt Doraine will teach you to sing a few ditties."

"Doraine!"

"Nothing but hymns, of course," the clerk laughed as she disappeared toward the back of the store with the baby.

Loop Hackett followed Martina out the front door and down the sidewalk. She rounded the corner of the two-story brick building and walked down the fairly narrow shaded alley. It wasn't until they reached the back of the building that she stopped to catch her breath. Finally, she sat down lightly on the edge of a discarded shipping crate and wiped the tears from her cheeks.

"I'm sorry for becoming so emotional, Mr.

Hackett. This necklace is very dear to me."

"I can see that. Forgive me for taking so long to get it to you. I didn't know it was so valuable."

"The value is strictly in sentiment. Over twenty years ago my father saved a young Indian girl's life by risking his own when he charged a large grizzly bear at old San Juan. The girl made him a necklace, which he divided and gave half back to her. He wore this half because he said it always reminded him of a day when he did the right thing, the thing the Lord wanted him to do, no matter what the outcome might have been.

"When I was twelve years old, my father gave me this necklace. He said he wanted it to remind me to always do the right thing, the thing the Lord wants me to do, no matter what the outcome. It was then, and still is, my most valued possession."

Hackett dragged his boot heel through the packed dirt of the alley and stared at the ground. "And you gave it to your husband?"

"When he left for a three-week trip to the Comstock last year, I sent it with him. It was to remind him to do the right thing. He promised to keep it with him at all times. If he gave it to you, he was obviously in great difficulty."

Although Martina sat in the shade, Hackett stood in the direct sunlight. He pulled his hat down to shade his eyes. "Do you mean you haven't heard from him since last summer?"

"I've received some correspondence. But I haven't heard from him since before Christmas.

41

Was he well? What was he doing? Where was he staying?" She stared straight into his soft blue eyes. "Why doesn't he come home to me and baby Christina?"

The words had hardly left her lips before she quickly covered her weeping eyes. *Control yourself, Doña Martina Patricia. You have held back the tears from your mother, your father, your brothers, your clerks, all of your friends — and now you are breaking down in front of an unknown drifter.* She looked up at Hackett. "I'm sorry," she mumbled. "I don't usually . . ." Then she broke out in sobs.

Loop Hackett stared down at his boots and rocked from one foot to the other. "I'm surely sorry, Mrs. Swan, to bring you such grief. I don't know what to say. I don't know what to do. If you were, you know, my sis, I'd, eh, just hug you till you were all cried out. But I know that isn't a proper thought since I'm not your brother and —"

"You could pretend," she whimpered.

His eyes widened. "What?"

"I have three brothers, none of whom are here right now." Martina stood and threw her arms around Hackett's neck. "Just pretend you're one of them," she repeated.

She felt his strong left arm circle her waist and his right hand pat her hair. "You just cry all you want, Mrs. Swan."

She did.

My brothers — Walter Tipton Merced, where are

42

you? Or Joseph, or Edward. Father — that's who I need. It's not just getting bucked off a horse, Daddy. It's like getting bucked off of life. My life. My family. My dreams. My husband. Why didn't you come back, Billy Swan?

Martina noticed that she had run out of tears, and she was still embracing a man she had never met until a few hours earlier. She pushed herself back.

"Please forgive me, Mr. Hackett. I'm sorry you had to see me in such a deplorable and inexcusable condition."

"No apologies, Mrs. Swan. My only regret is that I didn't make it through the snow in January. I realize my tardiness has added to your sorrow."

"Thank you for your kindness." She wiped her cheeks with the palms of her pale hands and then walked back toward the sidewalk and the front of the building. Loop Hackett trailed along behind in the ten-foot-wide alley. "I'm sure you didn't expect such an emotional response. Will you be going back to Virginia City?" she asked him.

"Yes. There seem to be more opportunities there than here. I plan on leaving next week," he said.

"I don't know if I have any money to send, but could you return in a couple of days?" They now strolled along side by side. "I might have something for you to take to my husband."

He ambled along with long, deliberate steps.

43

"Yes, ma'am. I can come back every day if you want me to."

Yes, please do! No, absolutely not! What am I thinking? Why am I thinking these things? "Give me a few days to consider how to respond to him." *Martina reviewed the contents of the safe and cash register. If I have another customer like Mrs. Arden, perhaps I could send something . . . but why $500, Billy Swan?*

Before they reached the street, a worried Doraine LaFlor appeared on the sidewalk. Her tumbling bangs drooped over one eye. "Miss Merced?" She stared at the two emerging from the shadows into the bright sunlight.

"What is it?" Martina quizzed.

"I hate to bother you, seeing you are so busy . . . walking. But Mr. Clayton is here, and he's brought Sheriff Anderson," Doraine fussed. "I didn't know what to do. I think they're going to arrest you or something. If we had a bouncer, we could just throw them out on their ear."

Arrest me? Clayton is going to have me arrested? Hah! You have no idea who you're up against, Mr. Banker. You aren't dealing with merely a Swan; you're dealing with a Merced.

"We'll see about that," Martina asserted. She turned back toward Loop. "Mr. Hackett, may I borrow your revolver? I left mine upstairs."

He unlatched the rawhide stay, pulled out the Remington army .45, and handed it to her, grip first. "You know how to use this type, Mrs. Swan?"

44

"I'm a child of Old California, Mr. Hackett. I can outride and outshoot any man in the valley, except for my father and Uncle Jack."

"Eh, yes, ma'am. Do you plan on shooting the sheriff?"

"Heavens no, but I can't guarantee the safety of Mr. Clayton," she threatened.

Doraine's eyes widened as the three returned to the front door of the store. "I haven't had this much excitement since New Year's Eve in Stockton."

Martina marched right over to the bank president and the lawman. Both gave a startled look at the gun in her hand. Loop Hackett and Doraine LaFlor scooted up beside her.

"Sheriff Anderson, I'm so glad you're here. I'd like for you to arrest Mr. Clayton," she demanded.

"What?" Clayton sputtered.

The gray-haired, gray-bearded lawman looked first at the bank president and then back at Martina. "Well, Mrs. Swan, don't that beat all? Clayton dragged me down here to arrest you."

"Oh." Her dark eyebrows raised. "For what reason?"

"Unpaid loan," Clayton groused. "You know that. I've been as patient as a man can be. This store is legally closed. The dispersal of assets cannot continue."

Martina turned and addressed the startled Miss LaFlor. "Doraine, would you go get Mrs. Arden's bank draft for me?"

The apron-clad clerk scurried to the back of the store.

"Mr. Clayton, I wish to make a $325 payment on my account. I'm sure you will accept a draft from Mrs. Arden."

"Only $325? You owe the bank over $6,000, and you know it. The day for payments is over. Sheriff, I insist you evict these people and padlock this building. This business and its contents belong to the Delta State Bank."

She waved the gun at the bank president as if it were a stick. "What I'm asking for is a sixty-day extension. I'm paying you over $300 for such a delay. I believe that's fair. Isn't it, Sheriff?"

Doraine returned and handed her the Arden bank draft.

"Mrs. Swan," implored Sheriff Anderson, "it's a little difficult to talk business with a revolver bouncing in your hand. Put it away and let's talk this through."

"Certainly not," she huffed. "I will not go disarmed with the likes of Landel Clayton standing right there."

"What do you mean by that?" Clayton roared.

"I am left with no alternative," she said. "Sheriff, I wish to press charges against Mr. Landel Clayton."

"What are the charges?" the lawman demanded.

Her brown eyes narrowed. There was no hint of humor in her voice. "Illegal imprisonment and enslavement of a woman and infant child."

46

"What?" Clayton shouted. "That's preposterous!"

"Last night Mr. Clayton and/or his agents imprisoned me and my one-year-old daughter in this building. I have no idea what heinous schemes he had planned for me or my daughter, but I had to shoot my way out."

"You did what?" Clayton gasped. "That's outlandish!"

"My daughter and I were asleep in our upstairs apartment when our doors were secured with heavy chains on the outside. We had absolutely no way to escape. We were imprisoned in our own home. Fortunately there was no fire, or we would have burned to death. The only way we could get out of the building was to shoot the chain. Mr. Hackett and Miss LaFlor can testify on my behalf."

The sheriff turned to Hackett. "Is that true?"

There was a sly grin in Loop's reply. "Yep. Both doors were secured by heavy chains. No one could enter or leave. Mrs. Swan and the baby were trapped inside." He nodded his head and stuck his thumbs into his suspenders. "It was a clear instance of imprisonment, all right."

"And I saw it all too," Doraine added. "It reminded me of the time Poco Renaldi chained Consuela to the piano . . . sort of."

"It is my legal right to impound the building and its contents and sell it at auction," Clayton fumed.

Hackett rocked on the heels of his spurless

boots. "Is it your legal right to chain women and children inside the building?"

"That was an accident. I had no knowledge that she was in the building. I'll gladly apologize for that. But it does not change the situation!"

"Sheriff Anderson, please arrest this man." She waved the revolver at the banker. "I wish to fill out formal charges."

"This is an outrage," Clayton screamed. "I did not imprison you."

"We will let a jury settle this," Martina insisted. "What do you think, Sheriff? Will a jury have sympathy for a mother and a baby?"

Sheriff Anderson turned to Landel Clayton. "There ain't a jury in this city that would rule in the bank's favor, Clayton. You can't go around locking women and babies in buildings nor tossin' them out into the street, no matter how much money they owe you. People won't stand for that. Not in this town. Not in any town."

"Good heavens, Sheriff, you can't let her hoodwink you!" Clayton fumed.

"Please remove this man from my store, Sheriff. He's disturbing my customers."

"Your store? You've lost this store to the bank!" Clayton insisted.

Sheriff Anderson leaned close to Martina. "Mrs. Swan, by any chance would you drop these charges if Mr. Clayton agreed to that sixty-day extension?"

"Oh . . . what a marvelous idea, Sheriff! I do believe in forgiving a man and allowing him to show the grace of God at work in his life."

"That's blackmail!" Clayton huffed as she handed him Mrs. Arden's bank note.

"Sheriff, how can it be blackmail when Mr. Clayton makes over $300? I thought a blackmailer extorted money from others, not gave it away."

"She's right, Landel," the sheriff concurred. "It ain't blackmail. Now are you agreeing to this extension?"

"What kind of law enforcement is this?" the bank manager barked.

"Do you agree or not?"

"I agree," he mumbled, "under protest and duress."

"And will you, Mrs. Swan, drop all charges?" the sheriff pressed.

"Certainly not!"

"What?" he gasped.

"I will drop charges only in sixty days. In the meantime, I do not want Mr. Clayton or any of his compatriots to come on these premises or be seen on this sidewalk for sixty days. Then, and only then, will I drop these charges. I'm not about to have my baby and myself enslaved again."

"That's laughable!" Clayton fumed. "She has no grounds to —"

"Arrest him, Sheriff," Loop Hackett put in. "I'll sign the statement of false imprisonment myself."

"Wait!" Clayton mumbled. "I can certainly

49

wait awhile to take over this prime corner location."

"Thank you, Mr. Clayton." Martina nodded and then handed the revolver, grip first, back to Hackett. "Now if you gentlemen will excuse me, I have a store to run and a baby to feed."

Martina checked on Christina, now sleeping in a playpen behind the store counter, and then counted the change in the cash register. *That Arden money would have caught me up on salaries and purchased our groceries. Mr. Clayton, I do not appreciate your taking food out of my baby's mouth!*

But he is right. I do owe him the money. At least, the store owes him money.

Send you $500, Billy? It was so nice of you to run up a debt on your way out of town. You know for a fact that I don't have that kind of money. That's why you went off to Nevada, remember? You said you'd go get more financing, open a new store. Whatever happened to those dreams?

Whatever happened to you?

There was commotion at the front of the store as several well-dressed, laughing men and women fluttered into Wm. Swan & Son. Martina caught the flashing smile and wavy amber hair of the woman in the center. Martina glanced down at the little sleeping redhead in the playpen and then breezed across the store into the crowd and right up to the woman.

"Mother! What brings you to Sacramento?" Martina called out.

Alena Louise Tipton Merced flashed a smile that had won her the name Red Dove of Monterey. "Oh, my darling Martina, you look tired. Those eyes are so red. Have you gotten enough rest? Your Uncle Jack and Maria Alexandra were coming to town, and I decided to ride along. Are you eating right? You must come to the ranch and let Piedra fatten you up. Now where is the most beautiful baby in Sacramento?" She looked around at the crowd of well-wishers. "Did I say Sacramento? Why, she's the most beautiful baby ever born in California!"

Martina felt her mother's arm slip into hers as she whisked her way to the back of the store. *I was born in California too. Remember me?*

"Oh, there's *mi dulcita*," Alena cooed as she reached in and scooped up the sleeping baby. "I think I will have to call you La Palomita Roja de Sacramento." With startled round, wide eyes Christina stared at her grandmother. "And when you are old enough, I will teach you to dance the fandango!"

Three

"Darling," Alena Merced purred as she waltzed down the store aisle, Christina in her arms, "we are all going to meet at the Grand Hotel for lunch. Have you been there since they brought in that new chef from Del Monico's?"

I have never been there, dear Mother. "No, but I'm sure it's wonderful. I can't leave the store, Mother. Mr. Chambers quit today, and I need to keep an eye on things."

Mrs. Merced's thick, wavy auburn hair kept its proper place even as she whipped her head around. "Winifred quit? He's such a dear man, always so helpful to me. He's been at Swan's for years."

All men are helpful to you, dear Mother. "Yes, well . . ." Martina bit her lip and paused. "I think Winifred found a job closer to family in Grass Valley." *I can't tell her about being chained inside the store. I will not let my parents see me fail. I will not let anyone see me fail.*

Mrs. Merced jiggled Christina on her hip and ran her hand across a bolt of forest-green velvet. "Isn't this pretty, little darling? Can you say, 'pretty'?"

The auburn-haired infant smiled widely at the

auburn-haired grandmother. "Me!" she giggled.

"Yes, you are pretty!" Alena turned to her daughter. "Now, Marti, can I help with anything in the store? I'll be in town all day. How would you like to have an old lady clerk?"

Mother dear, no one on earth has ever called you old. You are forty-three and look young enough to be my sister. Why, you don't even have one gray hair — a fact I must ask you about when I get the nerve. "Mother, you go on and enjoy your lunch. I know you haven't been to town much this month." Martina scooted a step back from her mother. *I always feel so plain and ugly standing next to her.*

"I've got a splendid idea." Mrs. Merced's green eyes sparkled. "You go to lunch at the Grand, and I'll stay here and baby-sit! Christina and I have a lot to talk about." She wrinkled her nose at the baby. "Did I ever tell you about the time your grandpa stopped a grizzly bear in his tracks with only a revolver and a lot of courage?"

"I believe she's heard that one a dozen times," Martina replied, "from me."

Martina relieved her mother of a now-squirming one-year-old. "Thanks for offering, Mother, but really I can't leave. Besides, Christina will need to be fed, and that's a job only a mother can do."

Mrs. Merced reached out and laid her hand on Martina's arm. "Yes, but she doesn't need to be fed all the time. You've got to step back from the store. It's wearing you out, darling. Look at you.

Surely you could break away for . . ."

Martina glanced down at her mother's perfectly smooth hand and long, straight fingers. *Mother, please don't tell me again how poorly I look.* "I'm really committed to the store. I've got to do the best management job possible."

"I know you are, honey. Your daddy and I are extremely proud of all you have accomplished here. We had no idea you had such business skill."

Martina glanced around at the store. *Will you be proud if I go bankrupt and am kicked out into the street?* "It is not exactly a field of my choosing."

Alena forced Martina to look her in the eye. "Yes, but it is where the Lord has placed you."

Martina caught a whiff of her mother's camellia perfume. *Or the place where He's abandoned me.* "You and Daddy taught me to work hard. That's what I'm trying to do."

"I know." Alena's long, thick eyelashes seemed to punctuate every word. "You should hear the way Daddy brags on you all the time."

Dear, sweet Daddy would brag on his little girl even if I were lying in a foot of mud. For him, all Merced women are beautiful and perfect. "Some days I miss Rancho Alazan," Martina admitted. When she realized her mother was again staring deep into her eyes, she glanced down.

Alena stepped closer. "Marti, is everything all right?" It was spoken in what Martina called her mother's tuck-me-in-on-a-stormy-night voice.

Does it show that much? Martina ran her fingers

through her bangs, brushing them out of her eyes, and then patted her mother's arm. "Oh, Mother . . . it's just with Mr. Chambers quitting, I'm trying to figure out the staffing. Then I need to order more inventory and balance accounts, and deal with . . ."

Alena stepped close and brushed a kiss across her daughter's ear and whispered, "I asked, is everything all right?"

Martina sucked in a deep breath, lifted her chin, and threw her shoulders back. "Mother, everything is fine. I just have to work. You and Father worked long, hard hours to build up the ranch. I know that. I watched you every day when I was young. Well, now it's my turn. Swan's is my 'ranch.' "

Alena slipped her arm around her daughter's waist and squeezed. "Well, I do wish you would take a little time off and come up to see us. Your daddy and I miss you terribly. As do your brothers. Did I tell you Edward has a new girlfriend?"

There was a twinge of sadness in Martina's heart when her mother withdrew her hand. "Oh, who is the lucky girl this week?" Martina managed a very small smile.

Sweeping auburn eyebrows punctuated the reply. "Angela Miller."

Martina's eyes widened. "The Angela Miller whose daddy owns most of the San Joaquin Valley?"

Mrs. Merced laughed. "Well, I don't think Mr. Miller's holdings are that vast . . . yet. She seems like a delightful young lady. She hasn't let that wealth go to her head. Just the other day she was out in the blacksmith's shop helping Edward."

Helping Eddie with what? It's a cinch she wasn't pounding horseshoes. "Do you think they're serious?"

"Oh, you know your little brother." Mrs. Merced shrugged. "When was Edward ever serious about anything?"

"Angela Miller might be a good time to begin," Martina reflected.

"That's what I tried to tell him. But Edward doesn't listen to Daddy or me very much anymore. Perhaps big sister ought to talk to him. Your brothers respect your word as much as mine. Why don't you come up to the ranch and . . ."

Why don't I just chuck it all and go home? You'll never know how many times I've thought about it. "Mother, I really can't —"

"Well, when Billy comes back from Nevada, you'll be able to break away more often. We're having a twenty-first birthday party for Walt in a couple of weeks. If Billy's home by then, you come up for the celebration."

Mother, I will not let you squeeze information from me. I'm not about to admit to my perfect mother that I don't know when or if my husband will return. "I just have to wait and see."

Doraine LaFlor scooted up the aisle toward them. "Miss Merced, may I go to lunch now?" Her bangs flopped down across her eyes.

"Certainly, Doraine."

The clerk began to untie her crisp white apron. "You won't be shorthanded, will you?"

"Evie and I will get along fine. I'll have her stay until you return."

Doraine slowly folded the apron. "When are you going to eat?"

"Oh, I'll slip upstairs as soon as I get a chance." She held the baby out in front of her. "I do believe this young lady needs to be changed."

Mrs. Merced held out her hands. "Let me go change her."

Martina pulled the baby back to herself. "No. I'm not going to send you to the Grand Hotel smelling like a dirty diaper. Now go on, Mother; go have your lunch."

Mrs. Merced hugged her daughter's shoulders. "I wish you were going with me."

I really, really wish I were too, Mother. "Perhaps next time you are in town."

Mrs. Merced glanced over at the departing Doraine LaFlor and then back at her daughter. "Young lady, I believe that's what you told me last time."

"I promise . . . one of these days I'll just show up at your front door." *With my daughter and all my belongings.*

"That would be delightful!" Alena swooshed over by Martina and bent low to the baby on her daughter's hip. She kissed the giggling round-cheeked baby.

"Palomita, you are a living doll! Your

grandma looks old and dull next to you."

"Mother, you have never looked old and dull in your entire life."

"Well," Alena beamed as she sauntered toward the front door, "I have certainly at times felt old and dull."

That, my dear mother, is how I feel almost every day of the year.

Evie Norman meandered up next to Martina. "Your mother is so beautiful. I would love to look that nice when I'm her age."

"I would love to look that nice at any age," Martina mumbled.

By 2:00 P.M. Christina was sound asleep, and the store was nearly void of customers. Martina finished a quick lunch of white cheese, stale crackers, and a cup of tea. She carried a small yellow apple in her pocket as she started down the stairs. The store felt stuffy and warm. September in Sacramento was not her favorite season. At the moment she couldn't think of any season that was a favorite.

Nothing can compare to springtime at Rancho Alazan. Riding horseback in the rolling green hills, a picnic lunch under the oak trees. She pulled out the apple and took a small crisp bite. *I do believe your lunch, dear Mother, was better than mine. But then your life is better than mine. Lord, I must be very tired. When I get tired, I get cranky and complain. I know that. My mother always told me it was so. But I am not criticizing her good fortune, just bemoaning*

*my misfortune. Straighten up, Martina Patricia —
self-pity does not look good on you. My father always tells me that.*

He is right.

Doraine LaFlor met her at the bottom of the
stairs. "Is our baby sleeping?"

"Yes, she's clutching the wooden horse her
Uncle Joey carved for her." Martina took another bite of apple. "Not many customers this
afternoon."

"Well, there's an impatient peddler here to see
you." Doraine nodded toward the front door.

Martina scanned the room. "A salesman?"

"No, a peddler with a wagon full of goods,"
Doraine said. "He's one of those types that when
I was at the dance hall, I always hoped would
dance with some other girl — if you know what I
mean."

The man with the dusty dark suit and black tie
stood anxiously by the front door of the store.
He kept glancing out at the street as if he were
expecting someone or something. He looked like
it had been a couple of days since he'd shaved
and a couple of weeks since he'd bathed. He was
slightly taller than Martina's five-foot-five.

"May I help you, Mr. —," she asked.

"Earl P. Touchet. But you can call me Burro.
Ever'one else does," he announced in a throaty
voice that revealed years of cheap whiskey damage.

Martina stepped away from the door, hoping
the peddler would follow her lead. "Mr.

59

Touchet, what can I do for you?"

He peeked out the front door and stood his ground. "Are you really Mrs. Swan?"

"Yes."

"Mrs. William Swan?" His deep-set dark eyes examined her as if sizing up the conformation of a horse.

"I'm Mrs. William Swan, Jr."

"Junior? Oh, that explains it." He glanced back out the open doorway into the street.

"Are you expecting someone?" she pressed.

"No!" he blurted out, his gaze slashing at the stale air in the store. "Are you?"

"Only customers," she said. "Perhaps we could step away from the door."

"Why?" His word was hurled like a rock.

"Just to let folks in." She stepped back, and he reluctantly followed. "What can I do for you?"

"I was hopin' to talk to Mr. Swan . . . Senior. But that girl with the purdy blue eyes and tickle in her voice said Mr. Swan done up and died over a year ago."

I've never noticed Evie's eyes or the tickle in her voice. "Yes, that's true. My husband and I own the store now. But he's, eh, out of town. So how can I help you?"

"Well, ma'am, I've got a wagon chucked full of goods I think you'll be interested in." He pointed toward the street.

I can't imagine your quality being up to Swan standards, but even if they were, I have no funds to buy anything. "Thank you for thinking of us, Mr.

60

Touchet. However, we are not buying inventory at this time," she announced.

"Buying?" he blustered. "I ain't goin' to sell you nothin'."

Martina folded her arms in front of her. "Then I'm afraid I don't understand what you're talking about."

"Well, here's the deal," he mumbled as he shifted weight from one foot to the other. "And I'll talk fast because I've got a steamboat to catch. I'm goin' to San Francisco tonight. San Francisco. Got me a hotel room right there on Market Street. A fine hotel room. In San Francisco!" He emphasized each word as if to impress Martina and stretched his neck toward the doorway as he glanced up and down J Street.

"Are you going by yourself?" she quizzed.

He stepped toward the door and waved his arm. "Did you see someone out there?" he demanded.

"No. Perhaps you should try to relax," she said.

"Hah!" he exploded, then dropped his arms to his sides. "Five years ago Mr. Swan, Sr., outfitted me with a wagon full of goods and sent me to the northern mines. I was supposed to come back down the following spring and settle up accounts. But one thing led to another, and I stayed up there in Plumas County. Now I want to settle my account."

Lord, have You provided me a deliverer? A ner-

vous, obnoxious-smelling deliverer? "Just how much money do you owe Swan's?" Martina pressed.

He pulled off his floppy hat and rolled the brim in his hands. "Eh, $500. But I don't got it."

"That's the story of my life." Martina rubbed the bridge of her nose and then glanced down at Touchet's battered brown boots. "How much do you have?"

"Mrs. Swan, I've got you a bargain of a deal."

"How much do I get, Mr. Touchet?" she demanded.

"Oh, you get your full due and more. Yes, ma'am. Ol' Burro Touchet keeps his pledges. I've got a wagon full of goods, and everything is yours, and it's worth a whole bunch more than $500. Plus you get the wagon and two mules."

Martina tried to peek through the window at the rig parked in the street. "A wagon?"

"And two mules. Them mules ain't a year over twelve. Don't let no one tell you different. They just got bad teeth from eatin' sugar, that's all," he insisted.

Martina surveyed the half-empty shelves in the store. "What kind of inventory do you have in the wagon?"

"Dry goods, yardage, clothing, and stuff. When Pit River diggin's dried up, I bought out a whole store for twenty cents on the dollar. And you get it all. I figured it was fair." Touchet stepped toward the door, his right hand resting on the buckhorn handle of a huge hunting knife sheathed in his belt. "I got to be goin', ma'am.

62

I'm headed for San Francisco. San Francisco!" His voice was embarrassingly loud. He whipped around and stuck his hand straight out toward her.

She reached out to shake it. He had a strong, slightly grimy grip.

"Now we is all square. Yes, ma'am. Burro Touchet pays his debts. You remember that in case they are ever lookin' for someone to say kind words over me."

Say words over you? Like at a grave? Martina followed him to the door and fought the urge to grab a towel and wipe off her hands. "Are you in trouble, Mr. Touchet?"

He spun around with a wild look in his eyes. "Who told you that?"

"It seems obvious." Martina folded her arms across her chest. "Is someone going to come looking for the contents of that wagon claiming they are stolen?"

"No, ma'am. It belongs to me fair and square."

"Then may I have a receipt and a bill of trade for the wagon and mules?" she insisted.

He dug in his vest pocket and yanked out several tightly folded papers. "I'm ahead of you on that. I got 'em signed right here." He shoved them into her hands. "What's the quickest way to the Embarcadero? I'm goin' by steamboat to San Francisco."

She pointed down the street. "Straight down J Street."

"Will the alley get me there?" he questioned.

"Yes, I suppose so."

"Ma'am, I reckon I could have overlooked some personals in the wagon. If you find any, stick them in a crate, and I'll pick them up when I get back from San Francisco. Provided I live that long." He tipped his broad-brimmed hat and scurried out the door.

"Good luck, Mr. Touchet."

"I'm goin' to need a whole lot more than luck, ma'am."

Martina watched him cut around the building and head for the back alley. She was still standing there when Doraine LaFlor meandered up beside her. "What did that nervous little man want?"

"To give us that." Martina pointed toward the street.

Doraine shaded her eyes with her hand. "What? The wagon?"

"The wagon, the mules, and the contents. Said he owed it to Mr. Swan, Sr., and was repaying an old loan."

Doraine wrinkled her nose, which accented the crow's feet around her brown eyes. "What's in the wagon?"

Martina walked out to the sidewalk. "I don't know. He said it was new dry goods."

Doraine followed her. "Those mules look fifty years old."

Martina laughed. "Maybe they're just tired like the rest of us. Looks like they've been pushed hard." The bright September California sun felt good on her pale face. *Mother's right. I've been in the store way too long. Of course, Mother's always right.* Martina stepped up and rubbed the lead mule's neck. "Doraine, why don't you drive the wagon around the block and down the alley to the back door. We'll investigate the goods and give these mules a little water and shade."

Doraine's eyes grew wide. "I can't drive a rig like this."

"There's nothing to it," Martina assured her. "You just —"

Doraine emphatically shook her head. "Really, Miss Merced, I can't. Don't make me do it. I'll wreck it for sure. I once wrecked a judge's carriage. I can't ever go back to San Francisco, or he'll have me arrested. I swore I'd never drive another rig."

"I was racing the grub wagon to town with Uncle Jack and Piedra when I was five. I'll drive it. You keep an ear open for Christina. She should have a good nap after her busy night."

Doraine's eyes relaxed, and she looked much younger than thirty. "Evie's right. You can do everything, Miss Merced."

Martina approached the worn freight wagon with high wooden sides and dusty canvas top. *Everything except keep my husband home.* The mules were motionless except for their tails. Both were still fairly lathered.

"You two been doing a little racing, have

65

you?" She pulled herself up into the seat of the wagon and unleashed the reins. She released the hand brake.

It's a good thing they are lathered. If they were in high spirits, and if Christina were in the seat beside me, I just might drive out of town and keep going.

She slapped the reins on the lead mule's rump. "Come on, mule. Giddiup, you two!" she roared.

The tired mules dutifully moved out into the street behind a shrouded ornate carriage pulled by two high-stepping Andalusian stallions.

Of course, I'm not sure where I would go. I'd be welcome at Rancho Alazan, but I'm not going home a failure in business and a failure in . . . Perhaps I should take the Dutch Flat Toll Road to Virginia City. I certainly could peddle these goods for enough to pay board and lodging for a while. At least I would know what happened to Billy.

But I won't do it, Lord. If he doesn't love me and the baby enough to come home, I'm not going to beg him to return. It's not right. I shouldn't have to beg. No woman should have to beg her husband to come home.

Martina turned the rig right on 6th Street. The mules plodded slowly.

You boys deserve to take it easy. That's okay. We'll get there soon enough. Monterey! That's where I'd go. I'd go visit Grandmother Cabrillo. She always asks me to come for a season, and she is all alone. She would enjoy my company. We could sit on the veranda as we did when I was a little girl, and she could tell me all about the Californios . . . and the war. That was before the gold rush. Before Sacramento. Before William Hays Swan, Jr. Grandmother Cabrillo, how I wish all the men were still honorable!

Lord, that's unfair. Perhaps something's happened to Billy. If this were happening to someone else, I could almost laugh. A young girl wants to prove she can make it without her parents' help, so she thinks she's marrying into a prominent Sacramento business family. And a young man in a failing family business marries into a legendary old California family, hoping the connection will be good for business. Perhaps, Billy Swan, we both got what we deserved. That, Lord, is a very depressing thought.

Gunfire rang out just as she turned the rig into the alley. "Whoa, mules," she shouted. "Settle down!" She could hear approaching horses thunder down the cobblestone street. Bullets buzzed several feet above her head.

They're shooting at me?

The now-panicked mules reared up, kicking at the wind. Martina lashed the reins on the brake handle and leaped from the wagon seat to the alley. She sprinted to the animals' heads and caught a harness in each hand when they lowered their heads. When they reared back up, they lifted her off her feet.

But when they came back down, they stayed down. She let her full weight hang from the harnesses. Three hard-looking men, guns in hand, reined up beside the wagon and leaped to the street.

"Where is he?" the tallest one shouted, waving his revolver.

Martina kept her grip on the mules' rigging, knowing any relaxation might cause them to bolt and run right over the top of her. "Mister," she hollered, "as soon as this team settles down, I intend to have all three of you arrested for attempted murder!"

"We didn't know you was a woman," the man with the foot-long black beard growled.

"Save your explanations for a judge," she yelled.

"Where's Burro? We aim to hang him!" the third man demanded. All three holstered their revolvers.

"I have no idea. He owed me money and paid me off with this wagon full of dry goods. Don't tell me he stole yardage and dresses from you."

"Dresses? Do we look like we want dry goods? Burro's got somethin' of ours, all right. But it sure ain't dresses and ribbons," the original spokesman insisted.

"I never met the man before a few minutes ago. I don't know where he is now," she shouted.

"And I say you're a liar!" the tallest man snarled as he stepped around the mules toward Martina.

Quickly and almost silently, a man stepped out of the shadows of the alley behind her. She had not even heard him approach. With his left hand clutching the gunman's shirt collar, he yanked the man to his knees as he drew his revolver and shoved it into the gunman's neck.

"Mr. Hackett!" Martina called out.

Loop Hackett stared down at the kneeling man. "Mister, you shot at this lady and made threatening remarks. That's a crime in this town!" Hackett boomed. "Now you other two lay those revolvers in the street and step back away from them, because I surely will plug this old boy if you don't."

The two gunmen bellyached but followed his instructions.

"You two in partnership with Burro Touchet?" one of them grumbled.

"I don't even know the man," Hackett informed him. "You can go hang him for all I care. But not until after we go talk to the judge."

"I ain't goin' to no judge," the man on his knees fumed.

"Mister, you can have your pick right now — a judge in Sacramento or the judgment of the Lord Almighty. Which is it goin' to be?"

"You can't shoot me!" the man cried.

"You were trying to murder Mrs. William Swan, one of Sacramento's leading ladies."

Martina could feel the mules and herself begin to relax. *Leading ladies? Don't push it, Mr. Hackett. Most people in this town don't even know I exist.*

"We didn't know that. We thought she was a man," one of the gunmen insisted.

"Are you willing to tell a judge that you

69

couldn't tell whether Mrs. Swan was male or female? They'll lock you up at the sanatorium in Stockton."

"Look . . . we made a mistake. . . . We're sorry," the kneeling man apologized.

"Mrs. Swan, how long before a lawman will show up?" Hackett quizzed.

Still holding the prancing mules, she called out, "I'd say any time now, Mr. Hackett."

He shoved the gun barrel hard against the man's temple. "Of course, if these three were to apologize to you, I suppose you could postpone filing the complaint."

"I was thinking the same thing," she called out.

"We're sorry," the kneeling man muttered.

"I didn't hear that too well," Hackett insisted. "Did you hear that, Mrs. Swan?" he shouted.

"Hear what, Mr. Hackett?"

"You see, partner," Hackett chided. "You've got to do better than that."

"I'm sorry," the man called out.

"For what?" Martina released the headstalls and began to stroke each mule's neck.

"I'm sorry for shooting at you by mistake. We was aiming over your head."

"And tell her you are sorry that you're so dumb you couldn't tell a fine-looking lady from a man!" Hackett didn't loosen his grip.

"I'm sorry I mistook you for Burro. It was a grievous error," the man admitted.

"A grievous error!" she hollered back. "I like

that. You can let him go, Mr. Hackett."

"Not until those other two apologize," he insisted.

"We're sorry," one groused.

"I didn't hear from both of you," Hackett persisted.

"I'm sorry for shootin' at you, ma'am." The one with the long beard tipped his hat.

"I accept your apology." Martina kept herself mostly hidden by the team of mules. "However, I suggest you hurry out of town, because if the sheriff catches you around here, I will have to tell him the truth."

All three men holstered their weapons, then mounted, and rode south.

"Mr. Hackett, I appreciate your help," Martina called out, "but I could have taken care of things myself."

"Yes, ma'am, I have no doubt of that. But I was riled at them. That's no way to treat any woman — even by mistake."

Hackett drove the wagon down the alley to the back door of the store where Doraine LaFlor and Evie Norman stood.

"What was that gunfire?" Doraine quizzed.

Hackett swung down off the wagon and reached up to help Martina. "Mrs. Swan was teachin' three ol' boys some manners."

"Doraine," Martina instructed, "you watch the store and listen for Christina to wake up. Evie and I will start to unload."

"You'll do nothin' of the kind," Hackett insisted. "I'll do the liftin'."

Martina rested her hands on her hips. "Mr. Hackett, your chivalry is commendable; however, this is my store, and we are quite capable of handling shipments and inventory."

"Mrs. Swan, I am sure there is nothing you can't do better without me. You have made that abundantly clear. But for some reason, I'm standin' here now, and I don't have it in my bones to allow women to do hard labor while I watch."

Martina glanced over at Doraine and Evie. They waited for her response. "If you put it that way, I'll allow you to unload the wagon, just so you won't have to spend the rest of the day feeling guilty."

"Good." There was an infectious grin on Hackett's smooth-shaven face. "Now where do you want me to pack it?"

Martina shook her head. *Lord, I don't think I've ever known a man I could get used to having around quite as rapidly as this one.* "Well, Mr. Hackett, since every bundle will be a complete surprise, stack it against the wall in the southwest corner of the store. We'll sort it from there. There must be something we can sell amongst all these bundles."

Four

When Martina was twelve, her parents had given her a surprise birthday party. There were twelve presents waiting for her, each one housed in the same size box and wrapped in brown paper. It was the most exciting birthday of her life.

She was beginning to feel the same excitement as she and Evie investigated the contents of Touchet's wagon.

They discovered bolts of bright-colored cotton cloth, Hudson Bay Company five-point blankets, ready-made children's clothes, buttons and beads, long underwear, stockings, dishcloths, and diapers. There was even a crate of French undergarments.

"We are not selling those," Martina laughed.

"What exactly are they?" Evie blushed as she turned the sheer garment upside down and held it out in front of her. "Is this the way it goes?"

Martina could feel the tension in her neck begin to relax for the first time in days. "I have no idea, but we aren't selling them, whatever they are! There is no moral reason for a woman ever to wear one of those." *Unless she was trying to keep her husband home.*

Sweat rolled off Loop Hackett's forehead as

he carried a wooden barrel over his shoulder. "You won't guess what's in here," he called out as Evie quickly shoved the French silk out of sight.

"Is it embarrassing?" Martina laughed.

"Embarrassing?" Hackett questioned.

"I was teasing you, Mr. Hackett."

"Why? Did you two find something embarrassing?"

"We certainly wouldn't tell you if we did." Martina tried to suppress the grin. "Now what's in the keg?"

"Black powder," he replied.

She unfastened her cuffs and shoved her sleeves up on her forearm. "Not exactly what I would call dry goods."

"Well, it's dry powder." Hackett showed clean teeth when he smiled.

Martina circled around Loop Hackett, gazing at the small wooden keg on his shoulder. "Mr. Touchet bought out a store in the north. It was probably mixed in with the goods, and he didn't know it."

"It's hard to miss a keg of powder."

"That depends upon how close to the keg of whiskey you've been standing," she said.

"You want this in the same place as the rest?" Loop quizzed as he stood next to the stacks of freight.

"I would prefer not to have black powder in the store, especially with Mr. Clayton on the warpath to repossess this building." She stopped her circling and parked herself directly in front of him. "Mr. Hackett, I would like you to keep the powder for your pay for unloading our wagon."

With his free hand he shoved his hat to the back of his head. "I don't want any pay, Mrs. Swan."

She laced her fingers together in front of her waist and batted her eyes. "I'm sure you don't. But I don't have it in my bones, Mr. Hackett, to have people work for me and not pay them their worth. You would be doing me a favor if you would accept it." *I can't believe I'm acting this way!*

Hackett set the keg at his feet, wiped his brow, and grinned. "Well, now, if you put it that way, Mrs. Swan, I'll take it off your hands so you don't go through the day with miserable bones."

Martina strolled alongside him toward the open back door. She smelled his leather vest and sweat. She laid her hand on his arm. "Besides, I have one more favor to ask of you."

Hackett placed his hand on hers. "What's that?"

She pulled back and pointed toward the mules. "Would you take the team and wagon to Mr. Brownsford's livery?"

Hackett wiped his callused hand across his forehead. "You want me to sell them for you?"

Doraine strolled close enough to hear the conversation. Martina thought it was perhaps too close. "No, I want you to board them."

Martina's voice was now loud enough for even the hip-swinging clerk to hear. "I just might like owning a rig even if the mules are old."

Hackett's eyes followed Doraine across the floor, but his words were addressed to Martina. "You plannin' on goin' somewhere?"

You certainly have a roving eye, Mr. Hackett. Not that it matters to me. You seem to like Doraine's strong perfume. Perhaps I should . . . Straighten up, Martina Patricia. "No, but I might save some money picking up my goods from the Embarcadero instead of having them freighted. It just seems like Swan's should have a rig. My husband took our carriage to Nevada, so I've had to rent."

He shoved his hat back. "I'll run those mules over to the livery right now."

"You are a real gentleman." She curtsied.

"Now you don't know me well enough to go guessin' on my character." Hackett's hat was cocked to one side. It gave his eyes a teasing look. "Why, I might be such a scoundrel that I just ride off with your team and don't come back."

"Then you would be a dolt as well as a scoundrel." She reached over and gripped his arm above the elbow. "No one with any brains would steal two broken-down mules." She quickly dropped her hand. *What am I doing? Has it been that long since I touched a man? That's no excuse.*

Hackett laughed as he exited the back door and crawled up on the rig. "You're right about that, Mrs. Swan," he shouted back. "I'll see you later." He tipped his hat as the team rolled on down the alley.

Martina closed the back door and then surveyed the goods at her feet. *I wonder if those mules could make it all the way to Nevada? Perhaps I'm the one who needs to make a trip.*

"Miss Merced," Evie called out, "I can't believe that all this inventory just walked into the store out of the blue. It's almost like a miracle. I mean, look at this lace. I had three ladies ask for this just last week. And the paramatta and the crepe and the cashmere and the French merino wool, not to mention the French —"

"Please don't!" Martina grinned. She began unwrapping a package she supposed was bolts of cloth. "It's certainly a pleasant surprise. We haven't had many pleasant surprises lately, have we?"

"I think we've had several pleasant surprises today," Evie commented. "Miss Merced, may I ask you a rather personal question?"

A noncommittal smile rolled across Martina's face. "As long as it's not about these French silks."

"Oh, no." Evie's eyes grew wide. "It's about Mr. Hackett."

Martina fussed with another package. "What about him?"

"Did you know him before?" Evie's voice was soft, almost musical.

"Before what?"

"You know, before you and Mr. Swan, Jr., got married?"

For a shy woman, you aren't bashful about getting to the point. "No. I just met him this morning."

"Well, are you . . . you know . . ." Evie cleared her throat. ". . . interested in him?"

"Evie Norman, what are you saying? I happen to be a married woman."

The young clerk rocked up on the toes of her lace-up boots. It made her as tall as Martina. "Does that mean you aren't interested in him?"

"Of course I'm not interested in him." Martina scowled.

"Good." Evie giggled. "That eliminates one."

"One what?"

"One competitor."

"Are you saying you're interested in Mr. Hackett?"

Evie puckered her lips as if trying to decide whether to kiss him or not and nodded. "I was thinking about it."

"What happened to your Bobby?" Martina chided.

"He went to Dos Palos to work for Mr. Miller." Evie shrugged.

"He's coming back in the fall, isn't he?"

"Oh, you know how men are. Who knows when he will come back?"

Martina stared at the young clerk. *I certainly know all about men who don't come back, if that's what you're implying.* "You think Mr. Hackett's worth pursuing?"

Evie Norman's eyes reflected enthusiasm for the subject. "Oh, yes, Miss Merced! And so does Doraine."

"Well, he seems to be quite popular."

Evie took hold of Martina's arm. "He is nice, isn't he, Miss Merced?"

Martina patted Evie's hand. *I feel like an old married woman giving a girl advice. She's barely two years younger than I am.* "He is a very helpful man. But he's going to return to Nevada in a day or two, so you better work fast."

"Yes, ma'am. I think I will." Evie turned and looked back at the stack of inventory. "If you don't sell those French silks, what will you do with them?"

Martina tossed her long hair to her back and rubbed her neck. "Toss them out, I suppose."

"Maybe Doraine and I could divide them up and —"

"I didn't mean you needed to act that fast!" Martina teased.

Evie put her hand to her mouth, but it failed to cover her blush. "No, ma'am, you're right. You'd better throw them away before I do something awful."

By the time most of the newly inherited goods were stashed on the shelves, it was time to dust mop the floor and close up. Martina, carrying Christina on her hip, walked both clerks to the door.

"Are you going to hire someone to take Mr.

Chambers's place?" Doraine asked.

"I'd like to, but I'm not sure about being able to pay someone. I was wondering if the three of us couldn't take care of it, at least for a while."

"It will mean you're stuck in the store all the time," Evie cautioned.

"That might be good," Martina sighed. "I don't think Mr. Clayton will be back as long as I'm inside the store."

Doraine put on her straw hat with its fashionable tilt and tied the pink ribbon under her chin. "But you can't hide out in the store forever."

"What do you mean, 'hide out'?" Martina snapped. "I'm not hiding."

"No, ma'am," Doraine mumbled as she purposely avoided looking at Martina.

Evie held the door open as the clerks stepped out on the boardwalk on J Street. "I wonder why Mr. Hackett didn't return?" she asked. "I thought for sure he would. You don't suppose he's been injured, do you? Should we go check on him?"

Martina watched the Feather River Stage roll by, leading a cloud of dust. "I'm sure he has other things to do in Sacramento besides come over here. And he doesn't need us spying on him."

"Oh, no! I didn't suggest that," Evie stammered. "Eh, exactly what kind of work is he in?"

Ladies, this conversation is getting tiring. "I didn't ask him."

"I heard he has a gold claim in the Comstock

and came back for financing and will one day be a very, very rich man," Evie announced.

"Where did you hear all that?" Martina pressed.

"From Doraine," Evie reported.

Doraine LaFlor held her smooth, pointed chin high. "Well, he might have a gold claim. And he seems like the type that might be rich someday. I should know. I've seen all types."

Martina's dress hung heavy on her shoulders. The balls of her feet ached. "Somehow I doubt that." *Someone that driven wouldn't stop to take care of a widow all winter long!*

Doraine shaded her eyes against the setting sun. There was absolutely no breeze. "He didn't happen to tell you where he was staying, did he?"

"Why on earth would Mr. Hackett give a married woman such information?" Martina sighed. *I've got to kick off these shoes! Maybe I'll just go barefoot tomorrow. That was a joke, Mother.* "In fact, why would he tell any respectable woman such private details? Good night, ladies."

Martina made one more pass along the shelves, now displaying new items, and then strolled up the stairs. "Well, Christina, a grubby angel brought us some treasures today. It's the nicest thing that's happened in quite a while. I have no idea for sure where the man came across such items, but I have a bill of trade, so I don't believe someone will show up claiming the goods. We should give the Lord thanks. Can you

81

say, 'Thank You, Jesus'?"

Martina stared into the baby's happy green eyes.

"Play?" the baby squealed.

"Your Grandma Alena is right, young lady. You are the most beautiful baby ever born in the state . . . or even before it was a state. And you like to play. You should have been born a Californio."

The large room felt hot and stuffy. Martina opened the two windows that overlooked J Street and the one by the table that faced the alley. A slight breeze drifted up from the river. She set Christina in the middle of a large deep blue quilt that covered the bed. It had been a wedding present from Doña María Martina Cabrillo, Martina's namesake and honorary grandmother.

"Well, young lady, what shall we have for supper? Oh, I know what you want, but what shall I have? You think I should have soup? What a splendid idea. Although I hate to build a fire in the stove; it's so warm up here anyway."

Martina tugged off her earrings and rubbed her earlobes. Then she unfastened the ribbons in her hair. The waist-length dark brown hair cascaded across her shoulders. The baby let out a brief squeal, and Martina dropped the ribbons into the grasping tiny hands of Christina Swan.

The green velvet settee showed a slickness caused by years of wear long before it was given to the young Swans. She tugged at the laces of her high-top black shoes. When she finally freed her feet from the white silk socks, she wiggled her toes on the cool wood flooring.

"Did I ever tell you how your daddy used to rub my feet at night, little darling? Well, he did. He always worried about me working, especially when I was carrying you."

The ribbons were now wadded up and stacked on the baby's head.

Martina waltzed to the bed and spoke in a deep voice. " 'Marti, as soon as we get things established, you aren't going to work anymore,' " she mimicked. "Yes, that's what your daddy said. In fact, he told me that on the day he left. 'Just hold on for three weeks, darlin', and I'll come back, and you can retire.' "

Did he know he wasn't coming back? Lord, I just can't accept that. It's too humiliating.

I'm not going to cry.

I've cried every night for almost a year.

My tears neither beckon him back nor greatly impress You, Lord, so they are useless. She reached up and wiped her eyes, trying to take a deep breath. *I don't know why I can't control my tears.*

Mother would not approve. She could remain composed in the most threatening of times, always so disarmingly poised. I cannot be like you, Mother. Never once in my life have I been like you.

She sat on the edge of the bed and closed her eyes. She felt movement on the bed, and then a tiny hand clutched at hers. Without opening her eyes, she plucked up the baby, set her in her lap, and began to rock back and forth.

Lord, I did something wrong. I want to go back and do it over, but I don't know what it was I did. Perhaps I shouldn't have wanted a child so soon after marriage. The bigger my tummy got, the more distant Billy became.

Her eyes popped open, and a smile flashed across her face. "Of course, he was more distant." She grinned at the baby. "My stomach was very, very big. You were a very healthy baby, young lady. I once told your father that I thought I might be having twins. I was afraid he was going to faint."

Twins? How could I ever take care of twins? Perhaps You have kept me from trials, Lord. Not many . . . but some.

"Well, young lady, if you weren't here, my evenings would be frightfully boring. I wouldn't have anything to do but lie back on that big bed and sleep." Martina gazed across the bed. *Which at the moment sounds inviting.*

"Billy, why don't you take Christina for a walk in the stroller, and I'll take a short nap. Then we can all go out to supper at some fine restaurant."

"Why, certainly, my dear. . . . By the way, you look ravishing today!"

"Thank you, my sweet."

"Is there anything else I can do for you?"

"Well, there is just one other thing."

"Oh?"

"Come home, you rogue."

"Mrs. Swan?" The voice filtered in through the J Street window.

Martina rebuttoned the top button on her dress and picked up the baby.

"Mrs. Swan, are you home?"

She padded barefoot to the open window and peered down at a smiling, square-jawed man who held a large crate.

"Mr. Hackett!"

"Evenin', Mrs. Swan. I was wonderin' if you and little Christina had eaten supper yet?"

"Actually we were . . . I mean, I was just about to start cooking."

"Well, don't even warm up the oven. I've got a surprise for you."

"What do you have?"

"Come down and take a look."

"Come down . . . now?" *I can't believe I'm yelling out the window at a man.* "I'm afraid everything's all locked up for the evening, and I'm not, well, properly dressed."

"You look properly dressed to me," he shouted.

People stopped on the sidewalk and stared up at her. "Wait right there, Mr. Hackett."

I can't believe the nerve. She walked back over to the settee and sat down, placing the baby beside her. *Come down and see what he brought?* She reached down and picked up her silk socks. *The store is closed.* She tugged the socks on slowly. *I've settled in for the night.* After slipping on her shoes, she bent over and began to lace them up. *I'm a married woman. I don't receive callers after hours.*

85

Martina picked up Christina and strolled over to the dresser. *I don't receive callers at all.* She slowly inserted the posts of the earrings into her lobes. *Especially ruggedly handsome ones.* Holding the baby on her hip, she glanced in the mirror. *It's not proper.* She glanced over at the bed and spotted the baby-mangled ribbons. *Avoid the appearance of evil.* She brushed her hair to her back with her hand and flipped her bangs out of her eyes. *That's exactly what I will tell him.* She shifted the baby to her other hip and started for the stair landing. *Three visits by one man in a single day is too many.* She took the stairs slowly. *Far too many.*

She paused when she reached the store level and could see the outline of a man through the opaque window of the front door. *I hope he realizes that all women are not as desperate as the lady in the cabin in the mountains.* She marched straight toward the locked entrance. *What will the neighbors say?* She set the baby on the floor and struggled to reach the deadbolts. *If I had any neighbors.*

She plucked up the grinning baby and slowly opened the door.

"Mr. Hackett, I do not appreciate this . . ."

He marched right past her carrying the large crate.

"I don't believe I invited you in."

"Oh, I reckoned you didn't want all those people in the street gawkin' at us." His grin was so natural that she found herself smiling in spite of her annoyance.

"What people?" she asked.

"The ones that were listening to you and me holler at each other."

Martina tried to look back out to the J Street sidewalk, but her view was blocked. "Now please tell me what is so incredibly important."

"Look what I have here." He opened the crate.

Martina watched as he folded back a deep blue tablecloth. "Dishes?"

"China, crystal, linen napkins, and a complete supper for two and a half — straight from the kitchen of the Grand Hotel," he triumphed.

Her hand flew to her cheek. "Where did you get this?"

"Well, I bought it, of course. I went in there to eat supper and thought about how lonely it is to eat alone. Then I thought of how you and Christina have had to eat all by yourself for a long time. Well, I wanted to invite you to have supper with me, but I figured you wouldn't chance leaving the store with the likes of Landel Clayton trying to lock it up, so . . . I did the next best thing." He made an arm-sweeping gesture at the crate. "I brought us all some supper. Christina likes her steaks rare, doesn't she?"

"She doesn't eat meat, you should know —"

"Do all the men tease you like this, or am I the only one?" he mimicked.

She shook her head. "I seem to be an easy target," she replied.

He waved his arms in feigned resignation.

"Well, ma'am, I'll eat Christina's meat if she'll eat my applesauce and mashed peas."

Martina peered down at the crate. "You got applesauce and mashed peas at the Grand Hotel?"

"Nope," he admitted. "I got baked apples and fresh garden peas, but I figure we can mash both of them." He started to close the front door behind them.

"That's very delightful of you, Mr. Hackett." Martina's boot blocked the closing of the door. "But I don't believe it's proper for you to call on a married woman."

His blue eyes flashed a timid, cautious expression. "I'm not courtin' you, Mrs. Swan. I just thought we would all enjoy not eatin' alone. Besides, I have it all figured out. This crate will make a handy table. We can set it up right in front of one of your big store windows in plain sight of the sidewalk. That way any fool could see that what we are doing is quite proper."

"I'm not going to eat with people on the street gawking at me." The aroma of warm, fresh bread filled the room. She stared down at the meal and gave a deep sigh. "We can sit at the back of the store. I believe that would be just fine."

"Sounds great to me. I haven't had good company for a meal since . . ." His voice trailed off.

"Since the widow died?" she asked.

"Somethin' like that. Shall I scoot some chairs up to the crate?"

"I have some chairs upstairs. Perhaps we should bring them down." She stared down at the crate. "But they will be a little tall. Perhaps we should bring the table down as well."

"It might work best," he concurred. "I'll go up and get them."

"No, wait!" She knew exactly what she was about to say and was shocked that she could not stop herself. "Let's save some labor and eat up in our kitchen. I'll just keep a gun on you all evening, and if you even hint at improper behavior, I'll gut-shoot you."

He stood frozen in place until she cracked a smile.

"For a minute I thought you were serious," he gulped.

She pranced up the stairs, carrying Christina, then turned back, batting her long brown eyelashes. "Believe me, Mr. Hackett, I am serious."

It was almost 10:00 P.M. when Mr. Loop Hackett left the front door of Swan's carrying a crate of dirty dishes back to the Grand Hotel. Martina Merced Swan locked the doors and carried a lantern with her back up the wide stairs to the second-floor apartment. She set the lantern on the now empty table and checked on a sleeping Christina.

She stood at the open window facing J Street and stared down at the near empty street. Somewhere in the dark a woman laughed. It was a deep, guttural laugh, the kind a woman makes when she knows she is about to do something wicked and is both nervous and thrilled at the same time.

Martina bit her lip and closed the window. She slowly got ready for bed and then found herself sitting at the vanity, half-dressed, combing her long brown hair. She couldn't remember how long she had been sitting there. Finally, she scooted off the bed, set the lantern on the nightstand, and flopped on her back on top of the covers. She reached over, turned the wick down, and watched the reflection of the dying light on the ceiling.

When the lantern grew dark, only the dimly reflected light from the street lamp below filtered through the thin curtains. It was then, and only then, that Martina began to cry.

Oh, Lord, what am I doing? I can't believe I did that. I had a man in my home . . . a single man . . . a handsome man. I'm a married woman, and I invited him up here. I ate his food and enjoyed his company. I talked nonstop about business, family, babies, food, and the progress of the transcontinental railroad, but never once in four hours did I mention my husband . . . or You.

Martina rolled on her side away from the crib and continued to sob.

And I liked it, Lord. Do You hear me? I sinned and I liked it. No, I didn't kiss. I didn't touch. I didn't even speak suggestive words . . . but I thought them. Lord, this isn't good. I'm losing control, and I don't know what to do.

I don't know if I should save the store . . . or save my marriage . . . or just walk away from both. This isn't life. This is survival. One day at a time. I can't dream of the future. I just struggle to survive one more dark, lonely night.

Forgive me, Lord Jesus.

In my mind today I believe I broke every one of the Ten Commandments.

All except to blaspheme You.

I didn't do that.

Did I?

I need my husband, Lord. You know I do. Some women seem to be able to survive quite nicely on their own. But that's not me. I love Billy. I really do. I've never loved anyone else — You know that.

But I can't beg him to come home. I want him to love me, not be stuck with me. I want him to run through that door because he can't live without me, not because I threaten to divorce him if he doesn't. I want my lips on his because he can't keep them off me. . . . Oh, Lord, how I want his lips on mine tonight.

You didn't marry Alena Merced, Billy Swan. I told you that on our wedding night. You married her daughter. Her plain, boring daughter.

But Mr. Loop Hackett did not find me boring. He said it was a delightful evening. I was charming and delightful. But I was with the wrong man!

Oh, Jesus, forgive me.

Martina slept on top of the comforter until early morning and then finally crawled under the covers. A hungry Christina woke her at daylight, and she struggled to her feet.

Change the baby.

Feed the baby.

Dress the baby.

Feed the lady.

Dress the lady.

It was Wednesday: green dress.

She could do it all without thinking. Sometimes it was better not to think.

The first two people through the front door were Evie Norman and Doraine LaFlor. The third was Burro Touchet.

"Mr. Touchet! I'm surprised to see you," Martina greeted the nervous man at the door. "I thought you'd be in San Francisco by now." She could still smell the months of dirt and dried sweat that clung to him.

He rubbed his broad nose with the back of his hand. "I, eh, had a little change in plans."

She slipped her hands into the pockets of her dress. She was expecting to find the security of the pocket revolver, but she didn't.

"Did you know there were three men looking for you?"

"Today?" He jerked his head around so quickly that he had to catch his tumbling dirty hat.

"No, yesterday. In fact, they took a shot at me." She put her hands on her hips and offered him her best glare. "I don't appreciate that very much."

"They are a mean bunch." He yanked off his hat, revealing matted, slightly gray hair. "My apologies, ma'am. I had no idea they was so low as to shoot at a lady like yourself."

"What were they after?" she questioned.

"Somethin' that is rightfully mine."

"If you don't mind my saying so, perhaps you should state your business and leave. I would rather those three didn't show up here again. I don't want your quarrel with them to continue in my store."

He leaned so close she could smell beans and coffee on his breath. "They're long gone by now. You told 'em I went to San Francisco, didn't you?"

"Of course not." She stepped straight back. "I wouldn't betray your confidence. I didn't tell them anything."

"Betray my confidence?" he boomed, startling both clerks. "I didn't tell you it was a secret. You didn't owe me any favors. Why didn't you tell them where I went?"

This little man is quite manipulative. "I assume you were counting on me to give in to a threat of violence and tell them your supposed location."

"I didn't know they would use violence. But you were supposed to tell them San Francisco! In a town like this, I have to run across a woman of integrity and honor. What are the odds of that happening?" Touchet moaned.

"Mr. Touchet, I don't believe we have anything further to discuss. I'd like for you either to make a purchase or leave the store."

"You're right about that. I don't intend on staying in town if they're still around. I'll just get my powder and leave."

Martina's hands dropped to her side. "Your what?"

"I forgot and left my keg of black powder in the wagon. I'm sure you found it when you unloaded. It didn't exactly fit the rest of the load, did it?"

"I thought it was part of the inventory."

"Inventory? Black powder with dry goods? It wasn't on the bill of sale, was it? Anyway, I'll take it with me now." He pranced from one worn brown boot to the other.

Martina took a deep breath and let it out slowly. "I'm afraid it's not here."

His bloodshot eyes glanced around the room. "What do you mean, it's not here?" he exploded.

"A gentleman by the name of Loop Hackett helped us unload the wagon, and I paid him off with the keg of powder."

"You paid him with my powder!" Touchet hollered.

"Mr. Touchet, you are disturbing my customers."

"You don't have any customers."

"Then you are disturbing me and my clerks. Would you please leave?"

"That was my powder! You cain't give it away! It wasn't on the bill of sale," he repeated, his face and neck completely flushed.

"Mr. Touchet, it was a logical mistake. You traded me your entire outfit for a past-due account. You made no comment about a keg of powder. However, I am an honest woman. A keg of black powder that size is worth about $20. I will give you $20 if you promise to leave my store and not return. You can go buy yourself another keg of black powder."

"I don't want any old keg of black powder!" he screamed. "I want *my* keg!"

Martina stared at his wild eyes. *I don't trust the sanity of this man. Lord, please get him out of the store. Now.* "I suspect there was something in that barrel in addition to black powder."

"Who told you that?" he howled.

"You did, by your nervous and excited behavior." She swept her hands toward the door. "I want you to leave the store."

He started to move and then spun around. "Where is this guy, Hackett, staying?"

"I do not know." Martina jabbed a finger in the back of his canvas vest, causing him to take several more steps toward the door. "Mr. Touchet, it is not proper to ask a gentleman where he is lodging. I know he's a traveling man."

Touchet resisted the shove. "Where was he going?"

"Perhaps he was going to San Francisco. . . . No, you were the one going to San Francisco. But you didn't mean that at all. Mr. Hackett didn't tell me where he was going, but if he had, perhaps it too would have been a lie. Although I must admit, Mr. Hackett does not have the looks of a scoundrel, like you do." She shoved him into the doorway.

Touchet resisted. "What does he look like?"

"Evie! Doraine!" she called to her clerks who had been huddled in a nearby aisle listening to the entire conversation. "How would you describe Mr. Hackett?"

"He is tall with broad shoulders!" Evie exclaimed.

"And a square chin, clean-shaven," Doraine added. "He's ruggedly handsome."

Evie blushed more crimson with each word. "And brown eyes that give you a real good look and make you feel sort of good and sort of embarrassed all at the same time."

"That don't tell me nothin'!" Touchet seethed as Martina finally got him out to the sidewalk.

"Well, if you run across the three men that are chasing you, ask them what Loop Hackett looks like." Martina's fingers felt gritty from touching the back of his jacket. "He disarmed all three of them."

Touchet's chin dropped. "One man got the drop on all three?"

"Yes, he's quite proficient with a revolver." Martina glanced down the street as if looking for someone. "If I were you, I'd inquire about the black powder in a very diplomatic manner. He is not a man to rile, is he, girls?"

"I'd like to rile him," Doraine mused.

One stern glance from Martina sent Miss LaFlor giggling her way across the store. Martina and Evie stood in the doorway as if blocking it. They watched until Touchet disappeared around the corner.

Evie Norman folded her arms across her thin chest. "Do you think he will be back?"

Martina raised her narrow brown eyebrows. "Mr. Touchet?"

"No! Mr. Hackett." Evie sounded startled. "I think he will be coming back today, don't you?"

Martina reentered the store. "If you two keep gushing over him, I imagine he will be back."

Evie tagged along behind. "Were we gushing? I hardly think it would be considered gushing. Do you? Well, perhaps just a little gush. It's fun, isn't it, Miss Merced?"

Martina's mind wandered to the long, enjoyable supper the night before. "Yes, I know what you mean," she mumbled.

"Oh." Evie put her hand over her mouth. "I mean with your husband."

"That's what I meant," Martina snapped.

"Well, Mr. Hackett doesn't pay me and Doraine much mind. I think he has his eye on you, Miss Merced," Evie insisted.

"Don't be foolish," Martina shot back. "I'm a married woman."

"I know that means a lot to you. But I'm not sure that means as much to Mr. Hackett," Evie suggested.

You might be more right than you know, Miss

Norman. "Well, I'll just have to tell him to place his gaze elsewhere, provided he comes back by the store."

Evie stopped in an aisle and straightened a stack of ducking trousers. "He's got to pick up his keg of black powder," she announced.

Martina gazed toward the back wall of the store. "He took that with him last night."

Evie jumped on the comment. "When?"

"Eh, yesterday evening . . . when he finished unloading. Didn't he take it with him then?" Martina stammered.

"Nope. He just took the rig to the livery and didn't come back, remember?" Evie led Martina toward the back of the store. "Look, it's right there next to the box of French lace giggles."

"The mysterious black powder was here all along?" Martina stared down at the crate. "And I told Touchet it wasn't here." Then she turned toward the young clerk. "What do you mean, 'French lace giggles'?"

Evie blushed. "Well, every time Doraine or I think about what's in that box, all we can do is giggle."

Five

Evie Norman's small hands rested on the narrow waist of her green and white gingham dress. Her brown eyes narrowed; her eyebrows rose in the middle to form a wide "m." "What do you mean, we aren't going to open it?"

Martina used both hands to lift her long brown hair off her back. "That's exactly what I mean." The air felt cool on her neck. "We are not going to open that keg." *I should get up the nerve and cut my hair.*

"But — but . . ." Evie's mouth dropped open as she shook her head. "You just said there was something important in that keg, so valuable that several men were ready to kill for it. It must be gold. A whole keg full of gold! Think of the inventory we could buy with that!"

"Whatever it is, it's not ours." Martina busied herself folding a stack of thin white cotton tea towels. "It probably doesn't belong to Mr. Touchet or those three gunmen either. But what if we did open it and find gold? We would be sorely tempted to confiscate it for ourselves. Then we would be no better than those brigands. And we would become accomplices to their deeds. The Bible says we should flee temptations." *I could cut it shoulder length like Mother's. Then it would look short and mousy, instead of long and mousy.*

Evie pointed at the wooden keg. "Yes, but doesn't the Bible also say that heaven helps those who help themselves?"

"No, that's not in the Bible," Martina lectured. "What it does say is that God helps the helpless." *Maybe I could dye it red and finally learn to dance the fandango.*

"Sometimes I feel helpless," Evie insisted.

You feel helpless? With that beautiful, thick black hair? "You open that keg, and you are going to feel guilty. No, it stays sealed."

Evie tugged a hank of black hair out from its comb and let it drape across her ear. "What are we going to do with it?"

Lord, coal black hair like Grandmother Cabrillo's would have been nice. I could have pinned it up on my head and worn a yellow flower behind my ear. Martina waved her hand toward the high store ceiling with slightly peeling light green paint. "For the moment, leave it over there by the French giggles. Whenever Mr. Hackett returns, I'll have him take it to the sheriff's office, and they may dispose of it as they wish."

Evie's shoulders drooped with her eyes. "You're really not even going to look inside?"

"No, I'm not." Martina bit her lip. *I could cut it very short like an actress or a . . .*

"Not even a little peek?" Evie continued to probe.

"There is no way to have a little peek into a wooden keg. You have to bust it open, and then it's impossible to close." *No, I will never cut it. At least, not until it turns gray.*

"Miss Merced, I've never met anyone with self-control like you. If it were my decision, I would rip right into that keg and forget about the consequences. I wish I had your discipline."

Martina pulled some of her long hair around in front of her shoulder. "It's a learned trait." *Of course, the way things are going, it may turn gray any day now.*

"Well, I've never learned it. Of course, if I had self-control, I would never have followed that scoundrel Oliver Raymond all the way to California."

"Oh, you must have some discipline," Martina challenged. "At least, you didn't follow him back to Missouri." *I could always try using a curling iron on it again.*

"That's only because he up and married that horrid Susan Booker," Evie moaned. "I don't think that counts for self-discipline."

"Well, let's all exhibit self-control by not opening that keg." *Of course, last time I did that Mother said it looked like a wagon train ran over my hair.* "I believe we have a store to run, Miss Norman."

"Yes, ma'am." Evie's bangs made her look about sixteen.

On some days Swan's was so quiet it was depressing. On those days Martina felt like a family member sitting in the parlor waiting for the doctor to come out from the bedroom and announce that the patient had died.

Then every once in a while, after payday at the mines and mills, the aisles would be so crowded Martina didn't know if they would ever catch up.

But other days . . . other days it was just a steady, constant flow of customers. Find a garment. Visit a bit. Take the money. Wrap the package. Walk them to the door. Then start all over again. Those were the days Martina liked best. She felt that she was sincerely helping people. Making money. And passing the time pleasantly.

Perhaps that last virtue was most important. When Martina was busy, she had a tendency to forget about overdue bank loans, or life in the shadow of famous parents, or husbands who are too preoccupied or disinterested to come home.

The morning sauntered by at a gratifying and comfortable gait.

Martina knew that the new merchandise had a lot to do with it. Doraine LaFlor plucked a fussing Christina out of the playpen and carried her out to the front of the store where Martina refolded a stack of men's tan cotton shirts.

"How's my baby?"

"I think she's a little hungry," Doraine reported. Her long white apron retained its starched crispness. "Why don't you go on up and take a lunch break?"

"We can wait, Doraine. You go to lunch first."

Doraine held the baby with the curly red hair straight out in front of her. "Maybe you can wait, Mama, but Miss Christina is very, very hungry."

Christina grinned at her mother and then offered a sheepish, "Me!"

"I see you've had a busy morning. I believe every customer in the store toted you around, young lady." Martina picked up the fidgeting infant and hugged her to her hip. "Well, punkin, Miss LaFlor is right. You're a hungry girl." She turned to her clerk. "Are you sure you don't mind waiting?"

"Evie and I brought basket lunches today. We kind of wanted to stick around in case any interesting men customers showed up during the noon hour."

Martina poked the round flat nose of the baby, who instantly giggled and grabbed her finger. "What do you think, young lady? Could Doraine possibly be talking about Mr. Hackett?"

Doraine straightened the collar of her blue gingham dress. "We figure we might have a chance at him if we keep you upstairs. It's sort of like the time I worked in a ballroom where Lola Montez was working. You had to tie them and drag them out into the street before they ever noticed you. Have you observed how Mr. Hackett's eyes seem to follow you everywhere?"

Martina glared and then broke into a smile.

"I'm sure he's just watching this red-haired cutie. Anyway, I'm going to be studying the old ledgers."

Doraine walked with Martina to the base of the wide stairway. "Are you looking for something?"

"I was curious to see if Mr. Swan, Sr., had any record of this Mr. Touchet." She pulled the baby's hand away from her dangling earrings.

"Maybe there are others who owe Swan's," Doraine suggested.

"That's exactly what I was thinking. I don't know what we'll do about it if there are. I'll be up in the apartment unless you get busy and need help." Holding the baby in front of her, Martina jogged up the light green wooden stairs.

"Eh . . . I was wondering," Doraine called out. "If Mr. Hackett shows up, can we tell him you are ill-disposed?"

Martina turned and grinned. "By all means."

"Miss Merced . . . if you don't mind me saying so . . . it's nice to see you smile again. You have a very nice smile."

"Thank you, Doraine. I assume you'd rather I didn't use it when Mr. Hackett is around."

Doraine beamed. "I knew you'd understand, Miss Merced."

The upstairs living quarters were stuffy. An aroma of a fine meal from the Grand Hotel lingered in the large room. Martina opened the windows and set Christina on the spotless wooden floor. The baby crawled over to the bed, pulled herself up on her feet, and tottered around the edge, giggling and clutching the comforter.

"What will I do when you start running around, young lady? Are you going to grow up running up and down the aisles of Swan's?" *That's a very optimistic prediction. Chances are she'll never remember a thing about the big, old store that carried her name. Where will you grow up, punkin? I wish I knew. Maybe you'll be out at Rancho Alazan. You could do a lot worse.*

Martina stoked the stove and then stared into the pantry cupboard that had been built against the south wall of the large room. *Nice to see me laugh and smile again? I didn't know that I ever stopped. . . . That's not true. I didn't know others knew it. I have no idea why I'm smiling more. I certainly hope it's not because of Mr. Hackett. That makes me feel even more guilty about last night.*

Christina let her mama know when she was through with lunch. She fell asleep in her highchair. Martina tucked her into the crib and then pulled out the thick, heavy, worn leather ledgers from an unpainted wooden cabinet without any doors. The record journals seemed to weigh about ten pounds each. The earliest one went back to January of 1849, the original ledger of William Swan, Sr. The paper was faded, but the ink remained dark and legible. Most of the names of the paid-in-full accounts were strangers that Martina had never heard of. Occasionally the name of a now-famous person would catch her eye.

Mr. Swan had three categories of accounts — those paid in full, those due and payable, and those he marked "forgiven." It was the third category that intrigued her most. *Forgiven? Did he just write them off? Did they trade something? Did they work it off in the warehouse?*

Martina unlaced her unwieldy shoes, let them drop to the floor, and then propped up the pillows and sat on the bed with her head against the headboard. The ponderous ledger lay open in her lap as she traced the names slowly down each column.

H. L. Pratt — $23.16? Isn't that the man with the livery? Why should he have a balance due for over fifteen years? Perhaps I should inquire. It won't exactly pay off the bank, but it would pay a week's wages for one clerk.

After several pages of closed accounts, Martina leaned her head back against the pillows and stretched her arms. She held her hands up in front of her. *I must trim my nails. They do look rather ragged. What has happened to my hands? At one time they were strong, brown, hardened from riding the ranch every day. Now they never see the sun. They are soft. Thin. Can two years really change one that much?*

She stared at the gold band on her left ring finger and then gazed across the room.

I am a married lady. I should not have allowed a gentleman in my home last night. My marriage does

106

not depend on my husband being present. It does not depend upon him supporting his family. It does not depend upon him keeping his word. My marriage depends upon me keeping the vow I made to You, Lord.

I haven't gone back on that vow.

It is not the marriage I hoped it would be.

But it is the marriage that has been assigned to me.

I thought I married a shopkeeper, but I married a dreamer and a drifter.

She shoved the heavy ledger to the side and then scooted down so that her head rested flat on the pillows.

Billy Swan burst through the door on a trot, and Martina leaped out of the rocking chair. Her growing stomach strained at the tiny buttons of the green dress. "They found gold up on Hat Creek!" he shouted.

Martina held on to the side of the chair and braced herself. Her head felt light, dizzy. "Where's that?"

"One of the tributaries of the Pit River."

"North of Mt. Lassen?"

"Yes . . . I just heard about it," he said.

"Where did you hear that?"

"At Sweeney's." Billy's white shirt was mostly untucked. His tie dangled loosely around his neck. "Three men from Plumas County came in and said they saw some of the nuggets with their very own eyes."

"I thought you were downstairs running the store," Martina lectured. "What were you doing at Sweeney's?"

"You aren't going to start that again, are you?"

"You look like you just wrestled a bear," she snapped. "Why were you at Sweeney's?"

"And you look fat as a toad, but what does that have to do with anything? And what difference does it make that I was at Sweeney's?"

Martina sucked in her breath and her stomach. "I would simply like to know where my husband is."

"We're adults. We don't have to report in like a grammar school pupil to his teacher." William Hays Swan, Jr., began to pace the wooden floor. "I don't ask where you go during the day."

"I don't go anywhere, and you know it."

"Well, maybe you should. That's your problem."

"I have a problem?"

"Why don't you go up and visit your folks or something? It could do you good to get out."

She folded her hands and locked her fingers to keep them from quivering. "I don't want to visit my parents. I married you, Billy Swan. You're the one I want to be with."

"And you're the one I want to be with. That's why I'm here now. It's really good news, and naturally I ran all the way back to the store just to share it with you."

"I thought you were running the store," she insisted.

"Business was slow this morning, and Chambers takes care of everything better than I — as you've often reminded me."

Martina took small breaths, trying to relax. *I only said that once, and it was during an argument over my mother.* "So why is this news so important? You surely haven't decided to be a prospector, have you? You promised me you wouldn't go off prospecting again."

"Of course not." Billy Swan's cool, blue eyes began to sparkle and dance. "But I thought I should go up and scout the area to see if it would be profitable to build a store. The first store in an area like that usually makes the best profit. This could be a very key business enterprise."

"But we already have a store, Billy. Why do we want another one?" she asked.

"You lack vision for the future. You can't help it; it's your upbringing."

"Just what do you mean by that?" she grumbled.

"Your family always lives in the past. It's the old Californio way of thinking. They just relax, sing, and dance. That's what I mean."

"I do not appreciate your insulting my family. We can't open another store. We're barely getting by with this one. If you remember, we owe the Delta State Bank $1,000."

"That's exactly the point, Marti. We need to expand. We need branch stores. Look at Stanford, Huntington, and Hopkins — that's the way people succeed in business. And they say there are nuggets lying right in the creekbed at Hat Creek."

"They were drinking when they said this, weren't they?"

"Of course they were drinking. They came to town to celebrate. No one would believe their story if they didn't celebrate."

Martina gripped the chair back with both hands and stared toward the J Street window. "You would think all the placer claims would be played out by now. I find it hard to imagine anything except hard-rock mining left in the whole state."

"That's the point." His excitement had reached a shout. "It will be the only rush going on in California. Everyone's been so preoccupied with the war, and now they will all run up there and try to strike it rich. We can't let this opportunity pass us by!"

Martina sat back down in the cushioned wooden rocking chair. Her feet felt swollen in her shoes. She felt dizzy. She leaned her head back and closed her eyes. "Maybe you're right, Billy."

"Really?" He stopped stalking. "You think I should go up and check it out?"

She opened her eyes and waved her index finger at him. "I have a better plan."

"Better plan?"

"Let's you and me rent a big freight wagon, fill it with dry goods that a camp would need, and both race up there. We could sell right from the back of the wagon. We wouldn't even need a store. Then when we're out of goods, we could determine if it's a substantial enough place to build a store. Or just come home with a sack of profits."

"You can't go up there. You're carrying that baby of yours. You shouldn't be traveling."

"This is not merely my baby. I'm carrying our baby . . . and I can make the trip just fine. Baby's not due until late August. Besides, you said I should get out and take a trip."

"No, that wouldn't work. I need to go check it out first by myself. Then maybe we'll send a wagon north."

She folded her arms and began to rock back and forth. "So you just want to take off and abandon me?"

"Don't get so dramatic, Marti. I'm not abandoning you. I said, it would be a good time for you to visit Rancho Alazan. We'll let Chambers run the store, and I'll go check out Hat Creek."

Martina stopped rocking. "I'm not going to my parents, and you aren't going to Hat Creek. Billy, we have a business right here on 5th and J. So forget that foolishness."

"That's it? Just like that? Your answer's no?"

She let out a deep sigh and held her hand out to him. "Billy, I've been stuck up here in this apartment for weeks. Why don't we both go up to Rancho Alazan for a few days?"

He turned his back to her and stalked toward the window. "I don't need to hear any more stories about the great old days of the Californios! That and the Bible are the only subjects ever discussed at your parents' house."

"Those stories are treasured memories in my family."

"Well, they aren't treasured memories to me. As far as I know, most of the stories were concocted by the Mexicans."

She stood up quickly, and her head began to spin. "William Hays Swan, Jr., I will not have you deride my parents and their heritage." She reached back down to hold on to the oak arms of the rocking chair. "I do not want you to go to Hat Creek. I want you here with me."

"But what am I going to tell them?" Billy's voice seemed distant, as if he were shouting down a long tunnel.

Martina's vision narrowed as if she were looking down a spyglass turned backward. "Tell whom . . . ?" The words floated out of her mouth but sounded as if someone else were speaking them.

"The three men waiting for me downstairs."

Martina felt her hands hit the hard wooden floor.

When she opened her eyes, she was on the bed, fully dressed. No one was in the room, but someone was knocking on the door and calling out, "Miss Merced . . . are you all right?"

The shout startled Christina. She sat up in the crib and bawled.

"Doraine, is that you? Come in," Martina called out.

The clerk stuck her head inside the door. "It's three o'clock, and we could use some help downstairs."

"I'll slip on my shoes. I had no idea it was so late."

"You were sound asleep."

"I was dreaming."

"We knew you needed the rest. That's why I told Mr. Hackett not to wake you."

"He came by?"

"And stayed for over an hour."

"Did you have him take the keg of powder to the sheriff?"

"Oh, no! We forgot all about that."

"Well, what did you do for that hour?"

"He helped us clerk, and . . . you know . . . we visited. But I better get downstairs and help Evie. She's a little flustered."

"Why?"

"Well, it was obvious that Mr. Hackett was more interested in me than in her. I don't think it sat too well with her."

"Is that what he said?" Martina asked.

"Oh no, he's much too polite to say something like that. But it was obvious." Doraine closed the door and then hollered back, "I'll tell you about it later."

Martina felt perspiration around the high collar of her dress, but the floor felt cool to her feet.

"Come on, baby, let's go to work." She hefted

113

Christina out of the crib and set her in the middle of the living room area of the huge one-room apartment. The baby quickly stood straight up and struggled to keep her balance. Her wide grin revealed all four teeth.

Martina sat down and tugged on her shoes. "Well, aren't you a big girl — standing up all on your own? Do you intend to walk some today, or is this one of your crawl-only days?"

The baby chewed on her tongue and watched a fly buzz high on the twelve-foot ceiling above her head. She tilted her head back and then staggered backwards. Her long white dress tangled around her legs, and she crashed to her seat.

"Ma-ma!" she cried out.

Martina scurried over and scooped up the baby. "Well, young lady, you might like to learn to walk forward before you learn to walk backward."

The baby studied Martina's face and then tugged on her mother's earlobe.

"You're right, darlin', I took off my earrings. But the girls need us to help out downstairs, and I doubt if any customer even notices."

It was after seven o'clock by the time they cleaned the store and restocked the shelves. Evie and Martina gathered at the counter near the cash register as Doraine finished washing the frosted glass on the front door. Evie Norman took off her white apron and folded it. "It was a good day."

"Are you talking about sales in general or one certain customer?" Martina chided.

"Mr. Hackett is *so* nice!" Evie swooned. "Some men just know how to treat women nice, and others are absolutely rotten. I tell you, he's one of those nice ones."

"You hardly know him."

"I grew up with a boy next door named Melvin, and by the time I was fourteen, I knew everything about him there was to know. He was simply horrid. Sometimes the most interesting men are the ones you barely know."

Martina stared at Evie's unblinking eyes. "I know exactly what you mean. But I think you're right. Mr. Hackett seems like a nice man."

"That makes three of us." Evie leaned close. "Don't tell Doraine I said this, but he made it obvious he was more interested in me than her."

"Oh?"

"Yes, it's just one of those things you can tell when a man looks at you. I hope Doraine takes it well."

Martina glanced toward the front of the store. Doraine hummed a lively tune as she finished the doors. "She seems to be doing fine so far."

Evie held her hand in front of her mouth. "I would imagine she's still trying to deny it. Anyway, I do know where he is staying."

Martina lowered her voice as well. "He told you that?"

"Well, not in so many words," Evie admitted. "But he tossed a hint. There was no doubt he wanted me to figure it out. Some men are that way, you know."

"What did he say?"

"He said that he had a grand supper last night."

Martina lifted her chin. "Oh, did he say anything else about it?" *If he told them about our supper upstairs, I will personally hang the man.*

"No, but if he had a 'grand' supper, then he's obviously staying at the Grand Hotel. He emphasized the 'grand' part. Now you have to admit it was an obvious hint."

"Or he might not be staying there. Perhaps he just ate one of those Grand Hotel meals," Martina suggested.

Evie Norman posed in front of the full-length mirror on the back wall and tried to straighten her hair. "Either way, I'll find out tonight." She brushed down her skirt and studied her rather flat profile.

Martina stood next to her, both of their backs to Miss LaFlor on the far side of the building. "What are you going to do?"

"Don't tell Doraine, but I'm going to go by the Grand on my way home. I have a friend who works there, so I'll just hang around the lobby as if waiting for someone. Then when Mr. Hackett shows up for supper all by himself and asks me to join him, I'll say, 'What a coincidence running into you tonight!' "

Martina studied Evie. She still showed flashes of teenage awkwardness, even though she was twenty. "What if he shows up for supper with some lady on his arm?"

With an exaggerated expression of shock, Evie covered her mouth with her hand. "What? My Mr. Hackett? He's not that type at all! Even a married lady like you can see that!"

Evie's last few words were almost a whisper. They both watched in the mirror as Doraine LaFlor approached.

"What are you two plotting back here?" Doraine quizzed as she yanked off her apron.

Martina spun around. "You girls are putting in long hours. I'm trying to figure out how I can operate with the present staff without running you both into the ground."

"I don't mind making more money," Doraine admitted.

"Yes, but we'll all be worn out at this pace, especially having to clean the store every night. I think that's when I miss Mr. Chambers most," Martina said. "Perhaps I'll hire someone to clean up for us."

"Oh, I'm not tired." Doraine spun a circle while studying herself in the mirror. "Why, I could dance all night, with the right man, of course."

Evie mouthed the word *denial*, then turned to the door. "I'll see you in the morning. I've got some, eh, errands to run before I go back to my place."

Martina scouted the store and found the baby holding onto the counter with one hand, toddling down the east aisle pulling a long red ribbon behind her. "I'll lock up, Doraine," she called to the clerk.

Doraine scooted down an aisle parallel to Martina's. "Is it all right if I'm a little late in the morning, Miss Merced?"

"What time would you like to come in?" Martina began to roll up the red ribbon.

Doraine stood on her tiptoes and peeked over the top of the stack of cotton sheets. "If things turn out like I think, I'll need an extra hour."

Martina didn't look up from the ribbon in her hand. "That's fine. You're expecting a big evening?"

"Could be." Doraine scooted to the end of her aisle and sauntered back toward Martina and Christina. "I happen to know where Mr. Loop Hackett is having dinner tonight," she boasted.

"And just where is that?"

"At Oh Fat Loo's."

"Did he tell you that?" Martina asked.

"No, but I learned a few things about men from those years in the dance hall. You see, he was talking to Mrs. Fairworth this afternoon. He asked her, in a voice that was obviously meant for me to hear, where the best Chinese restaurant in Sacramento was. And she told him Oh Fat Loo's. He said, 'Good, that's the place I'll go.'"

"She's right about Oh Fat Loo's," Martina remarked. "It has excellent cuisine."

"I know." Doraine grinned. "And I'm headed

over there right now. I think I'll do a little shopping in Chinatown. And if I happen to run into Mr. Hackett . . . well, what a coincidence!"

"And if he sees you, naturally he'll invite you to eat supper with him."

"Naturally." Doraine leaned close to Martina's ear to whisper even though the only other person in the store was a toddler sucking on four fingers. "It's destiny."

Martina patted her arm. "As my father always says, 'May all your righteous dreams come true.' "

"I wouldn't exactly say that mine are all that right . . ." Doraine's voice trailed off. "Anyway, I can just tell that something very unique is going to happen tonight."

I think you may be right about that. I just hope I have two clerks that are still speaking to each other by morning.

A pot of stew made chiefly from leftovers from the catered meal the night before sat on the stove as Martina and Christina changed into more comfortable clothing. Martina loved feeling the wooden floor with her bare feet. It reminded her of the cold, red tile floors at the big house at Rancho Alazan.

"Baby, did you know that when I was little, your grandpa let me go all summer without wearing shoes, except to church? That's right. Well, he also said I had to wear shoes if I was riding in a saddle, but I rode bareback all the time so it didn't matter. Look at you — you're over a year old, and you have never ridden a horse, let alone own one. We do have to get you to Grandma and Grandpa's. They'll teach you to ride like the wind. There is no one left in California who can ride like your Grandpa and Grandma."

The baby stuck a tiny index finger into her mouth and began to drool. "Horsey!" she finally squealed.

"Well . . . baby has a new word!" Martina beamed. "Let's see . . . *me, no, Mama, more, cry, play,* and now *horsey*. You are very precocious for a one-year-old. That's about all the words you are going to need, precious." *I suppose she should learn* Daddy, *but I don't have any idea how to teach it to her.*

Or why.

A young boy's voice filtered up from the street through the open window. "Mrs. Swan?"

Martina spied young Tapadera Andrews waving his floppy hat toward her window. "Mrs. Swan, there's a delivery at the back of your store."

Martina brushed her bangs back out of her eyes. "A delivery?"

The boy held his arms out wide. "Yes, ma'am. A big crate or somethin'."

"Thank you, Tapadera."

"Mrs. Swan, are you lookin' for any help in the store? I heard Mr. Chambers done quit ya. So if you need a man to fill in, I'm available."

"How old are you, Mr. Andrews?"

His head and shoulders drooped. "Ten."

"You need to be in school," she said.

"School's a lot of hard work, Mrs. Swan."

Martina rubbed her chin with her hand and studied the slightly scruffy, strong-shouldered boy on the sidewalk below. "I'll make you a deal, Tapadera. If you keep going to school, I'll hire you for an hour and a half every evening to clean the store. But if you quit school, you lose the job."

"You think school is that important?"

"Yes, I do."

"How much do I get paid?" he asked.

"Two dollars a week," she said.

"And all I have to do is go to school?"

"And sweep, mop, dust, and wash some windows."

He shoved his hat back on his head. "Can I start tonight?"

"We already cleaned the store tonight. Tomorrow evening will be fine."

"What time do you want me here?"

"Five-thirty," she instructed.

"Yes, ma'am. I'm goin' to tell my brother I've got me a job at Swan's. Ain't many men in this town can say that!"

Nor many boys. She watched as Tapadera Andrews ran down the wooden sidewalk, then spun around, and shouted, "Don't forget about your delivery in the alley, Mrs. Swan."

Martina went to the back window and looked down at the alley. She could see the edge of some type of small crate setting on her back step. *No one makes deliveries at this time of the night. Perhaps they left it there this afternoon. I was asleep a long time.*

She strolled back to Christina. "Well, come on, young lady. We have store business to do. There's a real drawback to living above the store. But it's after hours, and I believe I can drag a crate into the store without wearing my shoes."

She carried the baby in her arms and then paused at the top of the stairs. Martina turned around and reentered the apartment to retrieve her revolver from the end table drawer next to the bed.

"Mama's a little worried ever since we got locked in the other day," she told Christina.

Martina sauntered down the wooden steps barefoot and enjoyed the quietness of the empty store. "You play here, punkin." She plopped the baby down in the playpen next to the counter and then stole to the rear of the store. The solid oak door was secured by two deadbolts.

With her hand inside her dress pocket resting on the handle of her revolver, she cracked the door an inch and peeked at a good-sized vegetable crate on the step. She noticed Chinese writing across the end.

Someone delivered this to the wrong store.

She abandoned her gun to the pocket and opened the door.

I'll bring it inside for tonight and then —

"Evenin', ma'am!"

Martina jerked around. A man stood so close to the back wall that he had been out of sight from the upstairs window. She cracked her knee into the doorjamb and let out a panicked, "Oh!"

The man pulled off his hat and held it in front of him. "Hurt yourself?"

"Mr. Hackett!" she chafed. "What are you doing here?"

"I'm the supper delivery man, remember?"

"Supper?"

"I understand Oh Fat Loo's is the best Chinese restaurant in town. What I have in here is the Mandarin Dynasty for two and a half," he said.

"Mr. Hackett, I am wearing a housedress; I do not have on my earrings or my shoes. I have no intention of entertaining visitors dressed like this."

He pointed inside the store. "I'll wait . . . downstairs."

She stood straight up. By standing on the step, with him in the alley, they were nearly the same height. "No, you won't. I don't appreciate your using young Tapadera to get me to the back door. That was deceptive."

"It was not deceptive," he countered. "It was discreet. I just thought it was more judicious than me standing at your window and shouting at you like last night. I know how you treasure discretion."

"Mr. Hackett, I thanked you last night for

your generosity, thoughtfulness, and camaraderie. But I did not think that sharing that meal set a precedent." She could feel her chin begin to quiver.

"But you won't allow me to invite you out to eat," he said.

"No, I won't. And I do not like surprises."

The smile dropped off his face. He looked several years older. "You seemed to enjoy last evening."

Martina couldn't tell if she was shouting or crying the words. "I allowed you to do that just once. If I eat with anyone, it will be because I choose to eat with that person, not because they show up at my door unannounced with food in a crate. Do I make myself clear?"

Hackett's face flushed, and he took a step closer. "Are you mad at me for the way I behaved last night, or mad at the way you behaved?"

"The way I behaved?" she shouted. "I did nothing improper, and you know it!"

"Nor did I. That's the point," he hollered back. "We're just friends, that's all."

Both of them grew silent. From out on the street, the squeal of dry axles of a loaded freight wagon echoed off the brick.

"Do you have any idea why we're yelling at each other?" he asked her.

She tried to study his eyes.

"Maybe you are more than just friends!" Doraine LaFlor stepped out from the shadows.

"Miss LaFlor!" Hackett tipped his hat. "Are you still at work?"

"I just happened to be in the neighborhood and wondered what the shouting was about." The blonde's new straw hat was cocked to the right.

"In the neighborhood!" Evie Norman pouted as she stepped up behind Doraine. "You followed him all the way from Oh Fat Loo's!"

"And just how do you know that?" Doraine snapped.

Evie raised her chin and pronounced each word with deliberate haughtiness. "Because I followed him from the Grand Hotel."

Doraine put her hands on her hips and leaned nose to nose with Evie. She was two inches taller and twenty pounds heavier than the younger woman. "You what?"

Evie stepped back, bit her lip, then announced, "You heard me!"

"What's going on around here?" Hackett quizzed.

"I can tell you one thing that is not going on," Martina snapped. "You and I are not having supper together. I cannot explain why these two normally sane clerks are acting so presumptuous. Perhaps they can explain their behavior."

"We're acting presumptuous? At least we aren't married when we invite a man to come up to our place for supper," Doraine shot back.

Martina retreated into the store and slammed the back door.

"What about all this food?" he called to her.

"I hope the three of you enjoy it!" she shouted.

Martina marched over to the playpen, picked up a startled Christina, and then stomped up the stairs.

Six

Everything irritated Martina. The baby. The heat. The dress she wore. The lousy-tasting stew. The noise from the city. The laughter of people in the street. The whistle of the sternwheeler pulling up to the Embarcadero.

Everything.

By the time the street lamps were being lit, she had her hair combed out and her nightgown on. She meandered through the dimly lit apartment — from the table, to the sofa, to the crib, to the bed.

Lord, what have I done? I've alienated my clerks, compromised my honor, gotten angry at the only three people in this town that seem to care about me. This is berserk. Things were going well. More inventory. More sales. A postponement of the loan. How could I be so dumb?

How could I get upset at the girls? I knew they were going to try to find him. If last night was so innocent, why didn't I tell them about it? Why shouldn't Loop show up tonight? It worked the night before.

Doraine and Evie will quit me. They won't want to work with each other. I will have to run the store alone. I can't. It's too big. Maybe I'll just close it out. Sell off the stock. Maybe it's time to go home. I won't have men show up at my door at Rancho Alazan.

Daddy would run them off.

My brothers would shoot them.

What am I saying? Martina set the lantern by the nightstand and flopped on the bed. *I can't go home. I can't do anything. If Evie and Doraine don't show up tomorrow — I'll leave the store closed. I'll sleep all day.*

She stared at the dark ceiling for over an hour after the lamplight faded. Finally she turned, re-lit the lamp, and picked up her Bible.

I will read myself to sleep. Lord, I do not need a lecture tonight. I just need something soothing. Tell me about heaven, Lord. Tell me about a place where everyone is perfect and no one runs off and deserts his family.

A pressed, dried orange poppy creased her Bible at the beginning of Joshua. She flipped a couple of pages, and a short phrase caught her eye: "Get thee up." With her index finger tracing each word, she read all of verse 10. "And the Lord said unto Joshua, Get thee up; wherefore liest thou thus upon thy face?"

Lord, even Your Word irritates me! Get thee up? I've tried it, and I keep getting knocked down. This time I think I'll stay right here.

Martina sat in the old rocking chair and stared out the second-story window. The morning fog burned off the river as daylight broke into the streets of Sacramento. She had spent most of the night in the chair.

I would like a house in the country where I could see the sun come up over the Sierra Nevadas from my bedroom window . . . and the sunset on the Coast Range from my front porch.

Rancho Alazan.

It had everything. Fruit trees, vineyards, berry vines, vegetable gardens, cattle, horses . . . oh, Daddy's beautiful sorrels with blond manes. Sunrises with Piedra baking bread in the courtyard . . . sunsets with José playing the guitar and everyone singing and laughing.

The truth is, every day was not so delightful.

But many were.

I was surrounded by people who loved me and took care of me.

Lord, why do we have to grow up? Why couldn't I just have stayed that little ten-year-old girl without any cares and worries?

She heard the baby whimper. Christina had kicked off her covers. She slept with her knees tucked under her, her rear end in the air.

Okay, Lord, there's one reason I don't want to be ten. If I hadn't grown up, I'd never get to be a mother and never have the joy of little Christina.

But why was I in such a hurry to leave Rancho Alazan? I know . . . I wanted to make my own decisions. I wanted to show how mature I was. I wanted to show I didn't need beautiful red hair and stunning good looks to be successful. I left a perfect situation to prove I didn't need a perfect situation . . . and then found out I was wrong.

Lord, that little ten-year-old girl in me wants to pack the wagon, the baby, and drive those two mules home. But I can't. I can't fail. I can't fail my mother. I can't fail Daddy. I can't fail You.

She stood to stare down at J Street. Freight wagons had begun their morning trek up from the Embarcadero.

If both my clerks quit, I will need to hire new ones. But I cannot vacate the store to go hire someone because Mr. Clayton is just waiting to catch this building empty and lock it up tight. I'll go down to the sidewalk and see if someone on the street wants a job.

Of course, they won't know the store or the goods or the customers like Doraine and Evie. I can't hire a total stranger.

She left her perch at the window and shuffled over to the dresser, stopping to stare in the mirror.

Are you Alena Merced's daughter?

You look like her older spinster sister.

What would Mother do with a failed business?

I've heard the story over and over and over. Grandpa died; the warehouse in Monterey burned to the ground; all her family was 3,000 miles and six months' travel away. So what did you do, Miss Alena Louise Tipton?

You up and married Daddy and moved to the ends of the earth at Rancho Alazan to be a light in the darkness.

But I'm already married.

So what would you have done if Daddy had run

off and left you stranded at Rancho Alazan?

Daddy run off and leave Mother?

Martina began to laugh and laugh.

There has never been a man on the face of the earth more devoted to a woman than Daddy is to Mother. He would gladly give his life for hers . . . and proved it during more than one Indian raid, more than one flood, more than one stand against outlaws and cutthroats.

There is one thing my mother will never, ever have to face, and that is desertion of a husband. Sometimes he's a very simple man. Often he's a very stubborn man. But always and forever he is her man. And hers alone.

But what if Daddy had gotten killed? What if that arrow hadn't hit his hat but instead his heart? What if she were at Rancho Alazan with a one-year-old baby? Me. What if it were Mother, me, and the hired hands? What if the hired hands quit?

I cannot imagine her packing me up and going back to her brother in Boston. She would have stayed and made a go of it . . . or she would have died trying.

Martina wasn't sure when the tears had streamed down her cheeks, but she retrieved a linen handkerchief from the top drawer and dabbed her cheeks.

And Mother certainly wouldn't have flirted with some drifter.

She leaned close to the mirror, tugged at the skin under her eyes, and studied the red lines in her pupils.

I take that back. My mother flirts with every man. That's why they never take it personal. That's why they all love her. She makes every male feel good, important, manly. But she does it in such a subtle way. They all know she has eyes only for Daddy.

"Get thee up" — that's what You told me last night, Lord. Well, I'm up. And I've taken about every blow the Evil One can toss my way. If I'm going to fail, it will not be because I rolled over and refused to stand back up.

Someone is going to come through that door this morning, and I'll offer the person a job. Someone wants to work in this town. Young Mr. Tapadera Andrews wants to work; there must be others. If I have to, I'll hire a new crew, but this store is staying open.

At 7:00 A.M. Martina approached the big front doors of Swan's. She glanced around the store. Everything was in place, including Christina who sat in the playpen near the counter. She was content for the moment with six green wooden thread spools strung on a red ribbon and tied like a necklace.

Martina wondered who would be waiting when she flung open the front door. She climbed on the wooden chair and tugged on the brass deadbolts on top of the double doors. *Perhaps Mr. Hackett is here to apologize. Maybe Doraine or Evie, or both, thought about it and decided to come back to work in spite of last night. Perhaps there will be someone special. What if Winifred Chambers heard that we are still open and wants his old job back? Lord, that would be a wonderful blessing.*

She put her long, narrow fingers around the cold crystal glass doorknob. *Well, whoever is waiting to come in, Lord, I thank You for them!*

Martina swung the big door open to the silence of an empty sidewalk.

That's an answer to prayer?

She propped the door open with the huge rock and then opened the other one.

Lord, in case You forgot, I had Your day all planned out for You. I got off my face, Lord. I decided I could survive one more day. I had just enough hope to give it another try. And now this? I'm going to need some emotional, physical, and spiritual help today. Did I mention that? I guess I assumed You knew how totally helpless and pathetic I am without Your assistance.

She walked out to the edge of the sidewalk and looked up and down the street. There was no traffic in sight. No rigs. No carriages. No one walking. Nothing.

"Hello!" she called out. "It's morning! Swan's is open!"

Her words seemed to bounce along the empty street.

This is not Sunday. It's Thursday. It is September, so it cannot be danger from a flood. The war is over in the East. The hostiles have been subdued in California, for the most part. Where are the people?

Martina stomped back into the store, grabbed the back of the wooden chair, and dragged it, screeching on its back legs, all the way to the rear of the room next to the playpen. Then she plopped down in the chair and folded her arms.

Well, there's a possibility I didn't consider. I needed help in the store, and the Lord answered by keeping the people away. I won't need any clerks if it continues like this.

She stared down at the baby.

"You know what, honey? I think I'll just crawl into the playpen with you, and we'll play with necklaces today. Would you like Mommy to do that?"

The baby held up two chubby arms, bare from the elbows down. She wore a short-sleeved long dress. "Mama!" she squealed.

Martina plucked up the baby. "You might as well come play in the store. At this rate, you won't get in anyone's way."

"Hey . . . do you know where a cowboy can find a place to bunk?"

Martina spun toward the front door. At first glance the daylight behind the man made it impossible to detect who it was.

But the voice was familiar.

One step toward the front door revealed auburn hair curled out from under a wide-brimmed gray felt hat.

"Joey?" she called out. "Look, baby, it's your Uncle Joey!"

Martina's middle brother was two years younger and almost six inches taller. His thin, lanky frame was similar to their father's, but he had his mother's hair and his mother's eyes.

"Joey, I can't believe you showed up this morning!"

He snatched up the baby, kissed her round cheek, and then set her back on her feet.

"Mama says this big girl can walk now."

Christina sat down on the floor and immediately began to crawl.

"She only walks when she wants to. She's sort of stubborn."

"A trait of all Merced women."

"She's a Swan."

Joseph shook his head. "Look at that hair. That girl is a Merced, sis, and you know it." Joseph threw his arm around his sister and hugged tight.

It felt good. Very good.

When she finally let him go, Martina wiped a tear from her eye.

"Are you all right, Marti?"

"I'm doing a lot better since you walked in the door. What are you doing here?"

"It's a long story."

"I've got time." She pointed to the empty store. "No customers."

"It's seven o'clock in the morning. City folks don't get around this early anymore. It's a wonder you don't wait and open at 8:00," Joseph suggested.

"Swan's has always opened at 7:00 — you know that," she said.

"Yeah, but why?"

"Because . . . because that's the way things are done."

"Change your hours and you'd save money on clerks' salaries and give yourself more time to sleep in."

"If no customers show up, I could just sleep in the store." Martina slipped her arm into her brother's. "Would you like some coffee?"

"Thanks, sis, but I just ate down at The Coachman."

It feels so good to clutch a strong man's arm. "When did you get to town?"

His strong, callused hand patted hers. "I'll tell you everything if I get to hold my niece."

Martina released his arm. "She doesn't like men to hold her much."

He squatted down and held out his arms. "Come here, lil' darlin'. Come see Uncle Joey."

Christina grabbed onto a stack of ready-made gabardine curtains, pulled herself to her feet, and tottered over to Joseph Merced, flinging her arms out to him.

"See!" he crowed.

"Okay, Merced men are all charmers. Every girl in California knows that!"

Joseph carried the baby to the back of the store as Martina trailed along. "Sis, can I bunk with you and Christina a day or two?"

"Certainly. But did Mother send you to town to look after me?"

"Since when did big sister ever need someone

136

to look after her? Actually Dad sent me to town."

"How's he doing, Joey?" Martina queried.

"He won't complain. You know that. But he's slowin' down. Bound to happen. A man can't push himself that hard for that many years without wearing out. He misses his girl, of course. He prays for you, Billy, and Christina ever' evenin' at supper," Joseph said.

"This store has me tied down until Billy gets home from Nevada. I've hardly had time to go out to supper. Now why did Daddy send you to town?"

"He bought a bull from a rancher down at Visalia. The old man down there claims this bull and his sires are immune to Texas fever, and Daddy thinks it's worth investigating."

"Do we have Texas fever?"

"Nope. But you know how he is. Anyway, I was supposed to meet this man named Woods at the stockyards here in Sacramento. He was coming up early for the state fair. So I left home last night and rode down in the dark, only to find a telegram waiting for me sayin' he would be delayed a day or two."

Martina could smell what she called the Rancho Alazan aroma on her brother. "So you're going to stay with us for a few days."

He jiggled the baby and brushed a kiss across her chubby cheeks. "If it isn't too much bother."

"Bother? Joey, you are an answer to prayer. I'm having a little staff problem, and I could really use some help in the store."

"Mama said that Mr. Chambers quit." Joseph nodded.

"I'm not sure Doraine and Evie are going to show up today either."

"What happened?"

"I'd rather not talk about it. Anyway, can you help me out?"

"I'll do anything you want, sis. But do you really think anyone is going to buy dry goods from the likes of me?"

"Wash up, comb your hair, and leave your hat, chaps, and spurs on a peg. Then grab one of those new denim shirts, and you'll do just fine," she instructed. It felt a little like being at home where her word was always law to her brothers.

Joseph pulled off his hat and held it in his hand. His auburn hair shot out wildly in several directions. "Do I have to hang my hat?"

Christina stared at him and then began to giggle.

Martina laughed. "Joey, you definitely can leave a hat on. But you have to wear a better one than that. That old one smells like a well-used barn. Billy left one up on the shelf above the clothes rack in the apartment. Help yourself."

"What do you mean he left it?" Joseph probed. "Sounds like you don't expect him back."

"What do you mean by that?" she snapped.

"Hey, sis . . . relax. It's me, Joey. I'm on your side, remember?"

Martina took a deep breath. "Well, I am worried about Billy. How would I know if he got hurt and needed me?"

"You want me to take off a couple of weeks and go to Nevada and check on him?"

"No!" She tried to relax her shoulders. "Thanks, Joey, but the very best thing that has happened to me in a long time was you showing up this morning willing to help with the store."

"Big Sister, you know if you ever need help, you just say the word, and there will be three redheaded brothers standing alongside you."

"I know, Joey." She turned her head so he wouldn't see her brush back a tear. Then she spun back around. "Give me Christina. You trot upstairs and change your shirt."

"Yes, ma'am."

The baby whimpered when Martina took her away from Joseph. "Oh, sure, cry for your Uncle Joey. You redheads always stick together, don't you?"

Mrs. Gladys Moss and Mrs. Beatrice McMahn marched into the store and right over to the yardage goods. Martina carried the baby with her to wait on them.

"Ladies, do you need some quilt yardage today?"

"Yes, thank you," Mrs. Moss replied, her black leather purse clutched tightly in front of her. "Miss LaFlor usually waits on us."

"I'm sorry, Doraine isn't here at the moment. What can I do to help you?"

Mrs. McMahn looked at the baby, smiled, and then turned to Martina. "A mother should raise her children at home," she announced.

"This is my home, Mrs. McMahn."

"That is not what I meant."

I know exactly what you meant. "I consider hard work a virtue. And in order to make a business thrive, sometimes both husband and wife need to put in some hours. I'll bet when you ladies lived on farms in the East, you worked very hard alongside your husbands," Martina challenged.

"Yes, we did," Mrs. Moss replied.

"But that's different. We had a home on the farm," Mrs. McMahn countered.

"She already explained that, dear. They live upstairs," Mrs. Moss said.

"Well, you are going to move to a real home someday, aren't you?"

Martina gritted her teeth, then tried to relax. "That is certainly our plan, Mrs. McMahn. What can I get you ladies?"

"Well . . . I still say a store is a — a dangerous place to raise a child," Mrs. McMahn declared.

"My, it seems nice to me," Mrs. Moss countered. "Why, I raised six children for five months in that dreadful covered wagon along the trail. If we could have spent one night in a place like this, we'd have thought we'd died and went to heaven." She turned to Mrs. McMahn. "You came out in a wagon, didn't you, Beatrice?"

The sneer began to fade. "Well, I suppose we all have some months of difficulty."

Martina took a deep breath but tried to keep it from showing. She shifted the restless baby to her other hip. "What kind of material were you looking for today?"

"Miss LaFlor didn't quit on you, did she?" Mrs. McMahn probed. "We heard Mr. Chambers quit."

"He found a job in Grass Valley," Martina said.

Mrs. McMahn pushed her black hat back a little. "Who would want to live up there?"

"Now, dear." Mrs. Moss laid her hand on Mrs. McMahn's arm. "It's very lovely up in the mountains. Especially in the summer and fall." Then she turned to Martina. "We need a print with yellow and purple. Do you have any remnants like that?"

"Miss LaFlor's going to be in later?" Mrs. McMahn demanded.

"Well, how are my two favorite customers today?" The cheerful voice floated across from the front doorway.

Martina spun around. "Doraine!"

"Sorry I'm late, Miss Merced. I told you yesterday this might happen, didn't I?" Doraine sashayed toward the back of the room. "Let me get my apron. I'll be right with you."

The women watched as Doraine buzzed across the store. "Now I'm ready for work. I bet Miss Merced didn't tell you why I'm late."

Mrs. McMahn looked around with eager eyes. "No, she didn't mention it."

141

"That's just the kind of boss she is. Always covering up for us. Well, the truth is . . ."

Martina grimaced. *Do we want to know the truth, Doraine?*

"The truth is I had some of that hot mustard with Chinese food last night and could hardly sleep at all. I don't know how many trips I made to the little room out back. Does that ever happen to you, Mrs. McMahn?"

Mrs. McMahn's face paled. "Oh, I never touch the stuff."

"The mustard?" Doraine queried.

"No, Chinese food," Mrs. McMahn explained. "It's so . . . so foreign."

Mrs. Moss had a soft, quiet smile. "I think that's the point, dear."

Doraine folded her hands in front of her. "Did Miss Merced show you the purple and yellow parrot print we got in from the Sandwich Islands?"

"I was saving it for you to show," Martina sighed. "I'll leave you two in Doraine's capable hands."

Mrs. Moss stared across the store. "Did Billy Swan dye his hair red?"

"That man coming down from the apartment is not Billy Swan," Mrs. McMahn trumpeted.

Martina spun around. "Ladies, you know my brother Joseph, don't you?"

"Why, yes, dear. We met him at the wedding. Remember, Beatrice?" Mrs. Moss said. "Remember those three handsome young men with red hair like their mother's."

"Oh, yes, beautiful Alena's boys. Your brother. That's why he's in your home. Forgive my sullied thoughts," Mrs. McMahn demurred.

Just how sullied were they? "Joey's staying with us a few days to help out in the store," Martina announced.

"He is?" Doraine gulped. "Right here? All day?"

Martina tried to read Doraine's eyes. "Do you have a problem with that?"

"No, I don't." Doraine shrugged. "But Evie might."

"Evie's not here," Martina reminded her.

"Oh?" Mrs. McMahn pursued. "Don't tell me she had Chinese food too?"

"As a matter of fact . . . she did." Doraine shrugged at Martina and began digging through the remnant barrel.

Martina sent Joseph to purchase a rack of buttons from Huntington's wholesale warehouse while she and Doraine waited on customers. The baby seemed especially fussy, and Martina ended up carrying her around most of the morning. It was about eleven o'clock when Evie Norman scooted through the front door and up to Martina.

"Miss Merced, I'm sorry I'm late."

"You look pale. Are you ill?" Martina said.

Evie shook her head up and down. "It was that Chinese food."

"That's what Doraine told me. But I'm not

sure I got all the story."

"Good."

"What do you mean, 'good'?"

"Let me say this — after me and Doraine made complete idiots of ourselves in the alley, Mr. Hackett gave us the Chinese food and walked off," Evie reported.

"So you ate it?"

"Yes, but I don't think us Occidentals are supposed to eat those round peppers and the mustard sauce. I thought I was going to die all night long."

"I'm glad you're feeling better," Martina added. "I was afraid you'd both want to quit."

"You mean, because you didn't tell us that Mr. Hackett had supper with you in your apartment the night before last?"

Martina's shoulders slumped. "Something like that."

"Doraine and me talked that all out and decided that it had obviously meant a lot more to Mr. Hackett than to you. After you slammed the door on him, we figured you weren't really in the competition anymore."

"I was never in the competition."

"Well . . . anyway, we talked about it and got everything figured out."

"Oh, just what did you decide?" Martina questioned.

"We drew straws for him," Evie said.

"You what?"

"We decided that competing for the same man

was not a smart idea, so we drew straws to see who got Mr. Hackett."

"That was very democratic of you."

Evie's face lost expression. "It was? I didn't mean to be a Democrat. If they let women vote, I would have voted for Mr. Lincoln."

"What I meant was, that sounds like a fair solution. So who won?" Martina asked.

"Doraine."

"Are you disappointed?"

"I guess. But we did come to an agreement. The very next handsome bachelor who comes into the store is mine," Evie announced.

Martina tried to hold back a smile. "I suppose he'll have a little to say about that."

"Oh, yes, I suppose so. But you and Doraine cannot flirt with him."

"I promise."

Evie pointed to the redheaded man carrying several bundles through the front door. "Look! It's — it's your brother Walt!"

"No, it's Joseph. My middle brother."

"But he's so . . . so . . . so tall," Evie said.

"He's going to help us out at the store for a few days."

"He is?"

"Yes, isn't that nice?"

"He's not married, is he?"

"No, none of my brothers are ma—"

"He's mine," Evie insisted, as she brushed her hair back from her eyes.

"I promise I will not flirt," Martina giggled.

"Does he like Chinese food?" Evie grilled.

Martina locked her fingers and raised her brown eyebrows. "He absolutely hates it."

"I think I'm in love," Evie swooned. "If I live to be a hundred, I'll never eat Chinese food again. But having your brother here is great news. Isn't it strange how all night I kept fearing this day, and suddenly everything seems so nice?"

"Yes, it is nice that some days don't turn out as bad as we dread." Martina jiggled the baby on her hip. "Would you like to carry Christina while I help Joey? Or would you like to help Joey and let me —"

"Oh, by all means, I wouldn't want to separate a baby from her mother." Evie scooted toward Joseph.

Lord, what other surprises do You have for me today? I think You solved the short-lived staff problem. If Winifred Chambers shows up wanting his job back, I won't know what to tell him.

Christina spent most of the morning permanently attached to her Uncle Joey's leg, riding the store aisles on his boot. Evie hovered nearby while Doraine and Martina waited on the bulk of the customers.

Right after lunch Tapadera Andrews, Jr., trotted into the store with a huge cluster of white daisies and a note. "These are for you, Mrs. Swan."

"You should be in school, young man," she

146

scolded. "No school, no work."

"I'm on my nooner."

"And I believe you're telling a stretcher. Go to class."

"Yes, ma'am." Andrews trudged off down the street.

Doraine was drawn to the flowers faster than a honeybee. "Who are they from?" she quizzed.

Martina read the note. "Eh, from Mr. Hackett."

"I knew it. I knew it," Doraine fumed. "He can't keep his mind off you."

"Well, perhaps that will change." Martina read through the letter again. "He apologized for his behavior and is going back to Nevada tomorrow. He said he will not pester any of us again. And I should let him know if I want to send a note to Billy in Nevada. He's staying at the Grand Hotel."

"He won't pester us? He's not coming back? I traded away one of the Merced men for a drifter who isn't coming back?" Doraine moaned.

Martina rubbed her fingers across her lips. "I really should send Mr. Hackett a reply, shouldn't I?"

"Yes, you should," Doraine encouraged her.

"But it would be improper for a married woman to take a note to the Grand Hotel. So I'll have one of my employees do it. Do you suppose I could impose upon you, Miss LaFlor, to take a note by to Mr. Loop Hackett?"

"Right now?" Doraine grinned.

"I was thinking you could do it on your way home after work. About supper time." Martina tried to hide her grin.

"Oh . . . yes, well, so was I, of course. I'd be happy to convey your message," Doraine announced. "Strictly as a personal favor."

"Yes, most definitely."

A loud whistle came from the back of the store. Martina and Evie turned around to see Joseph tug a black silk garment out of Christina's little hand. "Where in the world did you find these, little darlin'?" he howled.

"Those are not to be opened up!" Martina huffed as she stomped to the back of the store.

"I should say not!" Joseph chuckled. "I believe you could sell those down in the badlands district."

"How would you know what the soiled doves wear in the badlands, Mr. Joseph Cabrillo Merced?" Martina contested.

"A man hears stories." His grin was contagious.

"Those garments are not for sale," Martina announced.

"They belong to you?" he asked.

Martina just glared.

"Eh, what about that keg of powder?" Joseph changed the subject. "Does it have unmentionables in it?"

"The powder keg!" Martina blurted out. "I need to do something about that."

Martina told Joseph the story about the pow-

148

der keg as she tied a heavy string around the package of French giggles and shoved it under the counter. By the time she finished, both Doraine and Evie were huddled next to them.

"What do you think I should do with that keg?" Martina asked her brother.

"Open it and see what's inside," he insisted. "Maybe you're all worked up over nothing."

"Those men were ready to shoot me for that keg. I'm not worked up over nothing," Martina snapped.

"Well, you promised it to this guy, Hackett. So why not give it to him and let him decide what to do with it?"

"He keeps forgetting to pick it up."

"I could take it to him," Doraine suggested.

"It's too heavy," Martina protested. "Perhaps Joey could take it."

"You promised me," Doraine pouted.

"I'll just tag along and tote the thing," Joseph said.

"No, you won't," Evie bristled. "I, eh, don't think we should be that shorthanded around the store. I'm still feeling weak and need Joey to help me straighten those top shelves."

"We straightened them last night," Doraine blustered.

"But we didn't do a very good job." Evie was almost shouting.

"I'll tell you what," Martina interjected. "I'll send Doraine to the Grand with a message for Mr. Hackett to stop by today."

"What's the point in that?" Doraine quizzed.

"So he can pick up the powder for himself."

"Oh, yes, of course. Do you want me to go right now?"

"Yes, go on."

"Well, I'll need to comb my hair and freshen up," Doraine insisted.

"Your hair looks like it always does," Evie announced.

"That's why I'm going to comb it." Doraine marched to the full-length mirror.

Doraine returned in about twenty minutes and informed them that Mr. Hackett would be over shortly. When an hour passed without his arrival, Doraine strolled over to Martina.

"I wonder what's keeping Mr. Hackett?"

"Relax, Doraine, you don't want to look over-anxious."

"I don't?"

"Of course not. I think you should be busy when he gets here."

"Don't tell me to ignore him. I've never made an impression on a man that way yet."

"No, but you want him to know you are a hard-working woman who has more to do than stand around and pine after him."

"I suppose I shouldn't go out on the street and look both ways," Doraine said.

"Definitely not," Martina insisted.

"Well, maybe you could go look since you're not interested in him anymore."

Anymore? Okay, Lord . . . she's right. "All right, I'll go look. If he's coming, do you want me to run back in here screaming, or should I act demure?"

"Demure would be better . . . I think."

Martina walked out the front door to the sidewalk and looked up and down J Street. She didn't see Loop Hackett, but she did spy three men galloping up the street toward Swan's.

It wasn't the first time she had seen them.

She sprinted into the store and shouted, "Joey, take Christina and that keg of gunpowder upstairs right now! Then bring your gun and come back down. Doraine, stay behind the counter and fetch the shotgun. Make sure it's loaded. Evie, get out the back door and go get the sheriff as fast as you can run!"

Seven

Martina marched right up to the front door as two of the three gunmen dismounted and stalked toward her. She studied their dirty and determined faces. *Lord, I'm not a heroic type. Mother is. And Father is the pattern for heroes. But I'm not going to be threatened by these men again. Not in my own store! Lord Jesus, deliver us!*

She startled the men as she swung open the door and blocked their passage with folded arms. "Are you two shopping? If not, you are not welcome here."

The man with a full black beard and scar above his right eye growled, "You ain't goin' to keep us out of there."

The skinny one with a huge knife hanging from a scabbard on his belt stepped closer. "You got our merchandise or know the whereabouts of the man who does. We ain't leavin' until we get some answers."

"Let me make this real understandable." Martina's brown eyes narrowed; her thin lips tightened. "If you come into this store, you will buy something." She could feel her heart beat through her tightly clenched fists. "If that is not your intention, you will have to leave."

"I reckon that old boy Hackett ain't here to protect you this time," the bearded one grumbled. "We ain't found him anywhere in town. He must have lit shuck when he heard we was lookin' for him. So we're goin' inside, darlin', and it's a fact you ain't goin' to stop us."

When Martina had been only nine, she had ridden a horse named Juany Boy to the edge of Little Oak Barranca. It was ten feet wide and thirty feet deep. She had backed Juany Boy up about fifty feet and jumped him across the ravine. In the middle of the jump she didn't know if she would live or die.

It was the riskiest adventure of her life.

Until this very moment.

The men barged into the store, one on her left, the other on her right. As she expected, they both purposely slammed against her, spinning her around. They both made sure their arms brushed the upper part of her torso.

Martina was surprised this distraction worked so well. *This is something Mother would be quite good at.*

Ten feet inside the front door, the men halted, and the skinny one bellowed, "Where is it?"

The click of a hammer being cocked on a revolver spun them both around, grabbing for their empty holsters.

"Are you looking for these, boys?" she challenged.

"What the —"

"How in the —"

"She picked us clean!"

"It wasn't much of a challenge," Martina boasted. "I don't allow shoppers to be armed. Now what can I sell you?"

"You cain't bluff us," the bearded one snarled. He took a step toward Martina.

"You ain't goin' to shoot no one," the skinny one derided.

"Don't count on it, boys. She's got a stubborn streak that won't let go." Joseph Merced called out from halfway down the stairway, his revolver pointed at the men.

"Who are you?" the bearded one called out. "You ain't Hackett."

"Nope. I happen to be the brother of the lady you just jostled coming into the store. You insulted my sister's honor. I reckon it would be fair to shoot you."

The skinny one pulled his knife and waved it wildly around the room. "Ain't no one shootin' me without a fight."

"Knives scare me, Miss Merced," Doraine called out from the back counter. The two men spun around to look down the barrels of a shotgun that Doraine held to her shoulders. "And when I get nervous, my hands twitch. Would it be a crime if I pulled the trigger now?"

Joseph Merced stomped down off the stairs. "As far as I'm concerned, it would be strictly self-defense."

"Self-defense?" the bearded one griped. "We're unarmed."

"You call that Arkansas toothpick being un-armed?" Joseph called.

"She ain't got it in her to pull the trigger!" the skinny one challenged.

"That is exactly what Red Ernie told me once," Doraine announced.

"You don't know Red Ernie. He died two years ago up at Angel's Camp," the skinny one argued.

"Yeah. From a double blast of a shotgun just like this," Doraine called out. "My shoulder was black and blue for a month."

Immediately the skinny one dropped his knife to the floor.

"Now that's better." Martina kept both re-volvers pointed at the men, but only the one in her right hand was cocked. "Doraine, try not to kill these men."

"Can I wound them?"

"Not on purpose," Martina replied. "Now what was it you two wanted to buy?"

"We ain't buyin' nothin'," the bearded one said.

"Oh, that's where you're wrong. I made it clear that if you came in here, you'd have to buy something. Now just what would you like?"

"We ain't got no money."

"Well, that is a problem. But this is a generous establishment. Joey, what do you think these two guns are worth?"

Joseph brushed some of the shaggy red hair off his ear and grinned. "About five dollars apiece if they're in good shape."

"We ain't selling our guns!"

"You have to buy something," she insisted. "And if you don't have any money, you'll have to trade. I can't imagine anything besides your guns that would be worth more than a dollar."

The skinny one reached into his black leather vest pocket and pulled out a gold coin. "Well, I'll be. I do have a half-eagle," he confessed.

"Oh, how nice." Martina waved the barrel of the cocked revolver at him. "Just put it on the floor."

The bearded one glanced around the room, then back at Martina. "What?"

When they were all young, Joseph and Martina would stand Walt and Edward in a tag game at Rancho Alazan. When she and Joseph won, his eyes would flash with excitement. It was the same look he had at the moment. "You heard her," Joseph pressured.

"I'm getting very, very nervous back here," Doraine called out. "Miss Merced, if you'd just step back a little so you're not in the line of fire."

The skinny one tossed the ten-dollar coin on the floor.

"Good. Now let's see . . . Doraine, get these men new cotton shirts and denim trousers. Better make it three sets. The one out in the saddle will be jealous if he is poorly dressed."

"We ain't buying new clothes."

"You just did. And Swan's would like to thank

156

you for giving us the business. But please do not come back again."

There was a commotion at the door. Martina turned. The skinny one stooped down for his knife. Joseph Merced emptied a .45 caliber lead ball into the wooden floor. The man jumped straight up, abandoning the knife. Gun smoke drifted across the store.

Loop Hackett, his drawn gun at the third rider's back, entered the store. "Looks like I just about missed the fun. I caught this old boy sneakin' up on the front door, gun in hand. Thought you might need some help, but it looks like you have it all taken care of."

"These customers just bought some goods and were leaving. However, I'm glad you came along. We can always use another clerk." Martina lowered the guns to her side. "Mr. Hackett, this is my brother Joey. And you know Miss LaFlor."

Hackett shoved the third gunman out into the center of the room near the bottom of the staircase with the others. His felt hat was tilted slightly to the right. "Looks like you boys got yourselves in a fine mess."

"There's a powder keg that's rightfully ours, and we want it," the bearded one demanded.

Joseph Merced scratched the back of his head but kept his revolver pointed at the men. Martina thought he looked thirty instead of only twenty. "Sis, did you ever notice how strange it is that men with guns pointed at them think they

157

can make demands?"

"What do you want me to do with these shirts and trousers?" Doraine called out.

"I've changed my mind," Martina called out. "No reason for them to be practical. Let's sell them that whole bundle of special items under the counter."

Doraine laid the shotgun on the counter and tried to cover her laughter with her hand. "You mean the French . . ."

"Yes. I believe that will make them a splendid purchase!" Martina tried to keep up her gruff, businesslike tone.

Doraine LaFlor toted the large brown-paper-wrapped bundle of silk garments toward the front of the store just as a winded Sheriff Anderson and Evie Norman burst through the door.

"What's goin' on in here?" the sheriff roared.

Martina lowered both revolvers and strolled over to the sheriff. "This is the second time these men have burst in on me, threatened me, and harassed me. I'd like them arrested."

The sheriff rubbed his mustache. "Did they steal anything?"

"No, but they did purchase a few items." Martina nodded toward the bundle in Doraine's hand.

The sheriff studied the men's faces. "What are they after?"

Martina tugged on her earlobe and then brushed her long brown hair off her shoulder. "I think it has something to do with a powder keg that contains more than just powder."

"It's our rightful goods, and she won't give it to us," the skinny man whined, his head low, the brim of his hat shading his eyes.

The sheriff stooped down and peered at the man. "Ain't I seen you before?"

"Nope. We're new in town," the bearded one insisted.

The sheriff stood up straight but kept his gun trained on them, as did Loop Hackett and Joseph Merced. "What's in the gunpowder keg?"

"I have no idea," Martina admitted, "but they seem ready to kill for it."

"You got the keg?" the sheriff quizzed.

"Yes, it's upstairs," Martina admitted.

"She's been holdin' out on us all along!" the bearded man roared. "It belongs to us! You jist let us have our goods, and we'll ride out of town. We told her that in the first place. She's just a troublemaker, Sheriff."

"What you three lack in intelligence, you certainly make up for in audacity," Martina fumed. "Sheriff, you might want to discuss the contents of that barrel with a Mr. Touchet. He seems to think it belongs to him."

Sheriff Anderson's square jaw tightened. "Burro Touchet? He's dead. We found him down on the Embarcadero this mornin' shot in the head three times. Someone said they seen three men in the area right before daybreak."

Martina felt her hands begin to quake. *Mr. Touchet dead? These men killers? What am I doing*

159

pulling a stunt like this? "I'm sorry for Mr. Touchet." She slipped her arm into her brother's. She felt her knees weaken. "Whatever else he did, he treated Swan's fair and square."

"What can I do to help?" Joseph offered.

"How about you and Mr. Hackett helping me get these hombres to jail?" the sheriff proposed. "And bring that powder keg with you."

Martina strolled over to Loop Hackett. "I trust you have time to assist. I appreciate your showing up when you did."

Hackett tipped his hat. "Figured I ought to say goodbye."

Doraine scooted up to the other side of Hackett. "Are you going somewhere?"

Loop Hackett tugged a slip of paper out of his vest pocket. "Bought a stage ticket all the way from Newcastle to Virginia City. Thought I'd go back."

Doraine chewed on her tongue, then said, "When will you be leaving?"

Hackett shoved the paper back into his pocket. "In the morning."

"Well." Martina tugged the cuffs down on her lavender dress and stood up straight. "I'd like for you to have supper with us tonight."

"You and Christina?" Hackett quizzed.

"Me, Christina, Joey, Doraine, and Evie," Martina announced.

"Really?" Evie shifted her weight from one foot to another as if waiting in line at a crowded privy.

Martina glanced around the room. "Yes, I think it's time we all had a discussion on the future of Swan's."

Doraine LaFlor hummed, and Evie Norman waltzed around the room as they assisted in cooking the meal. Loop Hackett and Joseph Merced toted shipping crates to the apartment to make the table bigger. The baby, barefoot and wearing a long yellow dress, was delighted to totter from one big person to another garnering a carousel of hugs and attention. She spent the bulk of her time in her Uncle Joey's lap, yanking on his braided horsehair watch bob.

When supper was finally served, it was dark outside. A slight breeze floated across the room from the open windows. The three lanterns gave a relaxed, easy feel to the gathering. The apartment filled with aromas of a fine meal, strong perfume, and expected conversation.

Pork chops, sweet potato pie, boiled red cabbage, and brown rice covered each plate — except the baby's. Most of her food was on the floor. Her head was braced on her folded chubby, slightly sticky arms, her eyes closed in innocent sleep.

Martina sliced her meat into thin bites and watched as Evie occupied Joseph and Doraine monopolized Loop Hackett. *On other days I'd be jealous — jealous of both of them. But, Lord, You said, "Get thee up." Well, I'm up. At least, for now. I've got other things to do. To think about. To plan. I've run out of mope.*

The pork was pleasantly moist yet thoroughly done as she let it rest on her tongue.

I should take some perfumes — it will be some miles between hot baths. And the bear-claw neck-lace, I'll take it too. It will remind me to do the right thing and allow God to intervene. I'm not sure how Christina will take to travel. She's never been far-ther than Rancho Alazan.

Her plate mostly empty, Martina retrieved the peach cobbler from the window sill. She started it around the table and then washed up the baby and tucked her into bed in the darkest corner of the one-room apartment.

When the dishes had been sufficiently cleaned, the entire party gathered in the part of the large room that served as a parlor. Loop Hackett and Joseph Merced dragged over kitchen table chairs. To their obvious dismay, Doraine and Evie were relegated to sitting next to each other on the worn green velvet settee. The men re-served the high-back rocking chair for Martina, but she chose to prowl the room instead.

Joseph rubbed his clean-shaven face and tilted the chair back. "Okay, sis, we're here for some discussion about the store, right?"

Martina locked her fingers behind her back as she strolled, her hands bouncing on the bustle of her dress. "Yes. Well, I have a plan. But this plan is going to be difficult for me to discuss. As Joey knows, I don't easily ask for help."

Joseph Merced picked his front teeth with his

thumbnail. "You don't ever ask for help."

"Well, that's going to change right now. I'm going to need to ask all four of you for special help for a couple of weeks."

Loop leaned back in the straight chair and stretched his arms. "All of us? I'm headed for Virginia City tomorrow."

Martina stopped in front of him and waved a long, narrow finger at him. "I have a special purpose for you, Mr. Hackett."

He laced his thumbs in his vest pockets. "Oh?"

"As you all know, Swan's is financially . . . about to go under. We've done well this week, thanks to unexpected inventory, but we'd have to keep this pace up for two solid months to meet our obligations. There is a big bank loan payment that I cannot stall any longer. Unless there is a major reversal, Swan's will close before Christmas."

"The $500 reward for returning that keg with the Central Pacific payroll will mean you can buy some new things," Joseph suggested.

Doraine brushed down her unaproned gingham skirt. "I can't believe we had a powder keg with $7,000 setting up against the back wall."

"That would have paid off Mr. Clayton," Evie added.

"I don't believe the Lord answers our prayers by sending stolen money," Martina replied.

Doraine fiddled with her sandy-blonde hair, trying to tuck it back into her combs. "So what are you going to do?"

Martina took a deep breath and stared down at her hands. "This is tough to talk about, so bear with me. I think one of the struggles facing Swan's is ownership."

Evie wrinkled her permanently upturned nose. "What do you mean?"

Martina dabbed at the corners of her eyes with the tips of her fingers.

"Are you all right, sis?" Joseph probed.

"Yes, and I'm going to continue." She ballooned her cheeks and puffed out the air. "I'm not sure I can plan any future for Swan's until I know the condition of my husband. As you all may or may not know, he has not seen fit to communicate with me in over six months." *Shoulders back. Chin held high. You will not break down and cry in front of these people, Martina Merced Swan. You may cry all night, but you will not cry now.*

"You want me to go to Nevada and track him down?" Joseph asked. "I reckon Walt and Ed would want to go along."

"I already have booked the stage," Hackett offered. "I could locate him and —"

"No," Martina interrupted. "I do not need my brothers to bushwhack my man for me." She sucked in another deep breath and began to pace the room once more. "Just let me explain. I believe I should take Christina and go to Nevada myself. I told myself I would never beg my husband to come home to me. And I won't. But I do want to know exactly what his intentions are. Perhaps he is injured . . . or worse. I must give him the benefit of a doubt."

She parked by the window facing J Street and continued the conversation with her back to them. "The last word I have from Billy came by way of Mr. Hackett. Billy needed some money. So I'm taking the reward money and going to find him. I have no idea where this will lead, but I know I must do it."

Doraine bit her lip and then glanced over at Evie. "What about the store?" she asked.

Martina spun around. "I'd like you and Evie to continue to work the store. I can't guarantee anything beyond the loan deadline, but until then we will operate as normal." She ambled toward her brother. "Joey, can you send word to Father that you need to stay in Sacramento for two weeks and help me out?"

Joseph Merced leaned forward so that the front legs of the chair struck the clean wooden floor. "I reckon so. What do you want me to do?"

Martina retied the lavender ribbon that kept her bangs out of her eyes. "I want you to live in this apartment and help the girls with the store, but you can't leave the building."

Joseph raised auburn eyebrows. "Why not?"

"Mr. Clayton at the Delta State Bank will board it up and repossess it if he ever finds it vacant. I want someone to be in the building all the time."

Joseph stretched long legs out in front of him. His boots almost reached to where Martina stood. "I can't even leave to have supper?"

Evie's hands became animated. "I could bring Joey, eh, Mr. Merced, his supper," she volunteered.

"Where do I come in?" Hackett pressed.

"I need you to spell Joey off some. That would let him get out of the store and stretch. But I really have a great favor to ask you." She walked over and stood in front of Loop Hackett.

He leaned forward, his elbows on his knees, his chin in his palm.

"I would like to purchase your ticket to Virginia City. The baby can ride in my lap for free."

"I could see that coming." Hackett nodded. "I reckon I could wait awhile to return."

"It would be nice to have Loop, I mean, Mr. Hackett around the store while you're gone. You know . . . to assist with things," Doraine gushed.

"I do have a proposition for you, Mr. Hackett." Martina pointed to a shelf in the shadows on the far side of the room. "Over there are four ledgers from Swan's. They go back to 1849. I marked 157 accounts that have never been paid that listed their original address as Sacramento or no more than half a day's ride from here."

Hackett scratched his dark brown hair behind his ear. "You'd like me to call in those accounts?"

Martina tugged at the ivory cameo pinned on the black lace collar that rose high on her neck. "Most are quite old. I know it's only a remote possibility. However, I'd like you to spend two weeks going to as many of these places as possible just to see what you can find. Take the ledgers with you. I'll pay you $100 for the two weeks, or 50 percent of what you collect, whichever is higher."

"I don't need more than the $100," Hackett insisted. "How much is represented in those unpaid accounts?"

Martina glanced over at the ledgers on the distant shelf. "I calculated over $7,000."

"That would be enough to pay off the bank!" Evie exclaimed.

"Yes, but I'm not sure we will be able to get even 20 or 30 percent of that . . . or any of it. Most every debtor may have left town. I know a few are still in business, but that doesn't mean they'll pay."

"Is litigation a possibility?" Hackett questioned.

"Not after all these years. I couldn't sue them. But I just feel that I would regret not having tried to collect. I know it's a thankless job, Mr. Hackett, and I have no right to ask you."

Hackett scratched his head and leaned back in the chair. "Well . . . $100 is more than I'd have if I left tomorrow. Besides, I'll be leavin' town sooner or later. Doesn't matter if they get mad at me." He glanced around the room. "Do you reckon I could bunk up here? The hotel is about to eat up my funds."

"Be happy to have you," Joseph offered.

"We could cook meals every day for Mr.

Merced and Mr. Hackett," Evie offered.

"I couldn't afford to pay you to clerk and cook too," Martina objected.

"Who's talking about getting paid?" Doraine insisted.

Martina looked straight at Loop Hackett's brown eyes. "You'll do it then?"

"I'll do it for you and little Christina," Hackett agreed. "But I have something I need to discuss with you first."

She brushed her fingers across her lips. "What's that?"

Hackett tugged his tie loose and unfastened the top button of his shirt. "It's sort of private. Perhaps we could . . . walk down to the Embarcadero or something."

"That sounds like fun," Doraine bubbled.

"I think he meant just the two of them," Evie informed her.

"Is it really that private?" Martina quizzed.

"Yes, ma'am . . . it is."

The late September evening felt cool but pleasant as Martina and Mr. Hackett stepped out onto the board sidewalk. Oil street lamps glowed in the star-filled darkness. The noises of a raucous party drifted from the next block. The saddle shop, furniture store, and meat market near Swan's were all closed, the sidewalks deserted. Carriages hurried to their destinations.

Loop Hackett strolled along the street side of

the sidewalk. When they reached the corner, he offered Martina his arm.

She hesitated.

"Mrs. Swan, I believe you righteously put me in my place last evening," he murmured. "But I would feel like I had abandoned my manners if I didn't assist you across a crowded street."

She took his arm, and they proceeded toward the Embarcadero. "Mr. Hackett, are you sure we need to walk this far for you to talk to me?"

"Probably not. I'm just screwin' up the courage to tell you what I need to," he admitted.

"It's about my husband, isn't it?"

He paused as they reached the far side of the street. "How did you know that?"

"What else would cause you such consternation? You seem to be dying a thousand deaths."

"I reckon you're right about that."

"And I suppose it has something to do with his behavior."

"It seems like you already know what I'm going to say before I say it," he suggested.

"No, but I couldn't think of any other topic that would cause you to be so discreet." Martina took a deep breath, looked straight ahead, and continued to clutch his arm. *I am not going to cry. I've cried this through before; I will not make a spectacle of myself now.* "Are you going to tell me Billy has taken up with another lady?"

His answer sounded sheepish. "No."

Like the first gentle spring breeze after a long, frigid winter, Martina felt her spirit lift. Her entire body relaxed. *Thank You, Lord.*

"Well, not exactly a lady . . . anyway," Hackett added.

Panic. Pain. Depression. Anger. They all hit Martina at the exact same moment. She dropped Hackett's arm as they continued to stroll. "What do you mean, 'not exactly'?" The words came choking out of her mouth as if they were to be her last.

"Ma'am . . . as I said before, I didn't know your husband real well. I saw him around town from time to time. We were both looking for a decent job other than in the tunnels. We were both on the same side of a scrape with The Bumble Bee."

"The Bumble Bee?"

"That's a silver mine over at Gold Hill," he explained. "Anyway, that's a long story. So when he heard I was headed for Sacramento, he looked me up and asked me to take the message to you."

Martina clutched her hands together. *Let's get this over with.* "Mr. Hackett, what about this other woman?"

"Well, I don't know if there is another woman . . . for sure."

Martina stared off across the Sacramento River. "Mr. Hackett, if you don't hurry up and tell me what you know, I'm going to gut-shoot you and stand and watch you die a horrible, painful death."

"Yes, ma'am, I believe you would. Now here's

170

the thing. I asked your Billy where I could find him when I came back from Sacramento with the money."

"Yes?"

"And he said he was stayin' at the Golden Slipper."

"Is that a hotel?"

"Eh . . . not exactly."

"Well, what is it . . . exactly?"

"A brothel."

One time, when Martina had been fourteen, she had raced her father eight miles from the Porter's Toll House to Hernandez's Ferry. She was riding a sixteen-hand sorrel stallion and was leading the race when a bear lumbered across the road, and the stallion bucked her high in the air. She landed flat on her back in the middle of a baked dirt road. When her father reached her side, her back ached with sharp pain, and the wind was knocked out of her so completely that she could open her mouth, but no words came out.

That was exactly how she felt at the moment.

"Mrs. Swan, are you all right?"

Martina stared straight ahead. *A brothel? Billy wouldn't even go to a brothel, let alone live in one. No one lives in a brothel . . . except the madam and the girls.*

She continued to stroll along the Embarcadero, each step like a forced march.

"Mrs. Swan, I surely am sorry to tell you that. It's just that I didn't want you and the world's cutest baby showing up in Virginia City and discoverin' it on your own. You deserve better treatment than that."

She could feel even the tiniest grains of sand and dirt grind into the soles of her shoes as they hiked up the ramp of an empty dock.

My Billy would not live in a brothel. There is some confusion here. That's it. Mr. Hackett does not know my husband at all. It's another William Swan. There must be others in the world. There's been a mix-up and . . .

But he sent Mr. Hackett to Swan's and gave him Father's bear-claw necklace. It has to be my Billy.

Hackett motioned to a long wooden bench at the end of the short dock. "Would you like to sit on this bench?"

She plopped down next to him and stared into the darkness. From the distant shore a lantern or two reflected on the meandering water of the Sacramento River.

My Billy is a Christian man. He doesn't do things like that. Of course, he hasn't been home for a year. But . . . even so. Well, he might reject me for some woman more beautiful and wealthier . . . but . . . not a common . . .

Her breath now came in short, shallow gasps, like a person who couldn't swim bobbing in the midst of a powerful river current.

Hackett's voice was deep and timorous. "Are you going to say anything, Mrs. Swan? Maybe I shouldn't have told you. Obviously I'm not too good at this sort of thing. That was six months ago. It doesn't mean he's still there. Maybe it was just a temporary thing. Some men are that way when they're away from home. I should just shut up, shouldn't I? I'm makin' this worse."

Perhaps he was just staying with a man he met who happened to live at a . . . What was he going to do with the money? Spend it on a . . .

In the darkness Loop Hackett pulled off his gray felt hat and held it in his hand. The dim light reflected off his white shirt, but his coat and tie were a shadowy blur.

Ill at ease with her silence, Hackett rambled on. "Now when you get to Virginia City, you can check around for your husband, but if you can't find him anywhere else, you can go to the Golden Slipper and ask for Pierced Katie. I hear she's the one that runs the place. But, like I said . . . that was six months ago. Who knows what's happened since then? There usually isn't much room at respectable places, especially for a man needin' funds."

Martina glanced down and realized that she had been wringing her hands as if washing them. She immediately stopped and let them rest on her dress, which had forfeited its color to the darkness. Her shoulders slumped. Her dress suddenly hung heavy on her thin shoulders. All of her clothing felt terribly uncomfortable. She felt extremely tired and extremely plain.

Pierced Katie? Do you mean Katie Pierce? Probably not. How would a woman get a name like Pierced Katie? I don't think I want to know. I could

173

never, ever ask a woman like that if she had seen my husband.

Lord, this is not happening to me. Not to Martina Patricia Merced Swan. It happens to women from the other side of town, but not to me. Ten minutes ago I had everything figured out. You told me to "get thee up." So I did. I figured out a plan. Got everyone to help me out. Now I'm going to leave with the baby in the morning to go to Nevada. If I had known this four hours ago, that my husband's living in a brothel, I would never have made such plans.

She took a slow, deep breath and held it. The night air was cool, almost fresh compared to the dust of the city street in the daytime. She let out the breath slowly. Under the right circumstances it would have been a pleasant evening.

These were not the right circumstances.

That's the point, isn't it, Lord? You want me to go to Nevada, but You held this back knowing that I would be so depressed I would never get up and get going. Well, I can't stop now. I've got the ticket. I've got the clerks lined up. I roped Joey and Mr. Hackett into the middle of this.

No matter what I hear about Billy — no matter what I find in Virginia City — I have to go there. I'm scared to death of what I'll find. But if I don't go, I'll spend my life regretting it.

I only hope I won't spend my life regretting that I did.

Eight

Born under Mexican rule, in the golden land before the war that shifted its political allegiance, before a gold rush that peopled it with pilgrims from every point on earth, Martina Merced Swan was proud to be a Californio.

Native born.

There weren't six fair-skinned women her age who could make that claim.

She often bragged that she had never been out of California. When she and Christina boarded the Central Pacific train in Sacramento, she knew that was about to change. The train took them a total of thirty-one miles to Newcastle. There she and ten others boarded a stagecoach headed up the Dutch Flat Toll Road toward Donner Lake.

Three days.

Two horrid nights.

Seven separate toll roads.

Eight mostly inedible meals.

Countless foul and blasphemous stories.

A seeming river of tobacco juice.

Clouds of cigar smoke.

And for the final sixteen miles, including the grind up Mt. Davidson, she was at the mercy of a

stage driver named Hank Monk who, she was informed, was the best in the entire West.

Martina arrived in Virginia City, Nevada, with
every bone in her body jarred from its original
position. She could only speculate that other less
competent drivers had passengers who never
lived to describe the horror.

Hank Monk tossed her carpetbag on the steps
in front of a three-story wood-framed hotel
called The International as Martina held the
wide-eyed, smudgy-faced, redheaded baby in
her arms.

Virginia City is not Sacramento.

It isn't level.

Nor organized in any recognizable pattern.

Across the street a man staggered out of the
Bucket of Blood Saloon, pulled a revolver, and
fired three shots at the swinging doors. Then he
tottered down the dusty, crowded street.

Martina clutched Christina close to her.

No one paid any attention to him.

Nor civilized.

But if a person went into business, there are cus-
tomers — plenty of customers.

"Excuse me, ma'am."

A man wearing a slightly soiled suit and dingy
cotton shirt, with a new silk tie, stood next to
her, his worn bowler cocked sideways.

She shifted the baby on her hip. "Yes?"

Christina broke out in a wide smile.

"Would you be interested in buying any mining claims? I have two feet of the Imperial, Cen-

tral, or Empire for only $200 a foot, and I have some footage on the Yellow Jacket and Ophir. But, of course, they're higher." He had rolled-up papers in his hand.

She glanced into the open door of the hotel lobby. "I'm not interested in any claims."

He spat tobacco into the street and wiped his mouth with the back of his hand. "Then why did you come to Virginia City?"

Martina scooted to the side of the boardwalk to allow three sweaty Greek-speaking miners to push their way by. "I came for my husband," she murmured.

He looked her up and down. "You came for a husband? You came to the right place, lady. There are twenty men to ever' woman in this town."

Martina brushed a fly off the baby's face. "I came to visit *my* husband."

"Yes, ma'am. I reckon he has red hair, don't he?" The man laughed as he stared at the baby.

"No, he doesn't."

The man glanced at Martina's long brown hair and shrugged.

She swatted a tiny stinging bug off her neck and tried to fan a cloud of dust away. "Perhaps you have seen him. My last address was rather vague."

The man rubbed his round, reddish nose. "What's his name?"

"William Swan. He usually goes by Billy Swan."

"Nope. Never heard of him. But he's probably here. It seems like the whole world is here." He slapped at a mosquito on his three-day-beard-covered cheek.

Martina glanced at the man's bloodshot eyes. *That insect has obviously no sense of smell and no discernment of taste.* "I'll find him."

"So many movin' in all the time." He looked across the street as if trying to locate a possible customer for his claims. "Ain't no one can keep track of folks except maybe ol' man Goodman."

Martina thought about her last night in Sacramento and the cool, clean breeze off the delta. "Who?" she asked.

"Mr. Joseph Goodman — editor of the *Territorial Enterprise*. That's our newspaper, you know," he boasted.

"Where would I find Mr. Goodman?" she inquired.

The man peered down the street to the east at a crowd of men surrounding a single-story unpainted building. "Down there."

"Why has that group gathered?"

"Must be someone readin' a paper to them who can't read. Why, there might be someone who wants to buy a claim." The man tipped his hat and shuffled out into the street. "Nice talkin' to you, ma'am."

Martina carried Christina in her left arm and the carpetbag in her right hand and entered the hotel. The lobby was crammed with men lounging on the sofas and chairs.

Most were talking, all of them smoking.

No one was at the counter, so she rang a small bell. The tinkle of the brass bell hardly sounded above the roar of the conversations.

She rang the bell again.

Certainly they are in no hurry to wait on customers. I trust the rooms are not as smoky as this lobby. I assume they will be able to draw me a hot bath.

She rang the bell again. No one looked in her direction. Finally a short, balding man with pinched glasses perched on his hawkish nose shuffled out of the back room carrying a stack of papers and an ink pen.

"Are you the one ringing the bell?" he asked.

"Yes."

"Well, stop it. It's bothering me." He turned to retreat.

"Wait! I want some service!" Martina demanded.

The man glanced over his shoulder. "You aren't looking for a room, are you?"

"I was. But I certainly am not impressed with the service here," she huffed.

The man turned around. "And I'm not terribly impressed with your intelligence."

Martina stiffened.

He waved his hand at the lobby. "I haven't had a room empty in months — not since The Sonnet came in halfway down Six Mile Canyon. I've got ever' room let, two and three men to a room."

"But . . . I need . . . my baby and I need . . ."

179

Martina was disgusted with herself for not finding the right words.

"Lady, I don't have room even if you was the Blessed Virgin and baby Jesus. You ain't goin' to find anyplace in town neither." The man disappeared behind a door marked Office.

Martina stared out the big lobby window at the crowded street.

Lord, I didn't even want to come here. I said I would never come looking for a husband who didn't want to come home. But here I am, trying to do what I thought You wanted me to do. . . . But this? This is a rude, dirty place.

What am I doing here?

Christina began to squirm.

What are we doing here?

She lowered the baby to her feet. Christina played with the handle on the satchel. A tall, broad-shouldered man who had been leaning on the stone hearth walked toward her. Clean-shaven except for a neatly trimmed dark mustache, he held his silk top hat in his hand. His crisp wool suit was trimmed with black silk cuffs and edging.

"Excuse me, ma'am." He ran his hand through neatly combed dark brown hair. "I noticed you at the counter. Are you by any chance looking for a room?"

"Yes, I am," she admitted. "I suppose it's rather naive of me. I was not informed that Virginia City was so crowded."

His smile was easy, relaxed, showing straight

white teeth. "There is always a room some-where."

"Would you be so kind as to tell me where I might find such a room?"

He swept his arm toward the hotel staircase. "I'll be gone for the night. You may have my room."

She shook her head. "Oh, I couldn't inconvenience you."

"It would be no inconvenience, I assure you."

"You're staying at this hotel?"

"Yes. I'm probably the only one in the International who has a room to himself. I have to pay double, of course."

"Thank you, but I really couldn't take your room. I'll look around."

"Well, if you don't find anything, look me up. I'll gladly let you have the key to my room."

Even when she stood up straight, he towered over her. "Thank you, Mr. —"

"Marsh. Quinten Marsh, but everyone calls me Quint."

"Well, thank you again for your kindness." Martina reached down to pick up the baby and then glanced at her carpetbag. "Mr. Marsh?"

"Ma'am?"

"Do you think I could leave my bag here in the lobby while I look for someone in town?"

"I'll keep an eye on it for you."

"Thank you very much." She walked with the baby halfway across the lobby.

"Ma'am, if you change your mind about that

room, come back and look me up. If I'm not here, I'll be across the street."

"Where?"

"At the Bucket of Blood."

"Why on earth would you be there?"

"That's where I work. I'm a faro dealer."

Martina pushed her way back out onto the crowded raised boardwalk in front of the porch.

"Well, darlin', it might be a little tougher than I thought to find your daddy. I bet you're as anxious to have a warm bath as I am. Let's go see this Mr. Goodman at the newspaper."

Joseph Goodman's long, dark beard swung up and joined his thick, drooping mustache, leaving a perfectly round circle that engulfed his small mouth. His eyes narrowed as he peered up at Martina.

"Are you looking for work?" he asked.

"No, I —"

"Good. I don't hire women reporters. Never have. Never will. They just don't have what it takes. No offense intended."

"Mr. Goodman, I will overlook for the moment your cursory dismissal of my abilities, of which you obviously know nothing. I am not here looking for a job. I was told you know more people in Virginia City by name than anyone else. I came to see if you could help me locate someone."

Goodman took off his silver-framed glasses and carefully laid them on the cluttered desk. He rolled his oak chair back and put his hands behind his head. "You obviously have a way with words. I like that. Whom are you looking for?"

"William Swan. Often he goes by the name Billy."

Goodman glanced at Christina. "You have a cute daughter."

"Thank you."

"I presume this Billy Swan has red hair."

"No, he doesn't."

"But he's your man?"

"He's my husband."

Goodman let out a deep sigh. "Lookin' for your husband, huh?"

"Yes, have you seen him?"

Goodman rolled his chair back up to his desk. "Did you come all the way out here from Iowa lookin' for your husband?"

"Iowa? No . . . I'm from Sacramento. Why did you say Iowa?"

He waved a stubby, ink-stained finger at the rolltop desk. "You see that stack of letters? Ever' one of them is from a lady back East who wrote to the paper to see if I know the whereabouts of her husband or her brother or her daddy."

Dozens of letters crammed a cubbyhole of the large oak desk.

"Gold fever does strange things to men," Goodman continued. "What can I say? I'm sorry he ran off and abandoned you. But he can't be much of a man to leave a handsome wife and a beautiful daughter."

"Mr. Goodman, I did not say my husband abandoned me. He came to Virginia City to start a business. We own a store in Sacramento."

"What did you say his name is?"

"William Swan."

"He owns Swan & Son Dry Goods?"

"That's our store."

"That William Swan. Why, I met him once in Placerville years ago." He looked down at Christina. "That old rascal . . . I thought he would be dead by now."

"He is. I married William Junior."

"Oh, yes . . . of course. Well, the fact remains, I don't know Billy. How long has he been in Nevada?"

"About a year."

"When did you hear from him last?"

"Around Christmas."

"Well, no wonder you're worried. All I can say is, he hasn't struck gold, been arrested for murder, or been lynched. I'd remember that. I don't want to sound depressing, but Hiram Conrad runs a furniture store down the street. You might check his list."

"His list?"

"He sells coffins and is the undertaker too. He has a list of nearly everyone buried in the cemetery. I don't say that to make you melancholy, but if I were you, I'd check it out. Of course, I'm not you."

"And if I were you, I'd hire a woman reporter — but then I'm not you either," she countered.

"Touché! I like that. You have spark. What was your husband's last known address? Where was he staying?"

Lord, You know I did not want to have to say this. Martina stared down at her shoes. "He had some, eh, friends at the Golden Slipper," she murmured.

"My word! . . . Do you know that it . . ."

"I know, Mr. Goodman, that the Golden Slipper is a brothel."

"Town's full of 'em, of course. If it's not a bar, it's a brothel. But what I was going to say is that the Golden Slipper burned to the ground late last January."

"It did?"

"Yep. No one was hurt though. We had over a foot of snow on the ground and some of the . . . occupants got mighty cold that night. Most of them who worked there left for Virgin Alley in Bodie, I heard. But I can tell you right now, you do not want to go to Bodie. I understand there's not a virtuous woman in the entire town."

"Tell me, Mr. Goodman, did the Golden Slipper have permanent boarders?"

"You mean, men?"

"Yes."

"Can't say I ever heard of any. But you might ask Pierced Katie. She used to work at . . . I mean, she resided at the Golden Slipper. I think she ran the joint for a while."

"Where would I find this woman?"

"Ever since the fire she sort of works on her

own. I don't rightly know where to find her, but you'll recognize her when you see her."

"How's that?" Martina questioned.

"Well, for a starter, she has a big diamond stud pierced through her nose, and the others . . . Well, they're only rumors."

Martina shifted the baby to the other hip. "Thank you, Mr. Goodman. Do you happen to know if there are any rooms for rent for the night? The baby and I took the stage from Dutch Flat."

"My word, you don't have any friends to stay with?"

"No, we don't. Are there rooms to let?"

"In this town? No, ma'am. There can't be a room left vacant anywhere. The miners are double-shifting beds as it is. Maybe you could take the stage down to Carson City. They could have a room."

Martina hugged the baby close. The room smelled of ink and raw alcohol. *Lord, my little apartment above the store certainly would seem like a castle right at the moment.* She nodded at the publisher and started toward the door. "We'll find something. Certainly there must be some charity even in a town like this."

Goodman studied her eyes. "Mrs. Swan, chances are I'll be working here late tonight, trying to put this paper out and keep my printers sober. I've got a big black leather couch over there." He waved an arm toward the front of the office. "You and that little redheaded princess are welcome to camp out here if you need to wait for the mornin' stage. It isn't much, but it will be safe and out of the wind."

"Thank you, Mr. Goodman. If nothing else succeeds, I might take you up on that offer."

The list at Hiram Conrad's Furniture Store and Undertaking Emporium revealed that one Swain, two Swopes, and a Swanstein had died. But no Billy Swan. Mr. Conrad was kind enough to allow Martina and the baby to wash up at a basin in the back of the store.

By the time they plunged back through the dust and grime of the street, Martina felt dirty again. She was determined to walk every street and glance at every establishment, but the steep flanks of Mt. Davidson quickly wore away her resolve. He legs ached. Her arm was numb from carrying the baby. Her eyes burned from the fine dust. Her face stung from bug bites. As the sun sank lower, a cold wind whipped up the draw.

Martina plodded by the blue-painted front door of Delaney's Fine Restaurant and went inside. Her first stroke of good fortune in Nevada came when they were seated at a tiny table by themselves in the back of the cafe. The second break was when Christina fell asleep in Martina's lap.

The beefsteak was almost cooked, the potatoes adequate, and the carrots boiled in such a way that left them rubbery. Martina picked at the food. She knew others would soon want the

187

table space, but she dallied, nonetheless, her back to the crowded room. She faced peeling wallpaper that had been painted a dull blue.

Even in the midst of a noisy restaurant, she found a slice of privacy — a time to gather thoughts. *" 'Get thee up'!" Lord, that's what You told me, so here I am. I obviously did something wrong. This surely can't be what You meant. You're punishing me, aren't You? But what did I do? What is my sin?*

Martina dabbed at her eyes with a mostly clean cotton napkin.

Get a hold on yourself, Mrs. Swan. What would Mother do in this situation?

Martina stabbed a carrot stub with her fork and dangled it in front of her mouth.

That's the problem, Lord. I've spent my entire life failing to live up to my mother's standards. I don't want to know what my mother would do. I want to know what Martina Patricia Merced Swan should do.

And what I'm going to do is find Billy. If he's going to reject a "handsome wife" and a "most beautiful baby," he'll have to do it face to face. And I certainly haven't finished looking around Virginia City. I will spend the night and search the town one more day. So, Mrs. Swan, find your best lodging for the night and get some rest.

She popped the carrot bite into her mouth and chewed.

And chewed.

I've had two offers, and I'll take the one that af-

fords the most rest. Whatever Mr. Marsh's quarters are like, as long as there is a bed to sleep on and a lock on the door, I'll be fine.

The noise in the Bucket of Blood ceased as Martina walked through the door carrying a smiling Christina Swan. The crowds of miners coming off their shift, professional gamblers, drifters, and working women parted like the Red Sea in front of her. Most of the men craned their heads to see the baby.

Quint Marsh, his Chinese starched white shirt sleeves rolled up to his elbows, met her midway. "Would you like to take a short stroll?" He nodded toward the door and offered her his arm.

"Thank you, Mr. Marsh. I'm not fond of this type of establishment," she admitted.

"Hey, Quint, that baby's got red hair!" someone shouted, and everyone laughed.

With his hand on the grip of a small revolver that protruded from his gold-flowered vest, Marsh whipped around and stared down at the man. "So does my mother. Are you questioning that?"

"Eh, no, sir . . . Mr. Marsh. No, sir. I was just about to say that is about the cutest baby on the face of the earth. That's what I was going to say."

"I couldn't agree with you more." Then he turned to Martina. "Come along, dear."

Even though the street was still dusty, it smelled fresh compared to the alcohol and smoke of the saloon. When they reached the raised boardwalk, Martina lowered her arm from his.

"You want to take me up on that room offer?" he asked.

"I'm afraid I do. Does your room have a soft bed and a lock on the door?"

"Yes, indeed." He reached into his vest pocket and pulled out a key. "I will not need the room until after breakfast in the morning. I work nights."

"Mr. Marsh, you are very kind for a . . ."

"For a gambler?"

"Well, I know that sounds highly prejudicial."

"Yes, it does. But I know how difficult a room in this town can be to find. I hate to tell you where I had to sleep the first several weeks I was here."

"I trust you didn't have to sleep out on the hillside."

"Oh no, I arrived in February. Too much snow for that." He looked around as if to see if anyone was listening. "I actually rented a cot in a brothel."

"The Golden Slipper?" Her voice was soft, as if not wanting the baby to hear.

He raised his eyebrows. "No, it was at the Mt. Davidson Sewing Club."

"Sewing Club?"

"That's what it was called. But I'm surprised that you know about the Golden Slipper. It burned down several weeks before I arrived. How did you know of it?"

"Some places are so notorious that many hear of their reputation." She looked down at the dust-caked hem of her long black dress.

"I suppose you're right. I'd walk you to the room, but I've got a table to run, and it might seem a tad improper. I'm up at the top of the stairs in Room 220. Your carpetbag is by the hearth. If there are any personal effects in your way, toss them to the side, and I'll straighten them up later."

She reached out to shake his hand. "Thank you again for your kindness. I'm not sure why you are so gracious to me, a total stranger."

He took her hand, shook it in a gentle way, and then reached over and tousled Christina's hair. "Like I told them in the saloon, my mother has red hair."

Martina looked him in the tired eyes bordered by slight creases. "Well, may the Lord reward you for your graciousness."

He winced.

"Did I say something wrong?" she queried.

"Oh, no, that's exactly what my mother would have said. Bless her soul."

She released her grip and readjusted the baby. "Where will you be having breakfast? I'll bring the key back to you."

"Just leave it at the desk."

"Won't that seem suspicious?"

"Oh, well, they're used to . . ." Marsh paused. "Just tell them you're my sister."

"I won't lie, but I'll leave the key."

His eyes relaxed, but he didn't smile. "Are you sure you aren't an angel from heaven sent by my mother to check up on me?"

"I don't think so. Few have ever called me an angel."

"I find that difficult to believe. Good evenin', ma'am." He tipped his tall, black hat.

"Good evening, Mr. Marsh."

She walked slowly across to the hotel. *This is a strange town. I walk into a common, vulgar saloon and borrow a room key from a professional gambler I've just met, and he seems like a nice man I'd like to get to know better. It's as if everyone lays convention aside and just takes people at face value. It seems like the right attitude in the wrong place.*

The first thing Martina did when she entered Quinten Marsh's room was light the lantern on the dresser. The second thing she did was lock the door. Then she set Christina in the middle of the high four-poster bed and gazed at the room.

"Well, baby, this room is the neatest I've ever seen for a single man. Look at this — everything exactly in place. Your uncles never kept their room this neat and organized at Rancho Alazan. Mother always said she had seen cleaner barns."

Christina crawled across the tan quilt and reached out to an object on the nightstand. "Me!" she squealed.

"That's a billiard ball, sweetheart. I don't think it's for you to play with."

"Me!" Christina insisted. She leaned so far

forward that she toppled off the bed.

Martina caught her, and they both sat on the side of the bed. She plucked up the white ball. "Look, punkin, it's engraved: 'To Capt. Quinten F. G. Marsh, from the girls of St. Antoine's.'"

Christina reached for the ball. "Me!"

"You can look at it, but don't throw it." Martina handed her the ball. *Capt. Marsh? Confederate, I would guess. Girls of St. Antoine's . . . I don't know if that's a girls' school — or a bordello. This man is difficult to figure out. Whichever, Lord, thank You for this room. I know that You provided it. And You'll take care of us. Keep us in Your will tonight, Lord.*

Diving straight out in front of the baby, Martina caught the white billiard ball. "Christina! I said don't throw it!"

"Mama!" The baby grinned.

"Yeah, you got me to play with you, didn't you, darlin'? Well, let's get ready for bed, and maybe I can play with you some more."

"Me!" Christina demanded, waving her chubby hands at the ball.

"Oh, no. You aren't going to throw this ball."

The baby puckered her tiny rose-colored lips.

"No pouting from you, young lady!" Martina snatched up the baby and dragged a heavy chair in front of the door. "Now, darlin', the Lord will take care of us tonight, but I thought I'd put this chair over here, just in case it's His will that we do so." She pulled her pocket revolver out of her carpetbag and laid it on the nightstand.

193

I know this doesn't look like I'm trusting You much, Lord. But I've never slept in a total stranger's room before. I'm not sure what to expect.

The baby squirmed and wanted to get down. "Darlin', you had a nice nap at supper, but Mommy didn't. So I'll let you run around for a minute. Then we sleep."

Within fifteen minutes both Martina and Christina were fast asleep in the soft featherbed with clean flannel sheets.

The first thing she heard was a curse in the dark, then a woman's voice hollering, "What's that chair doing there?"

Martina sat straight up on the bed. She reached for Christina with her left hand, the revolver with her right. "Who's there?" she called out at the silhouette in the doorway.

"I'm Katie. Who's in there?"

"What difference does that make to you? This room is occupied."

"You got someone with you?"

Martina pointed the revolver toward the doorway but didn't cock the hammer. "My baby."

"Well, hurry it up. When you are done, me and Mr. . . . eh, Mr. Smith need to use the room."

"My baby is one year old and sound asleep. Perhaps you have the wrong room."

"This is Quint Marsh's room, isn't it?" Alcohol sent the woman's voice down an octave.

"Yes."

"Is he in there?"

"Of course not!"

"Well, Quint told me if I ever needed to use his room while he was working, I could. And I need it. So who are you?"

"I'm merely borrowing his room for the night." Martina stroked the sleeping baby as she continued to point the gun.

"What for?"

"Because there aren't any others available. Did Mr. Marsh give you a key too?"

"Nah, I didn't want to bother him."

Martina's eyes had adjusted to the light coming through the doorway. She could see the ample profile of a woman with short yellow hair. "How did you unlock the door?"

"Are you kidding? Entering hotel rooms is my specialty. There ain't a door in Virginia City that Pierced Katie can't open."

"You're Pierced Katie?" Martina's gun began to sag.

"Yeah, so what?"

"I, eh, need to speak with you." *Lord, if it's Your purpose to totally humiliate me, then I believe You've accomplished that.*

"Well, can you take a walk first? I don't intend to lose cash money."

Rising anger seemed to settle Martina's nerves. "It's the middle of the night, and I have an infant with me. I'm not going for a walk."

"You really have a baby in there?"

"Yes."

The voice in the shadows softened. "Maybe you two can just wait down in the lobby."

"That's preposterous." Martina felt the need to clutch Christina but hugged her own chest instead. "But I do need to ask you a question." Martina had to force out each individual word. "Do you know William Swan?"

"Billy?"

Martina's heart leaped with fear and excitement. "Yes."

"Maybe I do, and maybe I don't," came a hardened reply.

"What do you mean?"

"I mean, I'll tell you what I know about Billy Swan if I get this room for an hour or so."

"I can't believe you want to use this room for such purposes."

"Would you hurry it up? I want to get in there before Mr. Smith dozes off in a drunken stupor and I lose five dollars."

Christina quickly fell asleep on the leather couch in the office of the *Territorial Enterprise*. Mr. Goodman brought Martina a cup of hot chocolate.

"So you found out something about your husband?" he asked.

Martina took a sip and nodded. "Yes, but it was not a pleasant experience."

Goodman's black tie dangled loosely around the unbuttoned collar of his white shirt. "Is he still in town?"

"No," she said. "It seems that when he got to Virginia City, he immediately invested our money in a mine called The Wasp."

"The Wasp! Why, that whole thing was a swindle. There isn't an ounce of silver in that hole."

"That's what I understand. I suppose Billy was too ashamed to come back and admit he had squandered everything." Martina took another sip of chocolate.

Goodman pulled off his soiled leather apron and hung it on a peg by the door. "So he kept hanging around, hoping he'd find a way to get the money back?"

She leaned back on the soft leather couch. "Yes. How did you know?"

"It's a fairly common occurrence in this town." He reached for a long, dark wool topcoat. "They either gamble their funds away at the faro table or in buying mining certificates."

"Well, according to Pierced Katie, he —"

"So you met her?" Even in the shadow of the single oil lantern, she could sense his stare.

"Eh, yes," Martina said, "we had a quick discussion."

"That's quite a diamond she has tacked in her nose."

Martina couldn't help but raise her hand to her own nose. "Which one?"

"My word, she had more than one?" he gasped.

"Oh, yes."

"Well, what did she tell you?"

"That Billy got a job driving ore wagons down to the mills at Empire."

Goodman fastened the top button on his coat and hoisted his silk top hat. "A man doesn't get rich doin' that."

"Yes, I think he was barely able to survive. But after the Golden Slipper burned, he took a wagon down to Empire and didn't come back. Pierced Katie heard he went to Carson City."

Goodman opened the front door. "I assume you'll be heading that way tomorrow?"

"Yes, but I'll need your couch until then."

"Help yourself. But I'm going home now, so lock the door behind me."

"Gladly."

He stepped back inside the building. "You know anyone in Carson?"

"No, I don't," she admitted.

"Let me give you a couple of names. Check with Mr. Orion Clemens. He was Territorial Secretary until statehood. His brother worked for me for a while. Young Sam was a little too sarcastic for folks around here. They sort of ran him off. Some folks just aren't cut out to write. But Orion is a square shooter."

Martina set the cup of chocolate on the wooden floor beside the couch, then stood, and walked toward the door. "Thank you very much."

"And if you can't locate Orion, go talk to Judith and the Judge," Goodman suggested.

"Whom?"

"The Kingstons. That lady knows everyone in the state of Nevada on a first-name basis. They live on . . . eh, I think it's the corner of Nevada and Musser. Ask anyone in town. They'll point them out."

"Thanks for your kindness, Mr. Goodman."

Goodman once again started through the door. "You're luckier than most."

"How's that?"

"At least you found some trace of him. Most women looking for their husbands come west and find no trace of the men ever again. I don't know if the men fall off a cliff or just don't want to be found. But they are never heard from again. You know what I mean?"

Martina Swan closed the door behind him and flipped the deadbolt as the publisher disappeared into the early morning darkness.

Mr. Goodman, I know exactly what you mean.

Nine

Set in scenic Eagle Valley, sixteen miles from the nearest mine, Carson City projected a calmer, more manageable pace than Virginia City. The winding toll road down from the hills had flattened out as they reached the pass at Moundhouse. The final few miles into town were as smooth, although dusty, as any Martina had ridden since she left Sacramento.

The wide dirt avenue called Carson Street had been recently sprinkled. The breeze that filtered in through the stagecoach's open window smelled fresh. To the west the Carson Range drew her eyes to the east side of the magnificent Sierra Nevadas — the west side of which Martina had spent her entire life enjoying.

In the middle of town stood a huge, empty park. She was informed by a man carrying a glass jar of gold nuggets in one hand and a revolver in the other that this would someday be the site of Nevada's state capital. Across from the park, the stage halted at the St. Charles Hotel. The two-story red brick building seemed to be one of the most substantial in town and certainly offered a more hospitable prospect than any she had seen in Virginia City.

Christina sprawled on Martina's lap and had hardly moved for the entire trip. That troubled Martina. She rolled back the thin linen handkerchief that kept the dust out of the baby's face.

Punkin, you're getting sick, aren't you? You've never been quiet and still unless you're sick.

Martina tugged off her beige linen glove and laid her hand on Christina's forehead.

You're getting a fever. Tears welled up in her eyes. *What am I doing? This whole idea was crazy. Who knows what sickness she could catch on this trip. I shouldn't have dragged her with me over here. I shouldn't even be here myself. No . . . that's not right. I'm here because I thought You were leading me, Lord. Maybe I should have left the baby with Mother and . . . I couldn't do that. I have to settle this on my own. I don't know, Lord . . . I just don't.*

"Lady?" It was the persistent tone of impatience.

A stocky man in a neat dark suit and tie held his hand up for her.

"Everyone has to disembark the stage," he said.

"Oh, yes," she mumbled. "Excuse me."

With one arm cradling the baby and another in the man's strong grip, she climbed off the stage and onto the boardwalk. Her feet felt slightly swollen in the tightly laced high-top shoes.

"Where would you like this satchel?" He pointed to her carpetbag.

"In the lobby." She motioned. "I'll see if they

have a room." *I like this town. There's an open, friendly feel to it.*

The man wiped the dust from his forehead and then replaced his round, narrow-brimmed hat. "Well, good luck, ma'am. But with that emergency session of the legislature in town, I doubt that the St. Charles has any rooms."

She stepped out of the bright Nevada sunlight into the shaded confines of the hotel lobby. Pipe smoke swirled with perfume as she picked her way across the room. Well-dressed men and a few women huddled in spirited conversation at every corner and chair.

The baby rode her hip with expressionless eyes. "Well, darlin', we'll get you a nice place to sleep, and Mama will put a cold rag on that forehead."

A short man whose smile was only exceeded by his ample girth greeted them at the desk. A toupee balanced on his head like a thick fur doily. "Good afternoon, ma'am. My, what a beautiful child. Her complexion is as pink as her hair."

"I think she might have gotten a little overheated coming down on the stage. I realize you're quite busy, but is there any chance we could have a room?"

His smile dropped off his face like the last tree in the forest being downed. "Oh, my-oh-my, we don't have a thing. I feel terrible, ma'am. You and the baby needing a room, and the baby's sick, you say? I keep telling them to build on more rooms, but they don't listen to a lowly clerk."

He leaned across the counter as far as his stomach would allow and then whispered as if divulging a personal secret. "You know what I would do if I had the money? I'd build another hotel in this town — that's what I'd do."

Martina's bangs drooped across her forehead. "Might there be vacancies at other lodging houses?"

When he rocked back on his heels, Martina could tell he was standing on a wooden box. "No, ma'am," he said. "When the legislature comes to town, everything fills up."

"Are there people who rent rooms? We won't need much. Just a small room for a day or two. My daughter needs some rest."

The man wrung his hands and tugged at his crooked black bow tie. "I'm truly sorry, ma'am. I doubt if you can find one. I've got two assemblymen and one state senator sleeping in bedrolls on the roof because they couldn't find anything else. An auditor from San Francisco is sleeping in my own parlor. Carson City is growing. It's just not growing fast enough. You got any kin here? No, of course not. You wouldn't be asking me for a room if you did. Do you know anyone in town? Anyone at all? Just mention their name, and I'll help you locate them."

Martina looked down at the weak eyes of the baby who laid her head against her breast. *Lord, this is getting severe. It is like You led me to the wil-*

derness and abandoned me. I thought I was to be like Sarah, and now I feel like Hagar in the desert — alone with my child and abandoned.

The clerk lifted up the back of his toupee, scratched his head, and then lowered the hair-piece and patted it down. "I say, ma'am, do you have any contacts here in Carson City?"

Martina bit her tongue. *What were those names?* "Eh, I was told to check with a Mr. Clemens . . . Mr. Orion Clemens."

"Oh, my, this is not good timing. They've gone to Washington. Seeking an appointment, so I hear. They being good church folks, they would certainly have welcomed you in. Too bad about their daughter, wasn't it?"

Martina hugged the baby and rocked her back and forth. "I, eh, really don't know the Clemens. We just have a mutual, er . . . friend."

The clerk pulled a pair of wire-framed spectacles out of his vest pocket and strapped them onto his ears and nose. "Yep, that sweet Jenny of theirs just up and died last year."

Martina looked down at the pained eyes of silent Christina. The tears welled up. *If my baby has to get sick, she's going to get sick in Sacramento — at our home — not in some strange town among unknown people.*

"You know anyone else in town?" the clerk pressed.

"Well, there're the . . ." *What were their names? The lady who knows everyone in the state . . . Kingmans . . . Kingburys.* "Oh, the

204

Kingstons!" she blurted out.

The wide smile returned to the clerk. He rocked up on his toes and looked a full inch taller. "Well, why didn't you say so? That's the ticket for you. I'm certainly relieved to know you have them for friends."

"Well, actually I just —"

"Charles!" the clerk hollered to a tall, thin man smoking a long clay pipe as he leaned against the railing at the foot of the stairs. "Bring the buggy around and give this nice lady and her child a ride over to Judith and the Judge's house."

He turned back to Martina. "It's only a few blocks, but I imagine you're tuckered from the trip."

Martina tried waving off the clerk. "Oh, no . . . I mean, thank you very much, but I don't —"

The clerk leaned over the desk and whispered, as if someone in the room might actually be interested in their conversation. "Let me tell you something about those two. If Judge Kingston ever wanted to run for governor, he'd get 90 percent of the votes in this state. And if they'd wise up and let a woman run for governor, Judith would get 100 percent of the votes! Fine couple." He stood back up and resumed his normal tone of voice. "Yes, ma'am, they are the kind of folks you could leave your dog, your bank account, or your baby with, and every one of them would be in better shape when you returned. There's Charles out front. Hope your baby gets better soon."

The man with the pipe was holding her carpet-bag and waiting. *Perhaps Mrs. Kingston knows someone with a spare room. I don't have many choices left.* She looked back at the clerk. "Thank you. I was wondering, does Carson City have a doctor?"

"Yes, ma'am. And a fine one. Got an office just up Carson Street. Doc Jacobs should be back late today or tomorrow."

She stepped back toward the desk. "He's gone?"

"Word came down that there was a knife fight up at one of the wood camps near Lake Tahoe. He went up there to patch up some wounds or bury some men — I don't know which."

She paid the crowd in the lobby even less mind than they paid her as she circled through them and scurried out the door. *Lord, isn't it about time for something to go right? No rooms, no Billy, no doctor, sick baby . . . I can only take so much, and it's getting really, really close.*

The light blue wood-frame, two-story corner home of the Kingstons looked almost new. The picket fence was only half painted. The driver parked the rig by the concrete loading step, bounded off the rig, and trotted to the front door carrying the satchel. Martina, clutching the baby, eased down out of the carriage. She was halfway to the front porch when the door swung open and a small-framed woman with curly dark brown hair pinned to the back of her head, an

206

easy smile, and dancing eyes greeted the driver.

"Charles! How delightful. What brings you here? I trust your Carrie is doing well?" Martina watched the true concern reflect from the woman's smooth, attractive face.

"She's as healthy as a hog, Judith!" The driver grinned like a boy who had just been given a lollipop. "I'll tell her you was askin' about her. I jist brought you some company."

The woman in her late twenties or early thirties peered at Martina and the baby. Her puzzled gaze instantly turned into a welcoming glance. "Well, how nice. Please come in, dear!" Judith Kingston reached out her hand. "I've been expecting you."

Charles set the carpetbag inside the Kingstons' parlor. "I imagine you two need to get caught up on visitin'."

"Yes, we do!" Judith responded. She stood with her hand on the knob of the front door, the top of which included a large diamond-shaped leaded glass window curtained in off-white lace. "Now, Charles, if your Carrie feels house-ridden and needs to go for a walk, you have her come see me, and we'll have tea."

The driver bounded down the concrete steps toward the waiting carriage. "She'll like that, Judith. Tell the Judge hello for me."

"I'll do that," she said.

"And tell him I ain't been drunk in over three months!" He shouted as he drove off.

Judith Kingston pointed toward a slightly

worn brown leather settee. "Please come in and sit down."

"I realize you don't even know me," Martina tried to protest.

"Nonsense," Judith scoffed. "I don't know your name. But I certainly do know a few things. May I boil us some tea?"

Martina sat on the wide leather chair, rocking the baby back and forth. "Yes, thank you." She fought the urge to lie down on the arm of the chair and close her eyes. The travel tension seemed to be ebbing away, replaced by exhaustion.

Judith buzzed over to where they sat. "May I get a wet cloth for your baby? I see she has a temperature."

Martina looked up at this woman whom she had never seen before. "I would appreciate it very much. But why are you doing this for a stranger?"

"Do you think it's our Christian duty to be kind only to people we know?"

"No, I just can't imagine that you have time for all of this."

"Dear, the day I don't have time for a sick infant will be a sad day indeed." She retrieved a large silk pillow from a gray velvet settee. "Perhaps you'd like to lay your little one on this."

Martina took the pillow and propped the baby on it. She smelled lilac perfume. "What did you mean when you said you were expecting me?"

Judith Kingston scurried toward the kitchen

door. "We'll have plenty of time to chat in a minute. Just relax, and I'll stir us up some tea. The water is already warm."

Martina studied the parlor. Polished oak wainscoting covered the bottom half of the room's twelve-foot walls. Above the wainscoting, a textured wallpaper of the faintest blue stretched up to the ceiling. An oval portrait hung near the white brick fireplace, and a glass-covered brass clock spun away minutes on the mantel.

Martina slumped back into the soft chair and closed her eyes. *Lord, someday I'd love to have a house like this. Classy, yet comfortable. Smartly decorated, but livable. And I think I'd like to have a friend like Judith Kingston. Even if she doesn't know my name.*

With a small damp calico rag on Christina's forehead, the baby closed her eyes. She drifted off to sleep on the forest green silk pillow atop the brown leather sofa.

The orange Chinese tea smelled sweet and tasted mild. Martina felt the tension in her shoulders relax as she strolled through the arched walkway into the dining room.

Judith Kingston placed a china plate of cheese chunks and small octagon-shaped salt crackers on the lace tablecloth. She motioned for Martina to sit with her. Although her hostess was no more than ten years her senior, Martina felt as if she were in the presence of her mother. *Sit up straight, Martina Patricia. Lift your little finger when you sip tea. Smile. Make others feel at ease.*

"Now," Judith insisted, "I want to hear your whole story."

Martina set down her china cup with more clatter than she intended. "Mrs. Kingston, tell me what you know about me."

"Please. Call me Judith. Everyone does. I can't seem to function under any other name." She took another sip of tea. Her mouth was rather small but seemed to be puckered in a permanent expectant smile. "Here's what I know about you. First, you were sent here by the Lord."

Martina bit her tongue, then blurted out, "I was what?"

Judith Kingston waved a small cracker as she talked. "I don't know anything about your religious convictions, but this morning during devotions with the Judge, I prayed that the Lord would bring some wonderful surprises into our life today. And here you are on my doorstep. The Lord sent you." She popped the cracker into her mouth.

Martina sipped the tea and studied the delicate blue flowers on the thin cup. "Well, I do trust in the Lord's leading. So perhaps you are right about that. At the beginning I thought this whole trip was His idea, but sometimes I wonder. What else do you know?"

"I know you've been on the stagecoach. You've got road dust on your dress. Let's see . . .

210

you have an I-could-use-a-hot-bath look in your eyes. And you came here in the hotel carriage, so that means you couldn't find a place to stay in this town, which worries you immensely. But the thing that worries you the most is your sick daughter and whatever motivation has drawn you to Carson City."

Martina shook her head and sighed. "You are right about all of that. Mother always said I was very transparent."

Judith took a tiny chunk of white cheese and bit off half. "But there are some things I don't know, such as your name."

"I'm Martina Swan, and my daughter is Christina."

"Well, I'm very happy to meet Mrs. Swan and Miss Swan. You'll be spending the night with us, of course. We have a guest room upstairs, and I promise to keep the children quiet."

Martina tried to study the woman's eyes. But their penetrating glance forced her to look away. "But we've just met."

"Posh!" Judith Kingston's body seemed to bounce when she talked. "You did say the Lord led you here, didn't you?"

Martina looked down at the lace tablecloth. "Well . . . well, I think so."

"Then who are we to argue with what He wants to do? Divine Providence is not a force to trifle with, Martina. Now that's settled. You're staying here. But, of course, you know nothing about us. My husband came here as the judge of the First District Court in the Territory of Nevada. He was appointed by Mr. Lincoln. After statehood we moved down here from Virginia City, and he was elected judge of the First District. We have two children, who happen to be across the street in that stone schoolhouse attending classes at the moment. We are originally from Kentucky . . . but that seems so long ago. Please eat some cheese. I know you're hungry."

"Actually I could —"

"I know, I know, I'm sounding like your mother. The Judge says I try to mother everyone in town. That's not true. I can think of a couple of men I'd rather whack alongside the head than mother."

Martina leaned back in the straight oak chair. "I can't believe you'd open up your home to us."

"Nonsense. You'd do the exact same thing for me if the roles were reversed. Isn't that true?"

I'd like to think I would. "Yes, I suppose."

Judith set her cup down and folded her hands in her lap. "Now tell me about yourself. I would guess that with a beautiful Spanish name like Martina, you are from California."

Martina glanced across the room at a glass-fronted hutch filled with china and smiled. "Judith, is there anything about me you don't know? You're right — I was born and raised in California."

Judith retrieved her empty cup and ran her finger around the lip. "How delightful. I don't think I've met an adult that was a native-born

Californian. Did you grow up along the coast?"

"No, my parents have a ranch north of Capt. Sutter's Fort in the valley."

"The Judge has a friend who's been in that area forever. Moved in way before the gold rush. I don't think he's ever been to his ranch, but the Judge runs across him from time to time when he has government meetings in San Francisco. An interesting fellow from what I hear." Judith brushed at her hair as if something were out of place. Nothing was.

"What's his name?" Martina inquired. "Perhaps I know him. My folks know all the early pioneers."

Judith waited until she could look Martina in the eyes. "Wilson Merced."

On a good day in church when the organ is in tune and the hymn is uplifting, Martina sometimes felt as if her spirit were skipping right into the presence of the Lord. At this very moment, the joy in her spirit matched one of those days.

"Wilson Merced is my father!" she exclaimed.

Judith leaped to her feet, gave Martina a quick hug around the shoulders, and then sauntered toward the teakettle boiling on the stovetop. "A daughter of one of the Judge's friends! We would have been insulted if you wouldn't stay with us. What did I tell you? The Lord really did send you here, didn't He?"

Martina stood up. "Yes, I believe He did." From the other room she could hear the baby crying. "And right at the moment, He's sending me into your parlor."

By the time supper was served at the Kingston home, Martina and Christina had bathed and changed clothes. They settled into the small guest room that featured a huge featherbed and sported new wallpaper with stenciled tiny blue flowers. Christina whimpered for over an hour but nodded off to a fitful sleep just before supper.

Judge Kingston looked exactly as Martina had imagined. He was well over six feet tall, with square shoulders and solid face lined with thick chin whiskers and a mustache. His dark brown hair was streaked with gray. His nose was rather hawkish, and his eyes narrow but forgiving.

He wore a dark wool suit and vest, with starched white cotton shirt and solid black tie. His overcoat and hat were left on a hook near the side door leading to Nevada Street. There were gold cuff links on stiff cuffs. Even at the supper table he had a countenance of decorum and authority.

Martina guessed the Kingstons' son David to be about ten. He had wild hair and the penetrating glance of his father. Their daughter Roberta was about six. Her blue gingham dress was made from the same bolt of cloth as her mother's apron. Her smile was a miniature version of Judith Kingston's.

Both children finished eating quickly and asked politely to be excused. That left Martina with Judith and the Judge. The conversation around the table had been warm but light, as if all parties were waiting for a more serious moment. That time came when they settled into their second cup of coffee and tea.

"I met your mother once in San Francisco. It was during a state boundary meeting," the Judge stated, as if issuing a ruling from the bench.

"Father was not very happy to serve on that commission, as I remember," Martina commented.

"Nor was I." The Judge's smile was faint but unforced. "He and I both came to the conclusion that the California/Nevada border was staked out by drunken surveyors."

Martina was fascinated by the Judge's eyes. *Try as you wish, you can't hide a father's kind eyes, Judge Kingston.* "I don't know if Mother ever went to those meetings or not. She doesn't much care for San Francisco. When father went there, we usually traveled on down to Monterey to see Grandma Cabrillo."

"You are related to the Cabrillos?" the Judge quizzed.

"Not relatives, but so close I have always called her Grandma. I was named after Doña María Martína Cabrillo."

"Well, I remember your mother very well," the Judge continued. "You recall what I said about her, Judith?"

Mrs. Kingston cocked her head in the way a woman does when she knows she is the center of a man's attention. "I believe you called her 'the Judith Kingston of California.' But I wasn't sure if that was intended as a compliment."

"Of course it was," he lectured in a tone that would silence any thought of protest. He turned to Martina. "Now I'm sure you and Judith have visited all afternoon, but I've been stuck behind the bench in horribly boring mining litigation. So please do tell me what you are doing in Carson City and how long you can stay with us. How are your father and mother?"

Martina's shoulders slumped. "It's rather a long story."

"I'll fill you in later, dear," Judith explained as she put her hand on her husband's arm. "For now, Martina is trying to locate her husband."

"We own a store in Sacramento," Martina explained. "Billy — my husband — came to Nevada last year about this time to locate some property to begin a second store in Virginia City."

"And she's very worried about him," Judith added.

"I can imagine." The Judge nodded. "You haven't heard from him in a year? That's incredible."

"No, no . . . I heard from him for a while, but then the letters slacked off and . . . ." Martina's chin dropped to her chest.

"He's never seen that beautiful baby of his," Judith interrupted.

"Little Christina has her grandmother's hair,

doesn't she?" the Judge commented. "I shall never forget your mother's auburn hair."

"Oh?" Judith raised her eyebrows. "The Judge doesn't usually remember any woman's features."

"Everyone remembers my mother," Martina replied. "I've spent my life hearing compliments."

"Oh, do I detect a little jealousy?" Judith quizzed.

Martina shrugged. *I had hoped it was not so obvious.* "Being a rather plain daughter of a very attractive mother does have its difficulties."

"My dear," Judith countered, "you do not have auburn hair, but you are by no means plain."

"You are kind."

Judith sipped her tea and then lowered her cup. "Listen, why is it that when others pin their hair up on top of their head, you allow yours to flow to your waist?"

"Oh," Martina explained, "I just never —"

"It's because you have beautiful hair, that's why. I'll bet your mother never pins her hair either, does she?"

"Actually, no, she —"

"Ladies." The Judge cleared his throat as if about to pronounce a sentence. "If you don't mind, I'd like to hear more about Martina's husband."

"Yes, your honor," Judith teased. "I believe the witness was about to testify."

"Judith . . ." The Judge's voice came up at the end, expressing a paragraph of unspoken thoughts.

Judith winked at Martina. "Proceed, dear."

"Well, the reason I came to Carson City is that I discovered that sometime this spring Billy was driving an ore wagon from Virginia City to the mill at Empire and that he quit that job and came to Carson City. But I have no idea how long he stayed here."

"Naturally, Martina's concerned that something's happened to him," Judith explained.

"Yes, that's quite understandable." The Judge took a swig of coffee and tilted his head at Martina. "His name is Billy Swan?"

Martina glanced down to see that she was wringing her hands again. She immediately ceased. "His full name is William Hays Swan, Jr., but he goes by Billy."

The Judge rubbed his bearded chin and murmured, "Billy who drives an ore wagon? It sounds vaguely familiar."

Martina sat straight up. Her eyes and her mouth popped open. "Really? That is good news."

Judith leaned over and patted Martina's arm. "Not necessarily, dear. The Judge saves his best memory for court cases."

"Let me check on something in my office." Judge Kingston lifted his six-foot, two-inch frame out of the chair and carried his coffee cup with him to the next room.

"You really must stay with us for several days until the baby is better," Judith insisted.

"I might just do that. If she doesn't break out of this fever, I'll need her to see a doctor. I understand he's in the mountains." Martina stared at Judith's hands. *She's ten years older, and her hands look ten years younger. Like Mother's.*

"Oh, yes, it sounded like quite a ruckus up there at a wood camp. There just aren't enough women in Nevada yet."

"Oh?" Martina said.

"Some men alone behave rather badly. I believe the influence of a good woman can change a man's heart. Of course, that's something else Nevada is short of."

"What's that?"

Judith laughed. "Good women. Are you sure you wouldn't like to move to Carson City?"

Judge Kingston burst into the dining room carrying a thick brown leather journal.

"Did you find something, Judge?" Judith asked.

"Well . . . Mrs. Swan, I don't recall all the details, but I do have a Billy Hays on my court records. It could be that I was given an incomplete name. We have no method of ascertaining one's true identity, so we accept whatever name is given us. But he's right here in the journal."

"Heavens!" Judith murmured. "I trust he wasn't murdered."

The Judge shook his head. "No, that's not the record. Now, mind you, Mrs. Swan, I'm not sure this is your husband."

"Please, Judge," Martina braced her hands against the edge of the table, "read me the exact account."

"Well, on March 6, 1865, five men were arrested at Black's Saloon for public intoxication, resisting arrest, assault, destruction of property, and attempted murder."

"Attempted murder?" Martina gasped.

"Yes, and one of the five was Billy Hays, a teamster from Virginia City."

Martina found herself defending a husband she had not seen in over a year. "But — but — my Billy doesn't even drink!"

"Well, he did that night, I can assure you," the Judge decreed.

"Perhaps it was a different Billy Hays," Judith suggested.

"Yes, well that's always . . . . wait . . ." The Judge turned the ledger sideways. "There was an addendum penciled in . . . oh, my . . . Billy Hays, also known as William Hays Swan, Jr., from Sacramento, California."

"That's my husband! A drunken brawl? I can't believe it. Attempted murder?" Tears trickled out of the corners of Martina's eyes.

The Judge continued, "The Plaintiff, a Mr. Lawson McKee, had a mining claim that the other five asserted belonged to them as well. They got drunk and attempted to hang him and take the claim."

Martina's hand flew to her mouth. "Oh, no!"

The Judge wiped his wide forehead with his hand. "Fortunately they were all too drunk to be successful."

Martina stood and braced her hands against the back of the chair. "What happened to them?"

Judith handed her a clean linen handkerchief. "Did you send them out to the state prison?" she asked her husband.

The Judge rubbed the bridge of his nose. "No, remember, Judith, that was the first group I sentenced to a wood-making camp."

"How's that?" Martina asked.

"We're using almost 50,000 cords of firewood every year here in Ormsby and Storey Counties. There's money to be made for those willing to work hard and bring it down out of the Sierras."

Judith scurried to Martina's side. "So the Judge had a plan to send prisoners up to cut wood. After three months the business and the profits became theirs."

"You sentenced them to go into business?" Martina quizzed.

"Some of these bummers loafin' around Carson City just need some work. I told them if they stayed up in the mountains for three months without coming to town, all the wood they split would be theirs to sell."

"Tell me again when you sentenced him," Martina requested.

"March 8," the Judge replied.

"That was six months ago," Martina said. "He

hasn't been back to Carson City since then?"

The Judge closed his judicial journal. "I have no idea about that. I know he didn't return until after the three months were up. But beyond that, I haven't paid much attention."

Martina held on to Judith's arm. "I assume there's more than one wood camp up in the Sierras?"

"Must be dozens of them," Judith said.

"But they aren't all peopled by men convicted of crimes. Actually I've only done that three times," the Judge said. He reopened the ledger. "These five were sentenced to Camp Sixteen. I believe that's one of the camps right by the lake."

"You look worried, dear," Judith observed.

Martina let out a deep breath. "I was just thinking that the man at the hotel said the doctor went up to a wood camp. Some men were hurt, perhaps killed, in some sort of altercation."

The Judge laid his ledger on the table. "I hadn't heard anything about it."

"I did hear that someone was killed," Judith asserted. "Perhaps Rev. White knows about it."

"Rev. White?" Martina questioned.

"The Presbyterian church is just across the corner from the back door," Judith explained to Martina. "And early this morning I saw Dr. Jacobs and Rev. White visiting on the front steps. Naturally I assumed they were discussing theology. Perhaps they were talking about the feud in the mountains."

"That might be," the Judge mused.

"It's getting dark outside, and I need to straighten the kitchen, but I'd be willing to run across to the parsonage and ask Rev. White if he knows anything," Judith offered.

"Oh, I wouldn't want you to go to all that trouble," Martina protested.

The Judge straightened his tie and retrieved his hat. "Mrs. Swan, that was merely my wife's way of telling me to go across the street and see the Reverend."

"Oh, would you, dear?" Judith cooed and then turned to Martina. "The Judge is such a dear man."

Judge Kingston retrieved his long coat and sauntered out the Nevada Street door.

Martina shook her head. "I have never met a couple who looked so dissimilar to my parents and yet acted so identical."

"I just know I would love your mother if I ever get to meet her," Judith Kingston said.

"Yes, I'm sure you would," Martina replied. "Everyone does."

When the Judge returned, Judith and Martina were putting away dishes. The Judge's face was tense, like a man about to pronounce an unpopular verdict.

"Should we sit down to hear the news?" Judith asked him.

"Well, you were right about the doctor stopping by this morning. He had word that a man or two were killed at Camp Sixteen. Others might be critically injured."

"Camp Sixteen? That's where you sentenced my husband and the other rowdy men."

"That's the one."

"Oh, dear!" Martina gasped. "Perhaps I should sit down."

"The Reverend said Dr. Jacobs had no word of who was killed but had checked with the Reverend about overseeing the burial of the dead."

"Were there any names mentioned?"

"No. I don't even know if the original five men are still up there. They could have all headed for California and sold the business to some others."

"What was the cause of the altercation?" Judith asked.

"Well . . . my information is thirdhand at best and totally inadmissible —"

"We're not in a courtroom, Judge Kingston," Judith chided.

"One report was that a tree crashed on them, and the other said it was a knife fight over . . ." The Judge paused and glanced at Martina.

"Please go on, Judge," Martina insisted.

"Over an Indian woman." He blurted out the words as if they were sour grapes.

"Well, if that's true," Judith jumped in, "it certainly won't involve William Swan. I can't imagine a man with such a charming wife and beautiful baby fighting over any other woman."

Martina stared down at the tea towel she held in her hand. *I can imagine almost anything. Lord, the closer I get, the worse this drama becomes.*

Judith Kingston scooted over to Martina and slipped an arm around her waist. She held tight but turned to the Judge. "When is Dr. Jacobs returning?"

"The Reverend thought he would come back down by tomorrow sometime if it's possible to leave the wounded."

Judith hugged Martina. "What would you like to do?" she asked.

" 'Get thee up,' " Martina replied.

Judge Kingston hung his hat back on the peg and brushed the dust off the cuffs of his coat. " 'Get thee up; wherefore liest thou thus upon thy face'? From Joshua 7?" he asked.

"Yes, it seems to be the only thing the Lord's said to me lately. If it weren't for a sick baby, I'd load Christina in a wagon and go up to that wood camp at daylight. Perhaps she'll be better by then."

"Nonsense!" Judith scolded. "You are not taking a sick infant into the mountains. I'll keep the baby, and you go on up to the camp."

"Oh, no. I couldn't leave her," Martina protested.

Judith hugged her again. "I would love her and care for her like my own."

Martina stepped back. "Oh, no. I wasn't thinking of that. It's just that . . . well, in over a year I've never . . ."

"You've never been away from your baby?"

"That's right."

"Not even for a break?"

"No." Martina stepped closer to Judith. "Well . . . I left her with Mother while I rode with Father down to the river for about an hour this spring."

"Mrs. Swan," Judith lectured, "you will be so tense and nervous all day tomorrow that you will be of no help or comfort to Christina. Go to the camp. Find out about William. I will not let Christina out of my sight until you return."

"But — but — I can't ask you to do that. We haven't known each other for a day yet."

"What difference does that make? You must go and investigate, and you cannot take a sick baby with you." Judith Kingston paced the floor with her arms folded tightly against her thin chest. "I'm right about this matter, and you know it."

Martina stared into Judith's determined eyes. "If you had red hair and another twenty years, you could be my mother!"

"If I had red hair and *ten* more years, I could be your mother!" Judith repeated. She continued to pace but turned to the Judge. "Martina will need a rig and a driver. I assume the road to Camp Sixteen is horrid."

"It was the last time I was on it," the Judge said.

"Perhaps I should go to the livery, in the dark of night, and arrange for a wagon and a driver to pick up Martina at daylight," Judith offered.

The Judge rolled his narrow blue eyes to the ceiling and shook his head. "Oh, why don't I go do that, dear?"

Judith's face radiated with delight. "Why, thank you, Judge. Be sure to secure the very best driver in town."

Martina gazed across the room at an oval portrait of a long-legged black stallion. "How much will that cost? I do have to watch expenses," she murmured.

"It won't cost a thing," Judith informed her.

"I am not going to let you pay for —"

"Mr. Stevens at the livery owes me a favor or two." Judith's tone was like a song of triumph. "He simply refuses our money every time we ask for a rig."

Once again the Judge tugged on his long coat and hat. "I will return shortly."

"I'll have some warm apple pie and melted cheese waiting for you," Judith promised him.

"All I've ever needed is you waiting for me, dear." For the first time since she met him, Martina saw a wide, warm smile break across the Judge's face. She thought he looked ten years younger.

As soon as the Judge was out the door, Judith slipped her arm around Martina's waist. "My, that man certainly makes my heart skip a beat. Did I ever tell you what a sweetheart he is?"

Martina hugged her back. "I think you mentioned it . . . Mother."

Ten

The room was spotless, the bed soft. The slight drift of air from the partially open window refreshed her.

There was no jostling of a speeding stagecoach. No dust in the air. No fowl stories or horrid smoke. No bank manager lurking at the door. No outlaws prowling the street. No soiled doves needing to use her bed. It was completely quiet. Thoroughly peaceful.

But Martina slept very little.

The baby fussed and whimpered most of the night, so Martina sat in the needlepoint chair and rocked her. When Martina did drift off to sleep, she had frightening dreams of knives slashing, men cursing, blood flowing.

Just before daylight Judith Kingston relieved her at rocking the baby. Martina washed her face and dressed. She was much too nervous to eat, but she did drink some green tea and agreed to take a basket of food that Judith had prepared. At the sound of a wagon pulling up to the gate on Musser Street, Martina clutched the baby to her breast.

"Well, little punkin . . . Mama needs to go check up on Daddy. Mrs. Kingston will take care of you today." She rocked back and forth. "Mommy loves you, darling."

Judith glanced out through the crocheted lace curtain. "He's got you a wagon. The Judge said a light carriage would never make the trip."

Martina glanced across the room. "I don't know if I can . . ."

"If you can walk away from this baby?" Judith held out her arms to Christina. "I know exactly how you feel. The first time we had to leave our eldest with a neighbor, I felt the same way. The Judge pulled me aside and gave me a little lecture."

Martina fought back tears when she looked down into the baby's trusting blue eyes. "What did he say?"

"He took David in his arms and asked me whose baby this was."

"What?"

"Yes, he said, 'Whose baby is this?' I said, 'Mine.' He said, 'Whose baby is this?' I said, 'Ours.' He said, 'Whose baby is this?' Finally I said, 'The Lord's.' Then he said, 'Do you think we can trust Him to take care of His children?' Well, the Judge was right. I had to learn to trust the Lord."

"Did it help you get through the evening?"

"It helped me out the door . . . but I cried all evening." Judith's smile was barely discernible. "That's when I found out that raising children is daily, even hourly, trusting them into God's hands."

Martina kissed Christina's warm cheek and handed her to Judith Kingston. "I'm going to cry all the way up the mountain."

Judith carried the baby on her hip and walked with Martina to the front door. "Oh, I don't think so."

Martina peeked in the small mirror by the door and adjusted the purple ribbons in her long hair. "Why do you say that?"

Judith pointed out at the street. "Because Hank Monk's your driver. Chances are, you'll be praying for your life the entire way!"

The road into the Carson Range narrowed considerably at the top of King's Canyon. Martina was sure it wasn't wide enough for the farm wagon, but Hank Monk did not slow down enough for her to worry about specifics. The last words he said to her at the Kingstons' before he slapped the lead lines on the rump of the drive horse were, "Hold on, missy."

She held on.

To the rough wooden seat.

To the iron railing.

And to divine Providence.

Eight miles into the mountains, Monk abruptly stopped in a small green meadow, jumped down, and unhitched the team. Martina was still waiting for an explanation when he picketed the horses, threw himself down in the shade of a massive yellow pine, and went to sleep.

She climbed down off the wagon and retrieved

the basket Judith Kingston had prepared. *I assume this is a meal stop. Mr. Monk, what you lack in conversation, you make up for on the road. Every bone in my body has been rearranged. If I looked in a mirror, I'm not sure I'd recognize myself.*

That, dear Martina, might not be an entirely bad thing.

I felt the Judge's stare.

He didn't say it.

He didn't have to.

I look nothing like my mother.

No one who has met me only once will remember what I look like by the next day. But that's all right. One good thing about being nondescript — I don't have an image to maintain.

Martina pulled her waist-long hair off her back and let it drape across her left shoulder. She brushed the road dust off the long lavender dress.

At one time this was Billy's favorite. "You look like a princess in that dress," he said. An abandoned *princess. If I looked like my mother, I doubt he would have abandoned me.*

If I looked like my mother, I doubt I would have married William Hays Swan, Jr.

Lord, that's not true. I loved him dearly. I . . . I still love him. Perhaps not with the same intensity. But I love him. I really do.

Finding a stump near a wild-limbed aspen, she sat down and opened the basket. On top of several large jelly-covered biscuits was a neatly folded note. She opened it and stared at the perfect penmanship.

Dearest Martina,

Joshua also says, "Have not I commanded thee? Be strong and of a good courage; be not afraid, neither be thou dismayed: for the Lord thy God is with thee whithersoever thou goest" (1:9). Every time I look into sweet Christina's eyes, I will be praying for her mommy. I trust you find your husband well, and I pray that you find more than your husband. May your restless spirit find deep satisfaction in all the blessings the Lord has for you.

Your new friend,
Judith

Martina cried.

She didn't want to.

She couldn't help it.

Lord, she has only known me a few hours, and she reads me like a book. My restless spirit. I'm never content to be myself. Never content with Your calling for me. Never content to be Martina Patricia Merced Swan.

Tears dripped down on the biscuit as she chomped into the flaky dough and wild cherry preserves.

Judith has the Judge, the ultimate example of a straight arrow.

Mother has Daddy, everyone's image of a rugged hero.

And me — I have Billy Swan. He deserts his wife and baby, squanders our money, lives in a brothel, gets arrested for drunkenness and attempted murder, and perhaps has been in a knife fight over an Indian woman. Well, Billy, you aren't Daddy, and you aren't Judge Kingston. But you are mine. And it's time you started acting like it.

She folded her arms across her chest and stared at the imagined William Hays Swan, Jr. "All right, Mr. Billy Swan. Get in the wagon; we're going home. We have a sick daughter to retrieve and a sick business to bolster. You will not touch another drop of liquor the rest of your life. And you will certainly have to give up dalliance with other women. Don't argue with me. . . . Get in the wagon!"

Martina took a deep breath and let it out slowly.

Why is it I don't believe I'll ever be able to say that? I'll probably just whimper, beg, and cry.

She had just finished her second jellied biscuit when Hank Monk leaped to his feet like a frog out of a frying pan and waved his gun to the west.

"Someone's comin'!" he shouted.

Martina stared up the road. "I don't see anyone."

"Course you don't, missy. Cain't see 'em, but I kin hear 'em."

Within seconds Martina heard the rumble of hooves and the rattle of a wagon. In a cloud of dust, the buckboard drew up alongside Monk.

233

Martina ran over to it.

"Some of 'em dead, Doc?" Monk asked.

Dr. Jacobs's black bow tie hung loosely around his unbuttoned collar. "One dead. Three wounded. One disappeared."

"Disappeared?" Monk queried.

The doctor pointed toward a roll of canvas tarp in the back of the wagon. "The one that stabbed this ol' boy was last seen sprintin' through the forest toward the lake. Ever' last one of them got slashed up some." The doctor stared at Martina. "What are you two doing up here?"

Monk looped his thumbs into his battered leather vest pockets. "Judith and the Judge asked me to drive Missy up here to find her husband."

Martina felt uncomfortable as the doctor looked her over. "Your husband is at Camp Sixteen?" he questioned.

"That is my understanding," she replied. "His name is Billy — Billy Swan. Do you know if he's there?"

"I don't know any of their names. The ones that are up there are still feudin' over that woman. She grabbed up the one who's stabbed the worst and toted him to her tent like a sack of potatoes. They're all crazy. Sooner or later there'll only be one left alive, and I'm bettin' on the Indian woman. Don't go up there, Hank. No tellin' what they'll do." Then the doctor turned to Martina. "You want to take a look at the one I got rolled in the tarp? It could save you a trip."

Martina had won a spelling bee when she was

in the eighth grade. She remembered that the winning word was *chimerical*. It was one of the words she had memorized the night before the contest, and when she was asked to spell it, a wonderful deep peace flowed over her. At that exact moment, she had the same feeling. "Yes, I'll look, but I know it isn't my husband."

"How do you know without looking?" Hank Monk questioned.

"A wife knows."

She walked to the rear of the wagon, and Dr. Jacobs pulled back the tarp. A blond-headed man with scraggly beard and distorted, puffy face lay motionless. His brown leather vest was caked with dried blood.

"That's not him," she announced as she spun around to face the others. "We'll go on up to Camp Sixteen."

Dr. Jacobs pulled the tarp back over the body. "Well, carry your side arm in your hand, pard. I tell you, they're all mountain crazy. That woman might be the craziest."

"Dr. Jacobs," Martina urged as she boldly latched onto his arm, "if you make it to Carson City this afternoon, would you stop by the Kingstons'? I left my feverish baby with Judith, and I'm terribly worried about her."

"If she's with Judith, she can't be in more capable hands. I've begged her for two years to be my nurse."

"Yes, well . . . my baby's just a little over a year old, and we've been traveling for several days.

Could you check on her?"

The doctor pushed his round, wide-brimmed hat back and rubbed his graying beard. "I'll do that. Think I'll stop by Judith and the Judge's about suppertime — if you know what I mean."

Martina scooted over to the wagon. "Thank you, Doctor. Come on, Mr. Monk. I believe we still have a mountain or two to climb."

Hank Monk wiped his mouth on his sleeve and adjusted his battered black hat. "Yes, ma'am."

"Take it careful up there," Dr. Jacobs warned. "I don't want to come back and roll you in a tarp."

Martina watched the doctor drive down the mountain as she waited in the wagon for the teamster to hitch the horses. "Mr. Monk, would you explain the term 'mountain crazy'?"

He glanced up at her but continued to rig the horses. "Missy, that's when men have been cooped up in the high country so long they lose touch with what's real and what ain't. I don't know if it's isolation or what they et, or both. But they start seein' things that aren't there and hearin' sounds that ain't been made. Then they reckon that ever' one is out to steal their poke or kill 'em. Some say it's the devil livin' up in the Sierry peaks, but the only devil I ever seen was livin' in the hearts of men. Which might be the same thing — if you catch my drift."

"Was the doctor serious about us carrying guns in our hands?"

"I reckon he was serious. Doc Jacobs don't kid much. Now the Judge — he don't kid at all. But the Doc is mighty somber too."

It took almost three more hours of hard, rough, teeth-jarring riding to reach the pass that led down into Camp Sixteen. As they dropped over the tree-covered ridgeline, Martina could see a curl of smoke from a cabin next to a gigantic stack of logs that covered most of the small meadow. Reflecting through the ponderosas was the mirrorlike surface of Lake Tahoe. If it had been a lazy Sunday afternoon drive with her husband and infant by her side, it would have been a pristine, idyllic scene.

Instead, Martina shoved her long hair back over her shoulders, clutched folded hands to her mouth, and tried to still a pounding heart and throbbing head. *Perhaps I should have him stop so I can dust off and comb my hair. If Billy's here, he'll hardly recognize me. I should have worn larger earrings. Or carried some rosewater.*

Hank Monk kept his shotgun nestled in his lap as he pulled up next to a corral that contained six mules and countless days of unshoveled manure.

About 200 feet up a tree-covered incline behind the big log cabin, Martina spotted a white straight-walled tent and a thick twist of smoke. In the yard in front of the log cabin were several broken chairs, a blacksmith forge, and a pile of

237

garbage the size of a chicken coop.

"This is a foul-lookin' camp," Hank mumbled. "I ain't stayin' here long, Missy. Let's take a roll call and see if your man is here. I'm hopin' he was the one that had the good sense to run off into the woods."

She stared into the darkness of a cabin without coverings on the windows. A broken front door lay propped against the doorjamb. "How do we find anyone?" she asked.

The puff of gun smoke from one of the open front windows coincided with the report of a rifle. What sounded like a bumblebee whizzed above her head.

Monk threw the shotgun to his shoulder and pointed it toward the cabin. "Looks like they found us," he growled.

"Get out of here!" a man yelled from inside the cabin. "This here is private property!"

"You got a woman with you?" another voice yelled.

"You ain't blind, are ya?" Monk hollered, not lowering his shotgun.

"Is she your wife?"

"That don't matter," the other hidden assailant yelled. "I get her after we kill him."

"I seen her first!" a deep voice screamed back.

Monk stood on the wagon, shielding Martina and pointing the shotgun at the door. "Ain't no one touching this lady. Hank Monk ain't never had a passenger harmed yet. I ain't goin' to start now."

"Monk? Is that you?"

"It ain't the governor."

"You got Doc Jacobs with you, Hank?"

"He's takin' your buddy down to the grave-yard in Carson City," Monk declared.

"Ain't our buddy. He's a lyin', thievin' woman-stealer! And he deserved to die. He busted my leg with a bear trap!"

"How about you two showin' yourselves?" Monk called out. "I don't cotton much to yellin' at shadows."

Martina peeked around the teamster. An extremely thin man with uncombed dirty brown hair, a Henry repeating rifle in his hand, stepped out on the porch. His tattered flannel shirt was unbuttoned and untucked. Bloody bandages girdled his midsection. He was barefoot. He rubbed a dirty hand across his face and then pointed the rifle barrel out toward their wagon.

"Where is your *amigo?*" Monk questioned.

"I told you my leg is gnawed up," a gravelly voice called out from inside.

The wild-eyed man on the porch pointed the rifle barrel at Martina. "Who's the woman, Monk?"

The veteran teamster never lowered the shotgun. "Is that your man, Missy?" he asked beneath his breath.

"Heavens, no!" she gasped.

"I surely am glad for that," Monk replied.

"I said, who is that woman?" the man

screamed as he kept waving his rifle in their general direction.

Martina slipped her hand in her purse and pulled out her pocket revolver. She cocked the hammer but left it lying in her lap on the lavender dress.

"You shoot the one who comes to the window. I'll take this hombre on the porch," Monk whispered. Then he shouted, "You got a man named Billy Swan here?"

The man on the porch lowered the Henry a few inches. "Swan, you say?"

"That's what I said," Monk affirmed.

"Ain't got no Billy Swan." The man on the porch spat a wad of tobacco juice on the disabled door, and it slimed its way down to the porch. "We got a Billy Hays. He's the son-of-Hades up there in the tent with my sweet Carmela!"

"She's *my* sweet Carmela!" an angry voice from inside the cabin screamed.

Martina felt her heart leap. "That's him!"

"Who's him?" Monk quizzed.

"Billy Hays. My husband is Billy Hays Swan," Martina explained.

"This here missy is the wife of Mr. Billy Hays Swan," Monk called. "Where is he at?"

"He cain't have two women," the hidden voice challenged.

The man on the porch danced from one foot to the other as if standing on hot rocks. "We'll take that skinny one off your hands, Monk, for fifty cash dollars."

"Is she purdy?" the inside voice quizzed.

The man on the porch scratched under his arm and called back through the open window. "She's passable, Lamont, but ain't half the woman Carmela is."

"We're going up to the tent to see this Billy Hays," Monk declared.

"You'll be dead if you do. Carmela has a Sharps and can hit a chipmunk clean across the meadow. We wouldn't be down here with her and Billy up there if we could get close."

"You mean both of them is shootin' at you?" Monk said.

"Nope. Billy's knifed up pretty bad. Cletus did that after Billy plumb near bit his thumb off. But Cletus ran off in the woods. After Doc bandaged Billy up, Carmela carried him off to her tent. She said she'd kill the first one of us who came close."

"Is Billy Hays still alive?" Monk pressed.

"I reckon he is. She ain't throwed his body out." The man on the porch spat another wad of tobacco against the door.

Monk motioned for Martina to sit back down. "We're goin' up to the tent to visit with them."

"She told us she was closin' up the business, and Billy was her only man from now on. That didn't sit too well with us. If you want to haul him off, that's fine with us. But she won't give him up without a fight."

"We jist need to talk first off," Hank Monk explained.

241

"Yeah . . . well . . . we ain't goin' to bury your bodies, no sir. We might shove you off a cliff just to keep the bears away, but that's all," the man declared, his Henry rifle now dangling at his side.

Hank Monk sat down. "Keep that pistol of yours pointed at the one on the porch. I don't aim to get plugged in the back." He slapped the lead lines and drove the team past the cabin and up the hill. About fifty feet lower than the tent, the trees were so thick he had to park the rig.

"Missy, I'm not sure what we'll find up here," Monk declared.

"Nor am I," she said.

"I reckon you want to go through with it."

"Yes, I do."

"You know, missy, at some point this scoundrel Billy Hays Swan jist ain't worth it. You're too knobby a woman to have to put up with this kind of treatment. He don't deserve all this attention."

"Mr. Monk, you just might be the first man in the world to call me knobby. Thank you for your sincere concern. But there's the cutest little red-headed baby down at Judith and the Judge's who has never seen her daddy. You might be right. Billy Swan doesn't warrant this attention. And maybe I don't merit it either. But that baby deserves it."

Monk tied the lead lines to the hand brake. "I reckon you're right about that."

Martina stood, clutching the pistol in her

hand. "Mr. Monk, I don't want to continue to endanger your life. You've done more than any driver would ever want to already."

"I ain't sendin' you up there alone." He leaped to the ground, shotgun in hand.

"Mr. Monk, this is not your business." She shoved the pistol into the deep pocket of her dress.

"Shoot, missy, I cain't send you up there by yourself and then go back and tell Judith about it. She'd skin me alive." He reached up a hand to help Martina down.

"Judith Kingston seems to be quite a lady."

Monk studied the trail to the tent. "Missy, that Judith Kingston can see right through a man within the first ten seconds of meetin' him. She looks right past all a man's faults and picks out something positive that the good Lord's given him. And it's the strangest thing — most men break their backs in her presence trying to live up to her image of them."

"That's quite an accolade," she said.

"Most folks around Eagle Valley say you got to please the Lord, your mama, and Judith Kingston — and not necessarily in that order."

"Well, Mr. Monk, for my own sake, I need to do this mostly by myself. Let me lead the way up to the tent. I've gone through a lot to get to this point, and I can't let someone else do it for me. I need to confront my husband."

"Missy, where's your pistol?"

"In my pocket. But I don't intend to use it."

"Never carry a weapon unless you intend to use it."

"You sound like my father."

"He must be a smart man," Monk said.

"I will use it if I am forced to," she replied.

"That's fair enough."

The ground consisted of decomposed pine needles and a scattering of granite outcroppings. The largest trees had been logged off, leaving stumps and brush piles. The remaining trees were four to six inches in diameter. The path to the tent meandered between these spindly thirty-foot trees. Shade from the grove of ponderosas had kept any underbrush from growing. The incline was barren between the trees except for the fallen limbs, pine cones, and needles.

The first shot from the tent shattered a pine cone twenty feet in front of her. The second tore bark from the tree only three feet to her right. Martina halted and jammed her hand into her pocket. She could feel her sweaty palm reach around the walnut grip of the pistol.

Hank Monk scooted up to her side. "She didn't shoot us yet — that's good."

"What do you want?" A woman's deep voice boomed out of a gun-smoke-filled tent.

"I need to talk to Billy Swan," Martina called out. It was not until she spoke that she realized how shaky her voice had become. *Lord, help me.*

"Ain't no one here by that name," the woman screamed. "Go away."

Martina cleared her throat. This time her

voice was not nearly so squeaky. "His name is Billy Hays Swan."

"This is a different Billy Hays. Go on!"

Martina took two steps closer. There was no shot from the tent. This time she was surprised by the forcefulness of her reply. "He has a birthmark on his right side on the lower portion of his hip — a patch of freckles about the size of your palm."

The tent flap was thrown open, and an enormous woman strutted forward. Dark-skinned, with thick black hair cropped above her shoulders, she looked barely over five feet tall. Her hair was matted and in some places stood straight up.

Martina continued to walk toward the tent. *She must weigh over 250 pounds! This is the woman they were all fighting over?*

The woman wore a dirty Hudson Bay five-point blanket with a hole cut in the middle for her head to stick out. A rope belt gathered the blanket around her ample waist.

She doesn't look like she's had a bath in a week . . . a month. But then neither did the men I've seen up here. Martina stopped about ten feet in front of the woman, who toted a sawed-off Sharps in her hand. Martina's hand was on her pistol, still buried deep in the pocket of her long lavender dress.

"What are you starin' at?" the woman demanded.

"I want to talk to Billy," Martina replied.

"He don't want to talk to you."

"Tell him his wife is here. I wish to speak with him."

The woman's big brown eyes studied Martina. "He don't got no wife."

Martina bit her lip, then spoke. "He certainly does. And he has a beautiful redheaded daughter too."

"He ain't got red hair." The woman folded her thick arms across a thicker chest. "You got the wrong Billy Hays."

"I've already described him." Martina took a couple of steps toward the woman. "You know I'm right."

The woman didn't budge. "And I said, he don't want to talk to you."

"How do you know? Go ask him."

"Don't have to. He ain't talkin' to nobody."

"Is he dead?" Martina was surprised that she could be so calm while asking that question.

"Nope . . . but he might not come to for a week. Those are pretty deep knife wounds. He's lost a lot of blood."

Martina took a couple more steps. She was now no more than four feet from the woman. "Let me see my husband."

The woman at the tent raised the gun and pointed it at Martina's breast. "You ain't goin' to steal my man."

"I don't want your man. I want my husband." Martina stepped close to the barrel of the gun.

"Missy!" Hank Monk cautioned from somewhere behind her.

"I said, don't come any closer," the big woman warned.

Martina took another step. She could smell sweat, dirt, and rosewater perfume. *Lord, if I die, take care of my baby girl. But I can't ride away without going inside that tent.*

The woman shoved the barrel of the gun into Martina's chest.

I will not put up with this any longer! No one, not this — this woman will keep me down on my face! I am getting up right now! Martina shoved the barrel of the gun above her head. The gun fired, but Martina clutched the barrel, which flashed to hot steel. As the woman tried to wrest the gun back, Martina pulled out her pocket pistol, cocked the hammer, and shoved the barrel into the woman's substantial belly. "Lady, drop the rifle and get out of my way, or the boys in the cabin will be rolling your body over the cliff to the bears," Martina growled.

The startled woman stepped back and tugged at the gun still clutched in Martina's hand.

"Get over here!" Hank Monk called out, waving his shotgun at the woman.

The black-haired woman mumbled something in a language that Martina did not understand, then released the gun, and waddled over toward the teamster.

Martina took a deep breath, held it, and pulled open the tent flap.

In the middle of the long tent was a round iron barrel stove vented out the top with chimney pipe. A dirty piece of carpet had been laid across the dirt floor, and a wooden barrel with a tailgate of a wagon served as a table. Piled all over the table were dirty tin dishes, food scraps, and various utensils. The stench inside the stuffy tent was somewhere between an old barn, wet goat, and black powder.

Martina recognized Billy's tattered green carpetbag tossed, empty, at the side of the tent. Behind the stove was a large cot piled with blankets and bear skin rugs. As she waded through the garments piled on the floor, she noticed several of Billy's personal things.

The unconscious man on top of the bear skins wore only his canvas trousers and bandages wrapped around his midsection and right arm. His light brown hair was matted with dried blood. He sported a month-old beard and a fresh scar on his neck.

Even closed, his eyes looked sunken, his face thin, his skin smudged. Martina laid her fingers on the caked dirt around his neck and hunted for an artery. When she felt the beating of his heart, she began to cry.

Billy Swan, what have you done to yourself? Where is that handsome boy I married? Where is the man who made my throat tickle and my heart flutter when he told me all those sweet things? Where are those arms that held me tight when I fell asleep? How did you ever come to this?

She stroked his face. For a moment she stopped, then started again.

Billy Swan, for over a year I've been so mad at you I could hardly control my anger. But you are pitiful beyond anger. Nothing I could ever do to you would bring as much personal devastation as what you are doing to yourself. May God have mercy on your soul, William Hays Swan, Jr.

"Missy," Hank Monk called out, "is that him?"

"Yes, this is my husband — what there is left of him. Would you help me carry him to the wagon?"

"Over my dead body you're takin' my Billy," the rotund woman bellowed.

"Missy, she's pitchin' a fit out here," Monk called out. "What should I do with her?"

"Shoot her," Martina replied.

Eleven

Judith Kingston buzzed into the room carrying a large porcelain pitcher with steaming hot water. She wore a thick silver velvet robe with black stitching that looked like a fancy cloak. Her short, curly dark bangs and swept-up bun were perfectly in place, as were the small pearl earrings she managed to put on when awakened in the middle of the night. "What happened when you told Hank to shoot that woman?" she quizzed.

Martina gazed down at the unconscious face of her husband sprawled on top of the guest room bed in the Kingston home in Carson City. It had been twenty dusty, dirty hours since she had pulled on her dress.

It seemed like twenty years.

"She went screaming through the woods, running toward the cabin." Martina's voice showed very little emotion.

Judith poured the water into a huge white bowl on the nightstand next to the bed. She stuck a finger in to test the temperature. "Did you see her again?"

"No, but we heard gunshots from the cabin as we drove away." Martina laid her hand against the unshaven face of William Hays Swan, Jr.

He's like someone else. A stranger. As if I hardly know him.

"Were they shooting at you or each other?" Judith queried as she retrieved a shaving mug and a straight razor from a basket near the door.

Martina turned away from the bed. "Mr. Monk and I couldn't determine that." She faced Judith Kingston. "The camp was so . . . so squalid. It was a foul place beyond description."

"I intend to talk to the Judge about that in the morning. Perhaps they would be better off in prison. Mankind has a perverse ability to take the grandeur of God's creation and turn it into grime." She handed the straight razor to Martina. "Here you go, Mrs. Swan. You may shave your husband."

Martina laced her fingers together at her waist. She stared at the pearl-handled razor and bit her lip. "I, eh, have never done this before."

"There is always a first time." Judith plopped the closed razor into her hand. "We washed and cut his hair together, but you'll need to learn to shave him. It might be awhile before he recovers enough to take care of himself. You will need to get good at it."

Martina opened the razor and inspected the blade, touching the sharpened edge gently with her finger. "But — but what if I cut him?"

"Didn't I hear Dr. Jacobs say he didn't have enough blood left to bleed?" Judith reminded her. "Here." She took the razor from Martina's hand. "I'll get him started; then you finish. Lather him up."

Martina brushed the thick shaving soap onto Billy's sunken face. "Is this right?"

"Perfect. One thing about an unconscious subject — you don't get any complaints. I believe you're learning a new skill."

Martina continued to whiten the man's face. "Not a very useful one."

Judith tucked a towel across William Swan's shoulders. "Oh, I don't know. Perhaps you and I should open a shop to cut hair and give shaves."

"Women shaving men? That would cause quite a stir." Martina finished soaping Billy's face and returned the mug to the dresser.

"Yes," Judith mused. "That's what is so tempting about it."

Martina returned to the bedside. "Judith, I can't begin to thank you enough for your incredible hospitality to my family."

Judith Kingston leaned across the bed with a wet rag in her left hand, the razor in her right. She started at Billy's upper lip and, with practiced ease, stroked away several weeks of ragged mustache. "Now don't start in on that again. It's just common Christian hospitality."

Martina watched her every stroke. "There's nothing common about opening your home to total strangers, especially when one is half-dead, unconscious, and smelling like something that crawled out of a garbage dump."

"He'll be better once he gets a bath." Judith

rinsed off the razor in the basin by the nightstand and handed it to Martina. She glanced back at the man's half-shaved face and then tugged at the high collar of her silver bathrobe. "Do you know what I see when I look at him?"

"What?" Martina said.

Judith waved a finger at the man. "I see the father of one very precious little girl whom I took care of today. There's something about the bone structure of his face that looks like hers."

Martina studied the man who was beginning to look familiar. "You may be right, although he still looks ghastly. I can't thank you enough for taking care of Christina."

"Take care of her? Why, she took care of us. She spent the day entertaining everyone she met. My, does she like to dance. Every time I played a note on the piano, she would dance around the room."

"That's my mother's influence already."

"And I could hardly force the children to go to school this morning. They both decided they should stay home and assist me, as if I couldn't take care of a baby on my own." Judith washed the shaving soap off her hands in the basin. "I'm just glad the fever broke and she's recovering. I'll keep her in the room with the Judge and me tonight so you can concentrate on your Billy."

Martina jerked back. "Oh . . . I nicked him!" She pointed to a red droplet forming among the white soap.

Judith took the wet cloth and dabbed off the

spot of blood. "It's the least of his worries."

Martina rinsed off the razor and continued to shave her husband. "You know, Judith, I had a horrible thought on my way up to Camp Sixteen this morning."

"Let me guess." Judith handed her a clean white linen towel with a red stripe on it. "You thought, *What if something happens to me, and Christina is left an orphan and grows up never knowing her father or her mother?*"

Martina didn't answer.

Judith's reassuring smile preceded her words. "Don't worry, I had the same nightmare. But it didn't happen. That baby has a mommy and daddy right here."

Martina wiped off the excessive shaving soap. "Daddy is not in very good shape. How does his face look?"

"Perfect. Are you sure you haven't shaved men before?"

Martina allowed herself a slight grin. "No, but I have thought about chasing some with a straight razor."

"Yes, few men truly appreciate our amazing self-control," Judith mused. "Martina, you have a beautiful smile."

Martina blushed and turned back toward her husband. "Thank you. I haven't had too much reason to use it lately. Judith, I do appreciate your getting Dr. Jacobs out of bed to come check on Billy."

Mrs. Kingston gathered up soiled towels and

rags. "The man sat at our table tonight and ate our pot roast and walnut pie, so how could he not come when I asked?" Her tone was that of a queen acknowledging conquest. "What was the doctor's final word on Mr. Swan? I was putting the children back to bed and didn't get in on all the discussion."

Martina reached down and gripped the limp hand of her husband. "He said that Billy seemed to be healing up fine on the outside, but it could be weeks before the internal damage could be evaluated. He told me to look for signs of internal bleeding. Of course, he didn't tell me what those signs would be."

"You'll know." Judith scooted up beside her and rested her hand on Martina's shoulder. "Believe me, you'll know."

Martina pointed toward her husband's face. "Now that looks more like the Billy Swan I married."

Judith fussed about, straightening the room. "He's a very handsome man."

"He was a handsome man." Martina closed her eyes and tried to remember what he had looked like the year before. She opened her eyes and sighed. "At the moment he has shallow eyes and sunken cheeks."

"He will flesh out with some of my biscuits and gravy." Judith, an inch or two shorter, stood beside her with arms folded. "I assume it will be a few weeks before he can be moved. He'll have plenty of time to get used to my cooking."

"We are not usurping your guest room for weeks," Martina insisted. "That is out of the question."

"And why not? It is obvious that the Lord led you here and just as certain that your husband cannot be moved."

"Judith, your graciousness is already assuming legendary proportions. Dr. Jacobs said if Billy comes around and there's no internal bleeding, he could be taken back to Sacramento in five or six days."

"That's ludicrous," Judith insisted.

"The doctor assured me that whatever is going to heal will stabilize by that time. And he also implied that if it isn't going to heal . . . well . . ." Martina avoided looking at Judith's eyes.

"Enough said," Judith assured her. "But you know you are welcome to stay with us as long as it takes."

"We really need to get back to the store. If I'm gone much longer, there will be no business to return to. But that's another story."

"The Judge thinks the economy in the West should improve when the postwar crowd decides to come west."

"Yes, that's a common theme around the store. But I'm not sure we'll be in business that long." Martina dried the sweat from Billy's face with the red-striped white towel.

"Well, what is the next step with Mr. Swan?" Judith pointed to the reclining man.

"I trust that when he comes to, we can talk

awhile. I want him to get to know the baby. I want to hear what he has to say about the last twelve months. I want to be able to forgive him." She turned to Judith Kingston. Tears streamed down her cheeks. "I want so desperately for him to say he loves me . . . and I'm terrified that he doesn't."

Judith Kingston slipped an arm around Martina's waist.

"I'm sorry for losing control," Martina whimpered.

"Mrs. Swan, if you didn't break down and cry, I was going to myself, and I don't even know the man. You must be the person the Lord wants you to be. If Mr. William Swan rejects that, he'll have a much higher court to answer to than his own conscience."

Martina wiped her eyes and took a deep breath. "Well, there is one good thing about him being in such pitiful condition. He can't exactly run away from me for a while."

"Perhaps that's God's way of giving you time to work this through," Judith concurred.

Martina squeezed Judith's small waist. "I don't even know what to say to him when he wakes up. I've been preparing a speech for months, but now it doesn't fit."

"Just be yourself. You'll know when the time comes. Tell him what you feel about him now."

"I don't know what I feel about him now. I'm so confused. I don't know whether to shoot him or kiss him."

"Tell him that." Judith pointed at a gray flannel garment hanging on the back of a cherry-wood chair. "There's one of the Judge's nightshirts. After you give him a bath, just pile his clothes in that box. I'll have the Judge burn them in the morning. I do believe it's time he had some new ones, don't you?"

"Most definitely. In fact, perhaps these should be buried immediately." Martina looked at the unbuttoned shirt and filthy canvas trousers of the man on the bed. "You're going to help me with this bath, aren't you? I mean, I've never bathed a man before."

"Mrs. Swan, that is Mr. Swan. He's your husband, not mine. I make it a habit not to bathe other women's husbands. Besides, it's not much different than giving that baby a bath, except he's bigger and dirtier, and he won't kick and squeal." With those words Judith Kingston turned and waltzed out of the room and softly closed the door behind her.

Martina examined the bandaged man on the bed. *Lord, this is not how I thought it would be when we finally got back together. On my worst days, I thought he would be yelling at me. Telling me to go away. Swearing that he never wanted to see me again. That he didn't love me. That he didn't want me in his life.*

On my best days, I imagined his strong arms were holding me tight, and he was tearfully telling me how much he had missed me, how he would never leave me again, how he loved and cherished me, how beautiful I am, and how thoughts of me kept him alive in the bleakest of times.

But never did I think about finding him wounded, unconscious, and filthy — draped across another woman's squalid cot. This is like a Shakespearean tragedy, without a noble purpose or the sublime prose of Elizabethan English.

But it is tragic. And pathetic.

Perhaps Judith is right. This will force us together.

She fumbled with the button on his filthy, tattered canvas trousers. *Judith was wrong. It is not at all going to be like bathing Christina.*

For over an hour Martina fretted over her husband, letting nothing but the cleansing job enter her mind. *We slept in the same bed for months, and I never really looked at him like this. When the baby was born, I spent two days examining every square inch of her little body. But when you marry, you accept it all at face value.* Finally she tucked Billy under the covers, the Judge's flannel nightshirt draped around his bandaged body.

She toted the basket of dirty clothes downstairs to the back door and shoved them out into the cold fall air. As she hiked up the stairs to the guest room, she caught a glimpse of the Judge building a fire in the den.

It must be after 4:00 A.M. Judith said the Judge gets up at four every day of the year, but I had no idea he would be wearing his suit and tie at this hour.

She closed the door of the guest room softly behind her and dragged the cherry-wood chair up to Billy's right side.

Her voice was not much louder than a melodious whisper. "Well, Mr. William Hays Swan, Jr., what do you have to say for yourself? You deserted your wife, ignored your baby, squandered a bank loan, left your family business to go bankrupt, ran down your health, drank alcohol, attempted murder, and took up with I don't know how many women. You've been a very busy man."

She plucked up his limp hand and held it between her palms. "And not only that, it was obvious you hadn't had a bath in months. But you are scrubbed pink now."

At least on the outside.

Martina allowed the tears to trickle down her cheeks. "Billy, what happened to our dreams? You would come up to Rancho Alazan, and we would race Father's fast horses among the oak trees. Do you remember the picnics by the willows? We would lie on the quilt, and you would tell me about the store you wanted to buy in San Francisco and how one day you would build me that vacation house at Cypress Point. And we would be so wealthy you would donate land for a church, a university, a library — or all three."

Martina laid her head on the back of the chair and closed her eyes. "On those days among the willows in the late September sun, with the valley air still warm, you held my hand . . . and my heart. You were strong. I had never felt anything so exciting as your fingers laced in mine, nothing

260

so heart-stopping as your lips pressed against mine."

Martina sat up, dropped her chin to her chest, and patted his motionless hands. "I have still never felt anything so thrilling. But it's been a long time since those days, Billy. Has it been too long? That was only two years ago. I feel as if I've aged ten years over that time. You look like you've aged twenty. I have a feeling I'll age a whole lot more in the next few hours and days."

Martina raised her head. Her waist-length hair tumbled across the arms of the chair. She threw her shoulders back. "So I came to bring you home, Billy. I don't know if you want to go home or not. I suppose you don't, or you would have before now. But you're going home anyway. You're too injured to object. Home to Sacramento. Home to Swan's Dry Goods. Home to me. And home to a baby who's never seen her daddy. There's no use in your complaining or objecting. As soon as the doctor says we can move you, we're going home. Now what do you have to say for yourself?"

"Does she look like me?"

The voice was weak, raspy, barely audible, but it made Martina drop his hand and leap to her feet. She felt dizzy. Her heartbeat seemed out of control. Her lips quivered. "Billy!" she gasped.

He hadn't moved a muscle. Didn't open his eyes. Only the freshly shaved thin, tight lips moved. "Does she look like me?" he repeated.

Martina felt every muscle in her body lock up

at once. She had to force her lips to move. "She looks like Grandma Merced." The words had more the tone of a cough than a conversation.

His words were so faint that had she not been looking at his mouth, it would have been difficult to detect their origin. "Does she have your mother's red hair?"

Martina didn't move. Her voice still sounded stiff. "Yes. Would you like to see her now?"

"Not yet," he murmured. "I can't . . . I can't believe you're here. When I heard your voice, I thought it was another dream."

Well, I wasn't in his thoughts but perhaps in his dreams. But then they could have been nightmares. Martina took a deep breath and tried to relax her shoulders. "Would you like to see me now?"

"No . . . I mean . . . yes . . . but I don't even know where I am."

"You're in Carson City."

"Marti, would you do me a favor?"

"What do you want?"

"Would you stand on the other side of the room and glance away from me?"

"Why on earth?" she said.

"I want to look at you without you looking at me. Please, Marti. I just can't look you in the eyes. Not . . . yet."

"Billy, look at me," she demanded.

"I can't, Marti. Please . . . humor me. Just give me a minute. My head's spinning, the pain — it's like I have hot coals piled on top of me. Are

262

you sure this isn't a dream?"

"Open your eyes."

"Where did you say we are?"

Martina was surprised she didn't cry. *He hasn't seen me in a year, and now he won't open his eyes. Is this a tiny bit of how You felt on the cross, Lord? Rejected? Abandoned?* "Billy, we are in the upstairs guest room at Judge Kingston's home in Carson City."

He started to lift a bandaged right arm to his head but let it drop on the pillow. "Was I arrested again?"

"No." She rubbed her hand across the perspiration on her forehead. *Lord, maybe I shouldn't have come to Nevada. Speculation, even negative speculation, is sometimes easier than facing the truth.* "Did you commit another crime?"

"I'm not sure," he mumbled. "What am I doing here?"

"Recovering from extremely serious knife wounds you received while fighting four other men for the attention of a very large woman. At least one man died in the scuffle, but so far they have not charged you with the murder."

"Cletus did that. I saw him. He went crazy."

"I'm not sure any of you were sane. Billy, look at me!"

"Not yet . . . let me catch my breath. What are you doing here, Marti? Did they telegraph you and tell you I was here and wanted you to come watch me die?"

"No one sent for me, Billy. I came on my own.

263

I had no idea you were injured. I had no idea where you were at all. I am here because you are my husband."

Tears raced across his shaved and scrubbed cheeks. His lips were chapped and tight. "Did you go up to Camp Sixteen?"

The squalid condition of the camp flashed across her mind. "Yes, I did."

"Did you see . . ." He paused and turned his face away from her, his eyes still closed, his voice now no more than a whisper.

"Carmela? Oh, yes . . . we had quite a discussion. A confrontation actually. Of course, I was in Virginia City also and met a real beauty named Pierced Katie." Martina could feel her anger start to swell up in her throat. "When are you going to open your eyes?"

"In just a minute. Will you walk across the room now so I can look at you?"

Martina walked over to the dresser. "Just give me a minute to comb my hair. You do remember the color of my hair?" She ran the brush down her hair and then fussed to retie the purple ribbons. *This is ridiculous. Who am I trying to impress? A man with no greater taste in women than Carmela and Pierced Katie?*

"It's medium brown, slightly wavy, and tumbles down to your waist," he reported.

That's good. He is thinking about me . . . at the moment. But he has not needed to look at me for a year. I don't suppose I will impress him greatly now. I don't know why I feel like I'm trying out in an audition for a school play. Perhaps I'll give him my most flirtatious smile anyway. This is what you've been missing, Billy Swan.

Martina tilted her head, dropped her chin, smiled, and batted her long, dark lashes. Her eyes caught movement on the bed behind her, and she watched in the mirror as Billy reached his hand to brush his eyes. She spun around.

"You peeked at me, Billy Swan!"

"Marti . . . I'm . . . I can't . . . you shouldn't . . . why on earth did you come to me?" He tried to push himself up on his elbow but dropped back to the bed.

She scooted over to the chair next to the bed and sat down. Without turning toward her, he reached out his hand.

She hesitated.

"You held my hand when you thought I was unconscious," he protested.

"We have a lot to discuss," she insisted.

"Couldn't we start by holding hands?"

"I don't think so. But we could start by you looking at me."

Again he thrust his hand in her direction.

This time she took it, and he turned his head toward her.

His blue eyes were sad.

Defeated.

Pained.

She wanted to kiss his troubled forehead . . . and slap him on the clean-shaven face.

"Who fixed me up?" he asked.

"Judith helped me cut your hair and shave you."

"The Judge's wife?"

"Yes. And I was the one that gave you a bath. Dr. Jacobs will be back tomorrow to change the bandages. How do you feel?"

"Like a hunk of raw meat that's been turned inside out and shoved into the grinder. I can't seem to catch my breath."

"The doctor said you have a collapsed lung. But he also said that was minor compared to several other wounds."

"I wish Cletus would have killed me." He swung his head back toward the ceiling and closed his eyes. "Did you sell the store, Marti?"

"No."

"Why not?"

"First, it is in your name. I have no legal right to sell it, and as Mr. Clayton is quick to inform me, we now owe him more money than the store is worth."

"You could have walked away from it."

"Unlike some, I do not quit anything easily," Martina replied. She pulled her hand back and dropped it in her lap.

He was silent for so long Martina thought he had passed out again. She could smell the vanilla candle Judith had left burning on the table in the hall. Somewhere in the street, a wagon wheel creaked, and horse hooves plopped.

His voice was now barely above a croak. "How did you find me?"

"A man named Loop Hackett showed up at the store about a month ago."

"Who?"

"Loop Hackett."

"Who's he?"

Martina rested both hands across the top of her head. *Lord, doesn't this ever simplify?* "He said he was a friend of yours."

"Oh?"

She dropped her hands into the folds of her dress. "He said you asked him to bring me a message last December, but he was delayed in reaching me."

"Oh . . . the professor. I forgot his name is Hackett."

"Professor? No, this man was the type —"

"Yep. He was a professor of mechanical engineering in Chicago. The Western Pacific brought him out here to design bridges, but he got mad at Charles Crocker and quit. I had forgotten all about him."

"He didn't forget you. He said you needed some money. What did you need the money for?"

"I don't remember." He turned toward her and barely opened his eyes, as if hiding their color — and intent. "Did you say you brought your baby with you?"

"Our baby," Martina corrected him.

"Where is she?"

"Down the hall. Would you like to see her now?"

"Is she sleeping?" he asked.

"I would imagine so."

"Let her sleep. I'm not worth losing sleep over."

Martina sprang to her feet. "Billy Swan, I lost countless nights of sleep over you. So don't tell me you aren't worth losing sleep over."

Again there was silence.

Martina sat back down and cleared her throat. "Billy, I don't want to be upset. I don't want to be angry. I am trying very hard. Now I want to hear your side of the story."

"I don't feel very good," he declared.

"Nor do I. But I still want to hear the entire account. I have waited a very long time, through much heartache, for this very moment."

"It's a very long, ignoble story. This might not be the time to tell it. I feel like I'm about to pass out."

"Give me the condensed version. If you black out, I'll get the smelling salts. My heart and my spirit cannot wait any longer."

He opened his blue eyes wide and stared into hers. "What do you want me to leave out?"

Martina turned away. "The accounts of other women."

"Where should I begin?" he sighed.

Now it was her turn to stare into his eyes. "How about when you left me pregnant, borrowed $6,000 from the bank without telling me, and ended up in Virginia City?"

His shallow breathing seemed to lengthen

each sentence. "I don't suppose . . . there is any way . . . I can justify my actions."

"I can't think of any," Martina agreed, "but try."

"I'm no good for you, Martina. You know that."

"You were good for me once, Billy Swan."

"Maybe we were just kidding ourselves."

"I wasn't."

"Sure you were. You were looking for a husband just like your daddy. I don't believe there's a man on the face of the earth that could measure up to Wilson Merced. I always felt like an inept child next to him."

"Are you saying you deserted your pregnant wife because I was disappointed you weren't more like my father? That drove you away?"

"I don't blame you for anything. I am responsible for my actions. I'm a Swan. I just can't be a Merced."

"I didn't marry you to be my father or my brothers. I married you to be my husband. What I wanted was Billy Swan."

"Oh? Well, you found Billy Swan passed out in Carmela's tent at Camp Sixteen. Did you like what you found?"

She could almost smell the stench of the tent. "Is that the Billy Swan you're happy with?" she pressed.

"On some days, yes," he said.

"How about on this day?"

"Today I'd like to forget I was ever up there.

I'd like to forget about Virginia City . . . and mining claims, and gambling, and smoky card rooms . . . and . . ."

"Would you like to forget about Pierced Katie and Carmela?"

"Them and the others most of all."

Martina bit her lip. *Others? How many others?*

"But I can't forget," he moaned. "The excruciating pain of these wounds keeps reminding me with every breath."

Martina rested her forehead on her fingers. *Lord, I'm tired of feeling sorry for myself. Tired of feeling sorry for Billy. Mainly . . . I'm just tired.* "Go on. Continue. You are not like my father. We agree on that point."

"Marti, be honest. I was failing at everything. I was never around at the store when you needed me. You didn't like my friends."

"I didn't like your friends who drank and lounged around saloons all day."

"I was attempting to expand our business. Trying to make the right contacts. But you didn't want to speculate. How could we ever find success unless we took a risk?"

"I didn't like risks that had very little chance of success," she countered.

His voice began to rise and gain strength. "My father risked everything by coming to California, and he made his mark. But what have I done? He died with me still riding on his shirttail."

"Would you like your father to see you now?"

"No. But I do think he'd understand."

"Deserting your family?"

Billy's voice dropped back to a whisper. "No. No, he would not approve of that. But he died. Mother was quick to walk away. I was not good at day-to-day store management. You told me many times that Mr. Chambers could run the store better than me."

"I regret having said that," she offered.

"It was true. We both knew it."

"So why couldn't you have waited until the baby was born? You have no idea the humiliation of having a child with no father in the home."

"I wanted to come back before the baby was born. . . . I planned to be back."

"I find that extremely difficult to believe."

"A few days before I left, I received a telegram from an old friend of Father's whom we knew in the East. In fact, the telegram was sent to Father. Obviously the man didn't know Father had died."

"What did it say?"

"He reported that he had moved to Nevada and that he had made a substantial discovery in the Comstock and was raising capital to develop the claim."

"And how much money did he need from your father?"

"He was trying to raise $25,000, but he said there were other interested investors."

"So you secretly took out a second mortgage on the store and went to invest without consulting me."

"You would have thrown a tantrum and re-fused to let me."

"Obviously, and I would have been correct to do so. But go on."

"When I got there, Father's friend, Zebul, said they just had to develop the claim to establish the value of the mine, and a big outfit from Chicago already wanted to buy it. Some of the other investors were friends of Father's from Philadelphia. He said I would get $50,000 within six weeks."

"Is there a collective insanity in mining towns or what? You lost all the money, didn't you?"

"Not all . . . but it didn't work out the way we thought. If we had just had another $50,000, I'm sure we could have sunk the shaft right into a huge vein of silver."

"As I said, you lost our money."

"I do own one-tenth of the Calistoga Mine."

"Which is worthless and abandoned, I assume."

"Worthless so far, but not abandoned."

"And what happened to Mr. Zebul?"

"He went back east to raise more capital."

"And you haven't heard from him since?"

"I couldn't come home to you and admit I lost the money."

"What makes you think money is more impor-tant to me than having you by my side?"

"The point is," he continued, ignoring her re-ply, "I had held back $1,000 and I —"

"That was wise of you."

"And I decided to try my luck at gambling."

"I don't believe this. Did you lose your mind?" She could hear her voice rise but could not hold it back. "Did you have some sort of spell in which your brain shut down? Is the air so thin in Virginia City that your rational thought and moral integrity dissipated?"

His voice was barely audible. "I didn't expect you'd understand. But I couldn't go back to you broke. Do you have any idea how that glare of yours can cut a man much worse than a knife?"

Martina folded her arms tight across her chest. "What glare of mine?" she snapped.

"The one you have right now. I'd rather die than face that every day for the rest of my life. I'm tired. Real tired." He turned his head away from her and closed his eyes.

"Billy Swan, you finish telling me this account."

"Why?" he mumbled. "What difference would it make? I committed every sin there is to commit. There is nothing left of me that you like. You should have left me at Camp Sixteen. I need to sleep."

"We need to talk."

"I'm tired of talking. I want to close my eyes and go to sleep."

"Then we'll finish this discussion when you wake up."

"If I wake up."

"The doctor said your recovery looks encouraging."

"A fact I will no doubt regret."

That was it.

He turned his head to the side and slipped off to sleep or unconsciousness, or he was just rejecting her. She was not sure which.

Martina was sound asleep in the chair by the bed when she heard a squeal and a faint "Mama." She spun around to see Christina decked out in a fancy long white dress, clutching Judith Kingston's outstretched finger.

"Hi, punkin! Come see Mama!"

With a grin as wide as her face, Christina toddled across the room, one careful step at a time.

Judith Kingston was dressed in a long green Irish poplin dress with a fresh white linen apron tied in front. There was no sign she had spent half the night assisting Martina with a wounded, filthy husband. "Little Christina's quite a walker," Judith declared.

"I've never seen her do this well. Have you been coaching her?"

"Well, the children played with her constantly after school yesterday."

Martina plucked up the baby and cradled her in her lap. "I missed you, darlin'."

"I'll bring you all up some breakfast," Judith announced as she proceeded down the hall.

"Oh, no, you don't have to do that," Martina called out.

Judith Kingston stuck her head back in the doorway. "I most certainly do. I'm not about to have that baby down in the kitchen when Mr. Swan wakes up again. This time he should see his daughter."

"I suppose you heard us talking earlier."

"It sounded like you got some things discussed."

"That's a pleasant way of phrasing it."

"Don't worry about us. The Judge and I have had a heated discussion or two."

Martina rocked the baby back and forth in her lap. Christina pointed to the bed. "Man!"

"Yes . . . well, young lady, let's get the introductions taken care of. Christina Swan, this is William Hays Swan, Jr., who just happens to be your father. This is your daddy, punkin."

Christina curled her little tongue in a circle and stuck it up toward her nose.

"Darlin', let's try this again. This man is your daddy. Can you try to say, 'Daddy'?"

"Big!" Christina squealed.

"Yes, Daddy's big. But you should try to say, 'Daddy.' "

With a quick swoop, Christina yanked the purple ribbon out of Martina's hair. "Me!" she squealed.

"All right . . . you play now, little princess. But when Daddy wakes up, I'll have to introduce you. I don't want you getting scared of him and crying."

With her mother's ribbon draped around her own neck, Christina stood on Martina's lap and leaned out toward the bed. "Ouchee!" she shouted, as she pointed to the bandage on Billy's right arm.

"Yes, Daddy has lots of ouchees."

The baby reached down and pulled her long dress up above her panties. "Me, ouchee!" She pointed to her knee.

"Did you get a scrape while Mommy was gone yesterday? Do you want Mama to kiss it?"

"Mama kiss!" Christina repeated.

Martina lowered her head and brushed a kiss on Christina's round, soft, talc-smelling knee. "Is that better?"

Christina let her dress flop back down and pointed to the man on the bed.

"Mama kiss!" she said.

"No, Mommy isn't going to kiss Daddy's . . ." *Lord, this isn't fair. This little girl has absolutely no concept of Daddy. She doesn't know what she's asking. She would say the same thing if this were an injured mule. Lord, there is no way I can kiss wounds he received fighting a man for the affection of another woman. This is not fair.*

"Mama kiss!" the baby insisted.

Still holding Christina in her lap, Martina leaned across to the bed and brushed a slight kiss across the back of Billy's hand.

Lord, I can't believe You made me do that.

They both finished a bowl of mush with dried cherries and a touch of molasses in the upstairs guest room. The baby sat in a highchair next to Martina and mauled a small piece of fried wheat bread. Most of the strawberry jam that had been on the bread now decorated the baby's face. Martina stood to retrieve a wet rag from the basin, and William Hays Swan opened his eyes.

"Man!" Christina shouted.

"Young lady, this is your daddy."

"Billy, this is Christina, your daughter. Her hair is red but not her face. I'll wash off the jam."

He opened his mouth. No words came out. Tears rolled down his cheeks.

"Billy, are you all right?"

"But — but," he stammered, "she's so — so beautiful!"

"Yes, she is. You look surprised. Did you think she would be plain like me?"

"I — I didn't say that. She does look just like your mother."

"There is a striking similarity."

"Can I . . . just touch her?" he asked.

"As soon as I clean her up. She is your daughter, but she doesn't do too well with men at first meeting. Unless they have red hair."

He tried to wipe the tears out of his eyes. "Bring her to me."

Martina washed the baby's face and picked her up. "Let's go see Daddy, punkin."

Martina set the baby at Billy's side. Christina clutched a finger that was thrust out of his bandaged right hand.

"Ouchee!" she exclaimed.

He loosed his finger and brushed it gently across her round little cheek. "Me kiss!" She reached over and planted an open-mouthed kiss on his hand.

"Oh, my, you get a kiss!" Martina exclaimed. "The only other men who get those are Grandpa Merced and Uncle Joey."

Billy Swan turned his head away from both of them. "You shouldn't have brought her here!"

"What?" Martina reached out to restrain Christina from climbing on Billy's wounds.

"If I had died at Camp Sixteen, you could have made up stories about me. Now she'll learn the truth. Having her here shames me."

"This baby doesn't shame you. I don't shame you. It's your conscience that hounds you, and you can't run away from it. Besides, she won't understand the truth for a long, long time. By then I'm sure she won't care." Martina hoisted the baby and plopped her back into the high-chair. "Little children are like puppies. They don't care what you've done in the past; they just want you to love them right now."

"And what do wives want?"

"The first thing I want is to apologize for snapping at you earlier."

"I deserved it."

"Yes, you did. But that does not give me a license to behave poorly. I regret that I did so."

"What's the second thing you want?"

"I want you to say . . ."

"What do you want me to say?"

"I think you know."

He turned away and looked at the wall.

"Anyway," she continued, "it's time for you to get something to eat."

"I'm not hungry. I don't think I have the energy to bring a fork to my mouth," Billy mumbled.

"I'll feed you. I've gotten good at it," Martina declared. "But you have to promise not to smear strawberry jam on your face."

Twelve

Hank Monk was right. He said that the return stage ride to California would neither be as crowded nor as frantic as the one to Nevada. Baby Christina's bright eyes charmed the drivers enough that they helped Martina move Billy from stage to station to stage. Several times she heard people murmur, "He must have been wounded in the war." Martina didn't bother to correct them.

The last leg of the journey was a train ride down from Newcastle. Billy slumped on Martina's shoulder, his eyes closed for most of the trip. Christina bounced on her lap, trying out her latest new word — *Daddy*.

The train car was half full as Martina watched the dry, brown grass on rolling hills and clumps of valley oaks that whizzed by the window. The "few days" of recovery at the Kingstons had stretched into ten days. Dr. Jacobs indicated that Billy was able to travel. Martina wanted to believe it, but as they bounced over the Sierras, she increasingly had her doubts.

Lord, please keep him safe. Our talks were not accomplishing much in Carson City. If I can just get him home, to our own place, then we can start rebuilding.

He says he's sorry.

I believe him.

But he claims he might up and do the same thing again someday.

I tend to believe that too.

Out the train window she spied a young girl galloping a long-legged black horse next to the river. *Enjoy it, sweetheart. The days will race by too quickly.*

Christina carefully studied the feathered hat of the woman in the seat ahead of them, and only Martina's quick hand prevented the woman from being plucked. *We've been gone over three weeks. It seems like a year. Is it still 1865? Is the war still over? Did Mr. Lincoln really get shot? Is this my husband? Am I still twenty-two?*

I feel old. I feel forty-two.

Martina reached down to the floor and snatched up the bear-claw necklace. "Be careful, darlin'. That's a family heirloom you're playing with."

"Daddy!" the baby yelped.

"No, the necklace belongs to Mama. It used to be Grandpa Merced's, but he gave it to me."

The baby studied her lips and wrinkled her nose. "Grumpa," she mouthed.

Martina laughed. It felt good to relax her face. "Grumpa? Well, that's close, punkin. But if you call him Grumpa, your uncles will tease him the rest of his life. Now if you want to be really smart, learn to say, 'Grandma Alena is pretty.' That, my dear, is not only true, but it will be like money in the bank."

"Me!" Christina struggled to pull the heavy necklace over her head.

Well, punkin, it's all confusing, isn't it? It doesn't get any easier when you grow up. For the last two weeks all I had to worry about was playing with you and tending your daddy's wounds. Judith insisted on cooking, washing, cleaning. Bless her, Lord. Bless her real good. But now there's a business barely hanging on and a marriage in not much better shape.

She brushed her hand across Billy's light brown hair. There were a few strands of gray. *I don't know if he was ready for this ride or not. Lord, I was afraid that if we waited any longer, there would be no business to return to.*

She glanced at the window and could see her own reflection scowling back at her. *Okay . . . the truth is, I was afraid if he got any healthier, he would run off again, leaving us stranded in Nevada.*

Lord, You told me to get up off my face. So I did. Now what? Everything's still a mess. Nothing's settled. Nothing's straightened out. When does something get fixed? Things can't continue like this.

At least, it can't get worse.

Martina stood next to a rough wooden bench on the train platform. The small terminal of the fledgling Western Pacific was more like a construction yard than a train station. She stared at the street, examining each carriage and wagon that rolled along.

"I can't imagine why Joey isn't here," she said

to William Hays Swan, Jr., who sat on the bench, leaning on a polished walnut cane. "I telegraphed him from Dutch Flat. Perhaps they are swamped with customers today."

Billy's breathing was heavy, his gaze toward his new boots. "You shouldn't have brought me back here," he grumbled. "I don't want to be here."

Martina stiffened her back. Her teeth ground against each osther. "Billy, I know you don't want to be with me or Christina but —"

"That's not what I meant," he said.

"That's what it sounded like."

His mouth hung open; his shoulders slumped. "Loosen your noose, Marti. I know I deserve to be hung. But not here. Not at home. Not in Sacramento. That's all I meant. I didn't mean I don't want to be with you and the baby. I just don't want to come back to Sacramento in this condition."

"You should have thought about that before," she said.

"I did. That's why I didn't come home. It's one thing being a pathetic failure where no one knows you. It's quite another thing to be one in your own hometown."

"Well, you are home. And it's time to do some things right. . . . I don't know where Joey is." She studied the dusty street.

"Now I get to face the wrath of another Merced."

"You haven't faced any Merceds yet. Christina and I are Swans, remember?"

"You know what I mean," he mumbled.

Martina paced around the bench, toting the baby on her hip, and continued to stare toward the street. "Perhaps we should rent a carriage." She stopped in front of him. "Billy, a hundred times during the past year I felt so melancholy I just wanted to lie down and die. Do you know why I didn't?"

"Christina?" he asked.

"That's right. She kept me going. I had to take care of her. But I spent a lot of time on my face — in sorrow, grief, and depression. Do you know what the Lord said to me?"

"He should have told you to divorce me."

"He told me, 'Get thee up; wherefore liest thou thus on thy face?' Now that's exactly what you have to do, Billy Swan. Just get up and start putting things together."

"Are you saying you can forgive me for all I've done?"

Martina brushed her waist-length hair over her shoulder. "I've been praying and praying about that. I know I should forgive you. And I think, with God's help, I can . . . someday. I need a little more assurance, I guess."

"Assurance that I won't ever sin again?"

"No. None of us can ever guarantee that. Billy, I need something else."

"What do you mean? What do you want me to do? Look at me. You want to beat me . . . shoot me . . . hang me? What is it?"

284

She shook her head.

"Well, what do you want?"

"I can't tell you," she murmured.

"What do you mean, you can't tell me?"

"If I tell you, you'll do it just to keep me still. But you won't mean it."

"You want me to get down on my knees and apologize? If I do that, I'll never get back up again."

"That's not what I had in mind." A black carriage caught her attention. "Look! There's Evie! I'll take the baby out to her and then come back for you."

"Just drive off and leave me," he suggested.

"Billy, I realize I could walk out of your life right now, and you'd have very few regrets. But I don't think you could abandon this precious little girl without it hounding you every day of your life. For your sake, as well as ours, I will not leave you here."

He nodded his head slowly. "Yeah, you're right, Marti. As always." He struggled to his feet.

"Just wait. I'll come back and help you."

"No," he insisted. "I want to greet Evie in my own strength. It's important to me." As he straightened his shoulders, he began to cough. He yanked a white handkerchief out of his suit pocket.

Martina stared at the stains on the handkerchief. "Billy . . . when did you start coughing up blood?"

"Last night."

"Why didn't you tell me?"

"Nothin' you can do, Marti."

"I can . . . I can pray," she blurted out.

"Don't waste the Lord's time. He's through with me."

"Nonsense. The Lord doesn't give up on anyone."

"The Bible says there's a 'sin unto death' that we should not pray about."

"Well, you haven't committed that."

"How do you know?" He carefully folded the handkerchief, clean sides out, and tucked it back into his pocket. "Okay, let's go meet the loquacious Miss Norman."

The pace was slow as Billy shuffled along. Martina carried their carpetbag in one hand and led the baby with the other.

"Look who's driving the carriage, punkin. It's Evie," Martina called out as they approached.

Christina gazed up at the dark-haired clerk and then pointed, wide-eyed, to Billy Swan. "Daddy," she squealed.

Martina studied Evie's expression as it turned from concern . . . to shock.

"Mr. Swan! I heard you were hurt, but you — you . . ."

"Hello, Miss Norman. Yes, I look terrible. Actually I looked much worse when Marti found me. This is my good view."

Evie held the palms of her gloved hands against her cheeks. "But — but — I . . ."

Martina handed up the grinning baby and

then assisted her husband as he struggled to climb into the backseat of the carriage. "Billy's not feeling too well today. I'll explain later." Martina pulled herself up into the carriage and plopped down on the black leather seat next to Evie Norman. "Now tell me how things are going at the store. Where's Joey?"

Evie slapped the lead line on the horse's rump. The carriage lurched forward. "You know how Doraine refuses to drive a carriage, so I was the one elected to come pick you up. Maybe I should have used that rig of yours with the mules, but I didn't think it would be —"

"Evie," Martina interrupted, "where's my brother?"

The clerk bit her lip and stared straight ahead. "Eh, Joey's in jail."

A familiar sense of gloom slid down Martina's back and slumped her shoulders. "Jail! Why?"

"The sheriff arrested him this morning. Doraine sent word to your folks. I'm sure they'll bail him out as soon as possible. He threatened to shoot Mr. Clayton."

Martina laid her hand on Evie's arm. "When? What happened?"

Evie Norman reached up to adjust her small, round, black straw hat. "This morning about ten o'clock. Mr. Clayton marched in and announced he was taking over the store immediately, and we had five minutes to gather our personals and vacate the premises."

"He can't do that. He gave me a sixty-day extension. We have a few more weeks."

"He claimed the bank policy forbade him to grant anything more than a final thirty-day extension. The earlier agreement was void."

"He obviously found out I was out of town. I paid him $300 for the extension."

Evie kept her eye on the street ahead of them. "He returned $100 of it."

"If I had been there, I'd have thrown it in his face," Martina fumed.

"That's exactly what your brother did. Joey told him to leave the premises and that if he ever came back, he would shoot him."

"I don't suppose that went over well." Martina released her hand and leaned back in the seat.

"Mr. Clayton got the sheriff and some deputies, and they came back and arrested Joey for threatening Mr. Clayton," Evie reported.

When does it get better, Lord? When does it end? "What about Mr. Hackett? Where was he?"

"He was out calling on your debtors. He's collected over $2,000 so far. He's such a forceful, determined man. Yet he's really nice. I don't think he and Doraine are hitting it off all that well. He really needs someone more demure," Evie said as she lowered her chin, "if you ask me. Isn't it grand about the money he's collected?"

"Yes, yes," Martina chafed, "but that's all a moot point if Clayton has closed the store and Joey is in jail."

"He hasn't closed the store exactly. When

they hauled off your brother, they started to give me and Doraine the boot, but we pitched such a yelling, screaming fit that the sheriff and the deputies backed away."

"The two of you pitched a fit?"

"We just asked each other, 'What would Miss Merced do if she were here?' "

I'm teaching my clerks to pitch a fit? "I appreciate your loyalty, Evie."

"Then Mr. Hackett showed up, but they said he couldn't enter the store."

Martina imagined an irate Loop Hackett — hat pulled down, jaw set, hair on the back of his neck bristling. "What did he do?"

"He is so brave, Miss Merced. I've never seen anything like it. He just handed them his revolver and strolled in anyway. He said shooting an unarmed man in the back is a crime in any state. Say, I'll bet you can't guess what Mr. Hackett used to do in the States?" Evie gushed. "Doraine just found out today."

"He was a professor of mechanical engineering at a university near Chicago."

Evie Norman's mouth dropped open. "Who told you?"

Martina continued to stare straight at the horses' heads. "My husband."

Evie shot a quick glance toward the backseat. "Oh . . . yes . . . well, Loop didn't want to leave the two of us ladies at the store by ourselves, so he sent me to pick you up."

The carriage hit a pothole, and Martina

clutched the baby. Billy let out a groan from the backseat. She reached her hand back to him, and he feebly gripped her fingers.

"I'm sorry, Mr. Swan," Evie apologized. "I'm not very good at this. I told Mr. Hackett that, but he makes a woman think she can do anything just by the way he grins."

Martina continued to hold Billy's hand but turned back to Evie Norman. "So the store's open after all?"

"Sort of," Evie replied. "Clayton has a man stationed in the alley so no one can make deliveries. He has two men out on J Street carrying shotguns. It looks more like a fort than a store."

"Why are they in front?"

"Intimidation, I assume."

"They won't let customers in?" Martina said.

"They don't force the customers away, but who would want to shop at a store under the barrel of a shotgun? I have no idea if they'll even move aside and let us back in there. I'm not as alarming as Loop Hackett."

"They'll move," Martina insisted. "We'll feed them. That's the kind of thing Judith would do."

"Who?"

"Judith Kingston. She's a very persuasive lady in Carson City. Her husband's a friend of my father's. And I do believe I learned a few things from her."

"Feed them? I never heard of anything like that before!" Evie exclaimed.

"Sure you have," Martina said. "The Bible

says that if your enemy is hungry, you should feed him."

"That's in the Bible!" Evie said.

Martina felt Billy release her hand, and she pulled it back into her lap. "Stop over there! At Oh Fat Loo's. Buy us two — no, make it three Mandarin Enchantments."

"You're going to feed them a first-class meal?"

"They work for Mr. Landel Clayton, and he's a first-class enemy."

"Perhaps you could buy extra yellow peppers and mustard." A knowing grin broke across Evie Norman's narrow face.

Billy Swan slept in the bed upstairs. The baby was conked out in her playpen behind the store counter. Doraine and Evie lounged on the bottom step of the wide staircase. Martina wandered the aisles of the empty store.

"If you hadn't given the store chairs to the men outside, you'd have somewhere to sit," Evie said. "Come sit with us."

"I don't want to sit." Martina continued to prowl the floor. "There has to be a way to save this store."

"Well, we did keep it open," Doraine popped off.

"Yes, and I'm very grateful. Grateful for your courage. Grateful that Mr. Hackett raised enough money to at least pay off my brother's fine. And grateful that Joey didn't shoot a banker. But can we say the store is open when there are no customers?"

"No one wants to come past the stooges with shotguns," Doraine said.

"Maybe they were less intimidating when they wandered back and forth, Miss Merced," Evie added. "They just sit by the door now."

"And eat their Chinese food," Doraine declared.

"Maybe I need a good lawyer," Martina pondered. "There must be something I can do."

"I don't think you can fight the likes of Landel Clayton," Doraine said. "He's determined to get this building and the location."

"Well, he can't have it," Martina asserted. "It's been Swan's ever since they abandoned Fort Sutter and moved town to the river. People like Clayton think they can buy out or force out anyone. That's not fair."

All three women looked up as an unarmed Joseph Merced strolled through the open doorway. Loop Hackett sauntered two steps behind him. "Well, big sister, I see you tamed the men at the door. I figured they'd fuss about letting us pass."

"Joey!" Martina scurried over and hugged her brother and then turned and held out her hand to Loop Hackett. "Mr. Hackett, I can't thank you enough for helping my brother get out of jail."

"I didn't do much. It was your money that I used for his fine." Hackett leaned up against an empty shipping crate. "I heard you were bringing back your husband."

"He's upstairs sleeping." Martina kept her arm laced in her brother's. "He has some serious knife wounds."

"What kind of scrape did he get in?" Joseph asked.

"I don't want to talk about it." She emphasized her words with her notorious glare.

"I bet he's mighty glad to be home," Loop Hackett said.

All eyes in the room were on her as everyone waited for her reply. *Glad to be home? If he could, he'd leave tonight.* "At the moment, he's hurting so bad I'm not sure he even knows if he's home. Since we have no customers, I need one of you to go find a doctor."

"Sheriff suggested I stay away from Clayton for a while," Joseph announced. "He said it was probably best if I don't wander around town tonight."

"I agree," Martina added. "In fact, I want you to go home."

Joseph Merced shoved his black hat to the back of his auburn head. "Do what?"

"Joey, Doraine sent word to Daddy that you're in jail."

"I didn't know what else to do," Doraine explained. "And we didn't know exactly when you would be back."

"No, no, that was fine," Martina insisted. "But now he'll come down here all steamed up. That's not good for him. So ride up to the ranch and tell him everything's all right."

"What do you mean, all right?" Joseph Merced barked. "The bank's foreclosing the business; there are two men with shotguns at the door scaring away customers —"

"Three men. There's one in the alley," Evie corrected.

Joseph waved his hands wildly. "And your husband is upstairs with serious knife wounds. Since when is that all right?"

Martina grabbed her brother's arm and waltzed him away from the others. "Joey . . . please," she begged. "Billy and I need to work some things through on our own. It would be absolutely disastrous for Mother and Father or any of you boys to be here at this time. He's ashamed, angry, and very seriously wounded. He's like an injured dog ready to snap at everything. You intimidate him. If I'm going to salvage anything out of this business . . . and this marriage, it will have to be on our own."

"Sis, all of that would be fine if you weren't in danger."

"I don't really think Mr. Clayton will try anything violent with me and the baby here."

"There are others besides Clayton, sis. You can hog-tie his type and cook supper at the same time. It's those others that I worry about."

"The ones that stole the payroll?"

"Yes. I was only in jail a few hours, but rumors were flyin' that if they ever got out, they were comin' after you, me, and Loop."

"Yes, well, let's worry about that in twenty

years when they get out of prison. 'Let today's own troubles be sufficient for today.' I need you to go to the ranch," she insisted.

"Why don't we all go to the ranch?" Joseph slipped his arm around his sister's shoulder. "You, Billy, and the baby could stay up at the cattle camp a few weeks. I'd make sure no one pesters you."

"But we'd lose the store." Martina laid her hand on Joseph's. *Lord, it's so nice to be touched by someone who really cares about me. Even a hug from a little brother.*

"Sis, some things aren't worth holding on to."

"Joey, remember that mahogany bay horse you boys said was unrideable? You kept wanting me to sell it, but I wouldn't do it. Not until I broke it anyway. I don't quit easy. You know that."

"Yeah, but I remember he drew blood when he bit you in the shoulder and blackened both your eyes when he bucked you off into the corral gate. But I'm not talking about quitting a marriage," Joseph said. "Or quitting business altogether. I'm talking about this particular store. Loop's dug up enough money for you and Billy to buy a little business somewhere else and start all over." His arm slid off her shoulder.

They stopped prowling the store and stood facing each other. "That sounds like quitting to me."

"Come on, sis." His tone was like a kid begging for stick candy. "This isn't Rancho Alazan. It's just Swan's."

"My husband is a Swan." Martina's tone was more like a schoolteacher grading a history exam.

"He didn't do you right, Marti. And you know it. He walked away from the business. He walked away from you . . . the baby . . . everything. It makes me furious to think about it."

"Joey, I'm aware of all of that. But the emotional battles are mine to fight and mine to live. He's here with me now."

Joseph put his hands on her shoulders. "Marti, look me in the eyes. If you had found Billy healthy, would he have come back with you?"

She stared up at Merced eyes. It was as if her entire family were huddled nearby waiting for her reply.

She choked out the words, "Probably not."

Joseph's hands dropped to his sides. "It's not worth saving the store for someone like that."

"Then I'm going to save it for Christina. She's not a Merced, Joey. She's a Swan. She might be the last Swan in Sacramento, but she is still a Swan."

Martina was relieved to see the tension in his face melt into tolerance. "I'm not going to convince you, am I?" he said.

A thin, tight smile broke across her face. "You know me better than that."

Joseph looped his thumbs in his pockets. "You're as stubborn as Mama. You know that, don't you?"

Martina reached over and brushed his wild red hair behind his ear. "It's about the only thing Mother and I have in common."

"Who are you kidding?" Joseph scoffed. "The only thing you don't have in common is the color of your hair. You two think exactly the same. You even sound alike."

She grabbed her brother's strong arm. "Joseph Cabrillo Merced, that's not true!"

"Oh, yeah? Ask Walt or Eddie. We all learned to say, 'Marti' before we ever said, 'Daddy.' "

"That's because I lined you up and coached you every day. Mother and I can both be bossy, I suppose. Now go home and tell Daddy not to come to town."

"Yes, Mama."

She threw her arms around her brother, hugged him tight, and kissed his smooth, tan face. "Joey, you boys spoiled me — you know that, don't you? I grew up wanting so much to marry a man just like my brothers. Billy was right. I always compared him to you three."

Joey's eyes dropped. "Maybe you should have set your standards higher than us."

"No, they were high enough." She released her hug. "Obviously, I just haven't learned how to bring out the best in Billy. Maybe there's still time."

Without any customers, Martina sent Evie and Doraine home at 4:00 P.M. The guards left when she hung the Closed sign in the front window. It was almost six when Loop Hackett showed up with a doctor. He and Martina played with the baby while they waited downstairs for the doctor to complete his examination.

Kerosene lanterns glowed across the store as Dr. Winstap plodded down the stairs.

"What's the report, Doc?" Loop called out. His voice always displayed the same controlled determination.

Dr. Winstap looked past Hackett. "Mrs. Swan, your husband is not doing well. He has some sort of internal infection."

"What does that mean?" Martina asked. Even with the doors of the store closed, it felt as if a cold breeze was drifting across the room.

"He will either be able to fight it off, or it will . . . well, it will slowly kill him."

She stood at the base of the stairs clutching the railing. "Can't you open him up and fix it? I understand they learned many new surgery techniques during the war."

The diminutive doctor with the white hat continued his slow descent of the stairs. "He can't stand any more shock to his system or loss of blood."

Martina closed her eyes and rubbed them. "I shouldn't have brought him back home so soon. It was too tough a trip. I just wanted him to be home so badly," she murmured.

The doctor shoved his gold-framed spectacles higher on his wide nose. "You did the right thing. A man heals better at home. Something about being where you belong that strengthens a man's resolve to get well. I doubt that it would have made any difference if you had stayed in Nevada. He's a young man. If anyone can fight this, perhaps he can."

For Billy, being at home means humiliation. He doesn't want to be here. I should have left him in that woman's bunk. "What should I do?" Martina furtively brushed tears from her eyes.

"Keep him in bed. Quiet. Give him something to look forward to. He seems to be a very depressed man at the moment. It was probably all that travel."

She walked the doctor to the front door, unlocked it, and let him out. *My prodigal husband has spent a year rejecting me, our child, and everything I hold important. He bears on his body the just consequences of his own choices, and I'm supposed to think of ways to cheer him up?*

She returned to Loop and the baby. "Well, Mr. Hackett . . . I think we should call it a day."

"Would you like me to stay here tonight?" He waved his arm toward the front door. "Downstairs, of course. Just in case Clayton tries something else?"

"No, we'll be fine. Besides, I might need some help from outside in the morning if he tries to lock us up again. You're a good friend, Loop. I'm afraid I've come to depend on you."

"I reckon I do my best when I'm around folks that need me."

She nodded slowly. "I believe that is true for all of us, Mr. Hackett."

"Do you surmise that's why the Lord puts us into scrapes like this?" he asked.

"I'm beginning to think that." She walked him to the door. "Let's see what tomorrow brings. If we can't get any customers into the store, we'll all be leaving town soon."

He stared at the empty chairs that now sat just inside the door. "I think you ought to advertise your guards."

"Do what?"

"Put it in the newspaper. Hang a big canvas sign out front. 'Shop at Swan & Son — the safest store in California! We keep armed guards posted to insure your tranquility.' "

Martina grinned. "I like that! It couldn't hurt. Let's work on that in the morning."

Loop tipped his hat as he exited the building. "You have a very handsome smile, Mrs. Swan. I'm glad you found your husband."

"Thank you, Mr. Hackett. I'm glad I found him too." *At least, I think I am.*

Billy hardly talked as she fed him beef soup. If his eyes were open, he lay on his back and stared at the ceiling. The only time she got him to smile was when she hummed "Clementine," and baby Christina danced around and around on the hooked rug next to the bed.

She thought he was sound asleep when she finally crawled under the covers and turned out the lantern. Martina lay on her back at the far edge of the bed, her hands folded across her long flannel gown.

His voice was low but pronounced. "I'm dyin', Marti."

"The doctor said a young, strong man like you has a very good chance of fighting this infection thing," she declared.

"I'm dyin'," he repeated, "and the strange thing is, I don't care."

The covers felt heavy and oppressive on top of her long flannel gown. Her voice was soft. "You'd rather die than live with me and Christina?"

His reply was weak in volume but clear. "That's not what I meant, and you know it," he said. "I just don't have the words to say it."

"Billy, let's give it a month. I know we can't keep the store past that time if we haven't paid Clayton off by then. But you'll be stronger. . . . Maybe then it will be clearer what we are to do." Her voice broke. "Please don't go running off on me for a month."

"I don't know if I can make it across the room. I'm not going to be running off. How about you? Don't you want to pack up and go back to your family at the ranch and leave me to die?"

"No, I don't." Every breath seemed to be labored. "My name is Swan. And my family is right here in this very room."

She flinched as she felt his hand reach over and touch her arm. "Marti, scoot over here," he beckoned.

She struggled to keep from shuddering at his touch. "I can't, Billy. Not yet. Give me time. My spirit is sliced up just as drastically as your body. We both need to heal a little first."

There was silence for several minutes.

"I was lyin'," he finally admitted. "I am afraid of dyin'. I need you close, Marti. For old times' sake. Come over."

Tears began to drip down her cheeks and drop onto the sheets. "And I need some distance." Her voice was now a barely controlled sob. "Some things have to happen first. When you touched me, the first thing I thought about was how I felt compared to the other women you touched."

"Don't think about those others," he said.

"Billy, that's an absurd notion. There's no way I can get them out of my mind so quickly. Perhaps someday."

"Well, I hope it's soon. Doc said if I don't fight this infection, it would take me in less than two weeks."

"You can fight it, Billy. I know you can fight it. Think of some things you look forward to."

"I destroyed everything good in my life."

"Billy, how many times did this store get destroyed?"

"It burned down once and was flooded out twice. Why?"

"Well, you and I are either going through a fire or a flood. But we can build it all back up again. The foundation's still solid."

"How's that?"

"Jesus is still Lord . . . and He is still on the throne."

Again he reached over and touched her arm. "Please, Marti, I'm cold. . . . Come warm me up."

"I've got to be more than just another blanket," she demanded.

"I don't know what you want from me!" he fumed. "I'm a sinner and a failure. What more can I say?"

Tears now flowed profusely down her cheeks. She reached over and pushed his hand away from her.

"Marti!" he pleaded.

"Billy, you know for sure what I need to hear." Her voice was so low she didn't know if he could hear her. "I still love you, William Hays Swan."

Her tears soaked the neck of her flannel gown. She waited.

And waited.

And waited for words she had not heard in over a year.

"I know," he finally managed to reply.

She turned away from him and hid her face in the feather pillow.

Those were not the words, William Hays Swan, Jr. Oh, Lord . . . He won't say it, will he? Have mercy on our souls.

Now we both want to die.

Thirteen

Martina had not slept through the night since the day of Christina's birth. Middle-of-the-night feedings were a thing of the past, and yet she continued to waken every few hours with a restless feeling that someone somewhere needed her.

For the past several months her response had been to listen for the baby, fluff the feather pillow, and then roll over and fall back to sleep.

This time when she woke up, she listened for the baby, fluffed the pillow, and lay perfectly still on her back.

She didn't attempt to roll over.

There was a man in her bed.

A wounded man.

A man whose soul was as critically mangled as his lacerated body.

Martina could hear his labored breathing.

I don't think I understand the full nature of sin, Lord. Has it so distorted Billy's heart that he has no true affection for me anymore? Did he day by day lose interest in me, or did he just decide all at once that it was over — not worth the work?

A person can only sustain the hard work of a relationship if the rewards are worth it.

What are the rewards for Billy in rebuilding our marriage?

What are the rewards for me?

It can never be like it was.

Can it, Lord?

The thin curtains in the upstairs apartment diffused the starlight of an early October night sky, but they could not restrain the quarter moon that seemed to hang just outside the window. It made a glow in the room similar to the few seconds between night and dawn, when everything in the room can be identified by its familiar silhouette, but nothing can be seen clearly.

A table. A coat rack. A chair. A crib. A lantern.

Everything was in place.

Arranged exactly by Martina's choosing.

She enjoyed the silence of the night. There was no baby fussing. No customers complaining. No clerks gossiping. No gunfire down the street. No freighters screaming profanity at mules. No stagecoaches roaring by. No shouts. No anger.

No laughter.

No teasing words.

No compliments.

No assurances of affection.

Nothing.

Nothing but silence.

The heat from the dying fire in the woodstove made the room feel warm and stuffy. There was a slight tinge of tonic water in the air, a remnant of the aroma she had splashed on Billy when she had shaved him early that morning. It mingled with a hint of fried onions.

Martina didn't know if it was the onions she had cooked for supper or the astringency in her soul that had left a bitter taste in her mouth. She ran her tongue around her straight teeth as if to wipe away the tang.

The pillow seemed lumpy beneath the back of her head. She could hear the feathers crinkle when she turned to look in Billy's direction. She thought she heard the faint hoofbeat of riders in the street below the window. She rolled to her side. The mattress felt hard, the sheets cold. A chill rolled down her back, and she reached up to make sure the high collar button on her long flannel gown was still secure.

It was.

Lord, I've spent a majority of my nights in this bed crying myself to sleep. I petitioned, implored, begged, and pleaded for You to bring Billy back home to me. Now he's back in my bed, and I'm still crying myself to sleep.

For months I promised that if You would bring him back, I would forgive him, no matter what the offense. Now he's right here beside me, and I realize forgiveness is not the problem. It's the inability to forget that plagues me. Every time he wants to touch me, I think about how my body compares with the other women. Every word that he speaks, I wonder if he's said those same words to others. And the few times he's smiled in the past two weeks, was he smil-

306

ing at me or at a memory of another?

Maybe that's why he doesn't say it. Maybe he knows how difficult it would be for me to believe it. Perhaps he's said it too often — to too many women. Perhaps the phrase means nothing to him anymore.

But it means the world to me.

Martina rolled over on her side and faced her sleeping husband. *I need some sleep, Lord. It was a tortuous trip across the Sierras. We arrived back to a crisis with the store.*

I haven't even prayed about Mr. Clayton and the store.

It doesn't seem to matter much anymore.

Only one crisis at a time. You can handle more . . . I can't. I really do need some sleep. Lord, take care of everything for me. I feel like a little stick floating down the rapids. I have absolutely no ability to change the course. I'm lucky if I can stay afloat.

What I'd really like is to wake up and have all of this past. My husband healthy. The store debt-free. Mr. Clayton confined to a leprosarium in the Sandwich Islands. And Billy cherishing me all the days of my life.

That would work, Lord.

That would definitely be the start of a good day.

A very good day.

Martina very slowly scooted across the flannel sheets to where Billy slept. She gently laid her cheek against his shoulder. She ran her hand down his limp left arm and then laced her fingers into his.

And cried herself to sleep.

The air chilled quickly when the sun dropped below the distant coastal range. Martina was glad she had worn her heaviest riding dress. Her mare Negrita raced down the eastern slope of Solamente Butte impervious to the tough day of gather they had just completed. Martina fastened the top button of her father's old ducking coat that she wore. She tightened the stampede string of the floppy-brimmed felt hat that she had begged off Uncle Echo Jack.

Somewhere, perhaps only a few yards back, she knew her brothers Walt, Joey, and Eddie raced behind her. They would not catch her, of course. They didn't have Negrita.

And they were mere lads.

I'm thirteen! More mature. A seasoned cowhand. It is the fifth gather that I've worked. Father has taught me everything!

Something happened to the time, but Martina did not know what. Instead of riding up to their cow camp near the creek, she was already there. With her back leaning against a saddle and her riding boots setting beside her, she wiggled her bare toes as they caught heat from the blazing campfire.

Father and Walter were drawing maps in the dirt and talking of a new trail to the summer range. Uncle Piedra and Mother were fussing about something he was cooking. Uncle Echo Jack was assisting Joey in repairing a broken stirrup. Eddie ran around with his slingshot hunting an imaginary grizzly, and Uncle Jose strummed his guitar and sang in Spanish about a girl named Juanita.

I think this might be the most perfect of all days, Lord. Mama calls these "Days of Heaven." Maybe she's right. Is this what heaven is like?

I don't want to go home.

I don't want to grow up.

I want to stay right here forever and ever and ever.

Martina rolled to her right side, and once again time was confused. It was dark. She was asleep in the bedroll. The camp was still . . . and quiet. Her head was tucked against the pommel of the saddle.

The fire had lost its heat but not its smoke.

Why does the smoke always blow toward me?

In the distance she heard a cough.

It's blowing toward Eddie too.

Then there was another cough.

Then a panicked, high-pitched cry, and the dream ended with a scream, "Mama!"

In the shadows and smoke, Martina could see the baby standing and clutching the railing of her bed. She could not see the expression on Christina's face, but the tone of her voice dramatized her anxiety.

Something's burning?

"Mommy will be right there, punkin. It must be soot in the chimney again. Remember how it caught fire last December? We smelled like smoke until New Year's."

She plucked up the baby. The crying stopped immediately, but the coughing continued.

Carrying the baby on her flannel-gowned hip, Martina scurried to the kitchen part of the apartment and over to the woodstove.

I don't remember stoking the fire much last night. Maybe Billy was cold and got up. . . . No, he didn't move all night. She grabbed the spiraled-wire flue handle and shut the vent tight. "See, baby, when we shut off the air, the fire has to die. We've got to get some fresh air in here! Mommy's going to open the windows. Then we'll bundle up in a blanket so we don't get cold."

When Martina shoved open the J Street windows, the sight across the street startled her.

Mr. Julian's meat market is on fire! Oh, dear, that's where the smoke is coming from!

Then she took a closer look. What she saw was a reflection in the meat market's big glass front windows.

"No, it's — it's our store! Oh, no . . . oh, no, baby, our store is on fire!"

Still carrying the crying baby, Martina ran barefoot across the wooden floor to the big double doors at the top of the stairway. Smoke boiled up the stairs as soon as she flung the doors open. She could see flames at the front of the store. The front doors blazed, as did the stacks of linens near the window.

Oh, Lord . . . no . . . he didn't do this. Surely Mr. Clayton didn't set this fire. That's criminal!

We've got to get out the back door to the alley!

The baby bawled. "Mommy will get you outside. It's okay . . . don't cry." Martina grabbed a tea towel from the table and covered the baby's head as she scurried through the swirling smoke on the staircase. *A brick building is not supposed to catch on fire. Right?*

Christina cried even harder and threw the towel to the floor. It was still a good hour before daylight, and the smoke made it impossible for Martina to see anything at all. But she could feel the intensity of the heat from the flaming merchandise.

The baby was now in hysterics.

"It's okay, punkin." Martina coughed. "You cry all you want. Cry for both of us, darlin'. Mommy's too scared to cry."

Martina stubbed her bare toes, stumbled, caught her balance, and scurried on through the smoke. She fumbled with deadbolts, grabbed the warm brass doorknob, and flung open the alley door. Fresh night air blasted through the doorway like a winter storm sweeping off the Sierras. She heard the flames, catching a fresh supply of air, roar at the front of the store.

Clutching the baby to her chest, she staggered out into the dark alley. A flash of gunpowder and an echoing explosion caused her to leap back inside the smoky store. Shattered chips of brick blasted their faces like a sandstorm in the desert.

The baby screamed uncontrollably.

Oh, God . . . no . . . they're shooting at us! Someone is trying to kill us!

Martina bit her lip to keep from screaming.

I've got to do something! They're in the alley!

311

Who's in the alley? Why, Lord? Why do they want me and my baby dead? I've got to get out.

Keeping her head low, she bumbled her way back toward the front of the store.

We've got to get out the front door. There'll be people in the street. They won't shoot us on J Street.

The intensity of the heat and flames caused her to stop at the bottom of the stairs. Above the screaming of the baby she heard a voice shout, "Marti!"

She couldn't see him, but she knew it was Billy's voice. She clutched the wooden railing and dashed up the stairway. She stumbled on the top stair. A weak arm caught her and the baby and dragged them into the apartment, slamming the doors behind her. Billy was on his hands and knees beside her.

"Get down, Marti. Get under the smoke!" he said coughing.

"They're trying to kill us, Billy!" Martina cried.

"Who is it?"

"I don't know . . . I don't know," Martina screamed above the roar of the fire and the cries of the baby. "We made it to the back door, and they shot at us. They're trying to kill me and Christina, Billy."

He was only a smoky shadow. "How's the front door?"

She coughed twice, then sucked in enough air to shout, "It's on fire."

The baby's howling slowed as Christina

gasped for fresh air. With every breath, Martina could feel smoke fill her lungs. "Billy, we've got to do something. I will not let my baby die like this!"

"Our baby." His voice was surprisingly clear.

"What are we going to do?" she wailed.

"Marti, where are your guns?"

"The pistol is in the nightstand; the shotgun's in the closet, I think."

"Pull a flannel sheet off the bed and soak it in the basin of water. I'll get the guns. Don't stand up, Marti. Stay under the smoke," he ordered.

She squeezed the baby to her shoulder, crawled across the floor to the bed, and yanked a flannel sheet to the floor. The baby stopped gasping long enough to cry, "Me, blankie!"

"No, punkin, we don't have time to go get your . . ." Martina crawled toward the crib. *Save us, Lord. Deliver us from all our enemies.*

She grabbed the small tattered quilt that was Christina's prized possession. She heard something crash to the floor. It was the bear-claw necklace. The baby grabbed it and tugged it over her neck and clutched her little quilt.

"Did you get it soaked?" Billy screamed from the smoky shadows. Then he began to cough.

"I'm doing it now!" she hollered through the darkness.

"Well, hurry up!" he yelled.

Anger flared up in Martina, but she didn't reply. *How dare you order me.* Still clutching the baby in her left arm, she sat on the floor and tried

to lower the big enameled tin basin. The flannel
sheet was crumpled at her knees.

Martina immediately lost her grip on the basin, and its contents poured over her head and
the baby's. It drenched their hair, their night-
gowns, and the blankets on the floor. The baby
was so startled she opened her mouth but
couldn't speak.

"Oh . . . no!" Martina moaned.

"What's the matter?" Billy yelled.

"The water's cold!" Martina shouted back
and then crawled toward the doorway.

She couldn't see him, but she felt his presence.
She reached in front of her and grabbed his
wounded shoulder. He winced, and she pulled
her hand back. Billy caught her hand and pulled
her close. His other hand clutched the back of
her soaked gown. He pulled her head toward his.

"Good!" he called out. "You soaked your
gown too. That was wise. Where's Christina?"

"Right here. She's too startled to cry, I think.
What do we do now, Billy?"

"We'll pull the sheet over our heads and go
back downstairs. At the bottom of the staircase,
I'll go to the back door with the revolver," he announced.

"They'll shoot you," she warned.

"I'll stay low. It's too dark to see much of a target. Anyway, I'll get them to think we're running
out into the alley."

"How about us?"

"Keep the sheet over your heads and make it

to the small stained-glass window in the corner."

"The 'Swan's since '49' window?"

"Yes. It's set in the brick wall. It can't be on fire. It's not in there very solid. I should know — I installed it. Bust it out with the butt of the shot-gun and get out on the street."

"What if they shoot at us?"

"I'm hoping they will all be around back with me. If not, use the other end of the shotgun. You'll hit something," he instructed.

Crawling out the door, he led them to the stair platform. The flames now roared so loudly she could barely hear his instructions.

"Keep the sheet over your head!" he screamed.

"When I get out, I'll come around and help you," she cried out.

"No!" he protested. "Get our baby away from here. Send the sheriff or others to the alley!"

They crept down the stairs on their knees, with a constant trio of coughs. They heard a crackle of dry ceiling timbers beginning to flame and explode. At the bottom of the stairs, he crawled out from under the nearly dry flannel sheet.

Martina clutched his hand and pulled it to her lips. The weak hand slipped around the back of her head and pulled her toward him. Even in the pitch-dark she closed her eyes and puckered. Like a veil, only the flannel sheet separated the soft touch of their lips.

Then he was gone.

With the flannel sheet still over them, Martina

crawled toward the corner window, clutching the baby in one hand and dragging the shotgun with the other.

Lord, deliver us. All three of us. For the first time in over a year, I feel like I have a husband!

When she reached the far corner of the store, the flannel sheet was bone dry. Sparks from the fire smoldered in its folds. She tossed it away from them.

Above the roar of the fire she heard gunshots from the back door. "Daddy's buying us some time, darlin'."

Martina set Christina against the brick wall and pulled the baby's wet quilt over her head. "Leave it there, baby, until Mommy busts this window. I don't want you to get glass in your face."

Coughing, the baby yanked the blanket off her head.

"No, punkin . . . leave it there. Peek-a-boo!" Martina cried. "Play peek-a-boo."

Instantly Christina pulled the quilt over her head. Martina slammed the brass butt plate of the shotgun into the leaded glass.

Nothing broke.

The quilt came down.

"Peek-a-boo!" Martina hollered.

The blanket went up. With both hands on the now-warm barrel of the shotgun, Martina slammed the butt plate into the stained glass.

Nothing shattered, snapped, or crashed.

There were three more gunshots from the alley.

"This isn't working, Billy. . . . This isn't working." Even in the panic of the moment, Martina could feel tears stream down her cheeks. The soles of her bare feet warmed. She heard a faint sound from the baby. She leaned over to Christina.

"Boo!" the baby shouted and dragged the wet quilt over her head.

It was either the heat of the fire or the heat of anger that rushed up the back of Martina's neck.

Satan, I don't know if you have something to do with this, but my baby is not going to die like this, and neither am I!

This time when the butt plate crashed into the window, the entire three-foot stained-glass window popped out of the brick casing and crashed to the boardwalk below. The blast of fresh air rushing in caused them both to gulp and cough.

It also caused the flames to race across the store. Martina glanced back. The flannel sheet only two feet behind them was now in flames. In the dim light of street lamps outside, she thought she saw people running up the street.

Lord, if these are the ones trying to kill us . . .

With the damp quilt over Christina's head, Martina thrust the baby straight out the round open portal. "Take my baby!" she screamed.

From somewhere, arms took the baby, and a strong grip held her fingers as she pulled herself out of the flaming dry goods store.

There was confusion for a minute. Then she

317

was sitting on the hard, grimy street in a wet flannel gown, clutching a wet flannel-covered baby. Her eyes still burning from smoke, Martina couldn't see the face of the tall man who had assisted her and now stood beside her. But she could see the street lamp reflect off black boots that were polished to a mirrorlike finish.

His voice was as deep as a river. "Are there more in there?"

"My husband!" she coughed and gasped. "He's in the alley. Someone's trying to shoot him!"

"I'll go check!" the man assured her as if this were a common event.

Martina struggled to her feet. She was suddenly surrounded by a crowd of people, including a volunteer brigade from the Young America Fire Company trying to save the adjoining buildings. The shouts and yells were so loud that she couldn't hear if there were any more gunshots from the alley or not.

Someone wrapped a heavy wool blanket over her shoulders. She staggered through the crowd on the street, clutching the baby and the blanket. At the corner of the alley a man lay sprawled on his back, revolver clutched in his hand. She couldn't see any wound, but she could tell that he wasn't breathing.

She studied the man's familiar face.

It's one of the payroll bandits! It was them! They're trying to kill us!

The fire from the building lit up the alley as if it were daylight. The heat was intense. Martina and the baby scurried down across the cobble-stones. Another of the payroll robbers lay stretched over empty shipping crates. His eyes were glazed. Both his hands clutched a bloody stomach wound that oozed through his canvas coat. Martina bent to retrieve the revolver discarded at the man's feet.

Only a few yards farther, the third outlaw lay facedown in the alley. She didn't have to search for a pulse on this man. He had been shot in the head.

She looked at the back step of the store. A hatless man was propped with his back against the brick wall. Sparks and flaming wood chips were showering off the roof around him.

"Billy!" she screamed.

His eyes were closed.

His right hand still gripped the small revolver.

Fresh blood appeared in several places on the flannel nightshirt.

"Billy! Oh, Billy!" she cried.

He mumbled something.

Martina stooped down next to him. "What?"

"Is our baby safe?" he asked.

"Yes! She's right here. . . . Come on, let me help you to the street. We've got to get away from the store."

"I can't move, Marti. I took some bullets. Go on."

"Billy Swan, I'll carry you over my shoulders if I have to! I'm not leaving my husband to die in an alley!"

He slowly reached up his arm. "Give me your hand!"

She reached down and laced her fingers into his.

She expected 165 pounds of dead weight. To her surprise, he struggled to his feet. With his arm around her and the baby, he limped his way out to the street. From out of the crowd now huddled in the middle of the street sprinted a winded Loop Hackett.

"Martina!" he shouted as he trotted toward them. "What happened?"

"They burned us out and shot Billy!" she wailed. "Help me get him across the street."

Hackett supported Billy's other side, and they navigated their way to the boardwalk on the far side of the street. "Who did this? Clayton?"

"No, it was the payroll robbers. They burned us out, Loop."

"What can I do?"

"Go get a doctor!" she pleaded.

Billy lost his grip and collapsed to the raised wooden sidewalk. Martina and the baby slumped down beside him. She noticed that Loop's black boots were heavily scuffed and covered with dirt.

"How about the outlaws?" he asked. "Are they still on the prowl?"

"No . . . two are dead. One is wounded bad. Hurry, Loop!"

Horses pulling water wagons galloped past on the street. Hundreds of people dashed about shouting, warning, and screaming commands.

Martina cradled Billy's head to her breast. Baby Christina stood next to her, a little hand balanced on her mother's shoulder. Martina tucked the dry blanket around all three of them. She rocked back and forth.

The baby's voice was faint but clear. "Daddy!"

Tears streamed down Martina's cheeks, and she could feel smoke still burning in her lungs. "Billy Swan . . . you hang on. There's a little girl here who loves you dearly."

He didn't open his eyes.

When he opened his mouth, dark blood trickled out across his chin. She wiped it clean with the blanket. "How about her mama?" he murmured.

Martina couldn't hold back the sobbing. "Her mama loves you dearly too!"

"I don't deserve your love," he coughed. "I never have."

Martina continued to rock — and sob. "That's ridiculous. No one deserves to be loved. That's the nature of love. We choose to love someone, just like the Lord chooses to love us even though we are sinners."

"You think He still chooses to love me?"

"Yes, I do," she sobbed. "And I chose to love you two years ago, Billy Swan. And I choose to love you today, no matter what you've done."

She looked around at the crowd and hollered to no one in particular, "Where's Loop? He went to find a doctor."

She turned back to her husband. "He'll be here soon, Billy. Don't cry, Christina. We'll get Daddy fixed up."

Suddenly Billy's raised finger found her lips and silenced her nervous chatter. She thought he mumbled something. Martina leaned close to his face. His eyes struggled open. His lips moved, but no sound came out.

"What?" she gasped and leaned closer. "What did you say?"

He closed his eyes.

"Billy, please. Please, darling, what did you say?"

The voice was suddenly so clear that it sent chills up the damp gown that clung to Martina's back. It was so forceful that the baby stopped her whimpering.

"I choose this day to love you, Martina Patricia Merced Swan."

His head slumped. His mouth closed. Another spot of dark red blood appeared at the corner of his lips.

"Daddy, ouchee!" the baby exclaimed. "Mommy kiss."

Martina bent low and pressed her lips against his still, lifeless ones. But even before they touched, she knew he was gone.

It was what they call an Indian summer.

It was the middle of October. The high Sierras were capped with a heavy fresh blanket of glistening white snow. The leaves on the deciduous trees had turned color and begun to drop. The garden plants had all died off except for the pumpkins scattered like bright orange boulders across the field.

But a warm west wind blew in from San Francisco Bay, and Sacramento and the Delta enjoyed a bright sunny day with seventy-two-degree weather.

One by one the carriages pulled out of the cemetery on the rolling hills east of the city. Joseph Merced, looking extremely uncomfortable in a new black suit and tie, held the lead lines for both of the remaining carriages.

Martina stood in front of the fresh mound of shoveled dirt and stared at the three-foot-tall marble headstone. In her arms baby Christina fingered the bear-claw necklace. Both wore long black dresses. A black felt hat with a violet ribbon was perched on Martina's head. Her long brown hair draped down her back to her waist.

Loop Hackett stood one step behind her and to the right. "Well, Martina, I believe it's time for me to leave too," he offered.

"Loop, you've been a dear friend to me — to all of us. Thank you."

"Just happened to be my time to show up, I suppose."

"You were heaven-sent right when I needed you."

"I reckon all of us have been in the Lord's hands," he said.

Martina shifted the baby's weight. "I think

you're right. Did you get a final report from the sheriff on those men?"

"The one talked a little before he died." Hackett stepped up a little closer, hat in hand. His clean-shaven, square-jawed face reflected years of outdoor work. "After they killed the sheriff's deputy and escaped jail, they were coming after me and Joey. I guess they heard we were livin' above the store."

Martina's eyes felt completely squeezed dry of tears. "So they weren't after me and the baby?"

"They were obviously ready to shoot anyone who ran out that door." Hackett glanced down at the tombstone. "I don't think they planned to be very discriminating."

She looked at the mound of dirt. "But Billy killed two of them."

"Yep, but it's that third man that's got me puzzled. Doc said he was stone-dead without a wound on his body. Must have had a heart attack or somethin'. Doesn't that sound rather bizarre?"

"Everything about that night was bizarre." She leaned over and planted a kiss on Christina's rosy cheek, and then received an enthusiastic but slobbery one in return. "I don't suppose you found the man with shiny black boots who helped me."

Hackett shook his head. In the bright sunlight of midday, Martina noticed several gray hairs. "Mrs. Swan, there isn't a man within 100 miles of Sacramento who can keep his boots clean."

"There was one." She reached back and held out her black-gloved hand to Hackett. "Thanks again, Loop."

He shook her hand. "What's next for you, Mrs. Swan?"

"Well, we don't have any belongings to move, so Joey's going to drive us north to my parents' home today at Rancho Alazan. I've decided to winter up there."

Loop Hackett jammed his hat on his head. "And in the spring?"

"Thanks to your collection of past debts, I have enough to open a small store somewhere. Perhaps just a millinery shop, something I could run by myself." Her brother impatiently held the carriages on the horizon.

"In Sacramento?" he asked.

"Oh, no. I'm looking for someplace much smaller than that."

Hackett nodded his head and also looked back at the carriages. "I know what you mean."

"How about you, Mr. Hackett?" She thought about setting Christina down, but the pile of bare dirt dissuaded her. "Are you headed back to Virginia City?"

"Nope. I'm lookin' for something a little more peaceful too. There's a railroad survey party going south into the San Joaquin Valley. They wanted me to hire on to give 'em a preliminary estimate on bridges. Some folks figure that land's about to open up, especially if they can figure out how to irrigate it. A nice little valley farm. That sounds peaceful, doesn't it?"

She nodded, and he stepped away.

"The Lord bless you, Mr. Hackett," Martina called out.

He tipped his new black felt hat. "You too, ma'am. And the Lord bless you, little punkin." He grinned at Christina.

"Man!" she squealed.

"A good man, darlin'," Martina added as they both watched him hike to the dirt trail where Joseph Merced held the carriages. "Mr. Loop Hackett is a very good man."

Martina turned back to the gray marble tombstone and read the words slowly to herself as if it were her first time, not her hundredth.

Husband & Father
Our Hero
William Hays Swan, Jr.
July 23, 1838 — October 11, 1865
The Last Swan in Sacramento